MW01139737

# *Cajun Fire*

## By
# RICK MURCER

PUBLISHED BY:
Murcer Press, LLC

Edited by
Janet Fix, www.thewordverve.com

Interior book design by
Bob Houston eBook Formatting

www.rickmurcer.com

Cajun Fire © 2016 Rick Murcer
All rights reserved

ISBN: 1539189880

For all of the storytellers out there.

Thank you.

# *Cajun Fire*

## A Novel

## By
## RICK MURCER

# CHAPTER-1

The two large men flanked the smallish one. They looked like Sequoias as they stood, stoic and erect, hands folded in front of them, impeccably dressed in customized suits that cost thousands.

The fact that this meeting was taking place in a musty, dank warehouse on New Orleans's east side at dusk only added to the bizarre contrast of the men's impeccable appearance and the less-than-desirable surroundings.

Rhodes crossed his legs and motioned for them to come closer.

They did, but only after the three exchanged glances. Caution was an understatement regarding this group. Good. That would make what was coming next easier to handle.

The man in the middle moved exactly one step in front of the other two, as if they'd performed this parade a thousand times before. Rhodes supposed, in this business, precision made sense. He'd been there a time or two.

None of them were particularly attractive; the two large men had shaved heads, large noses, and shaggy brows.

They might have been twins in another life.

Their employer, Mister Smith, as he'd communicated earlier, wore a white fedora with a black band. The hat hung low over his face, but even that couldn't mask the dark, beady eyes circled by gold wire-rim spectacles.

Rhodes couldn't help but think of the old line about makeup and pigs. Yet the two guards were hardly what he'd call swine. More like cobras in suits. Once more proving that money could only mask the man, not change him, at least for men like these.

The hard-ass, no-nonsense approach revealed something else. They weren't afraid.

That in itself was a wonderful trait when hiring men and women with their specialized skill sets. And Rhodes knew of such skills, didn't he? Had he not traveled a similar path in the wake of his journey to the here and now?

Pointing to the three chairs on the other side of his worn mahogany desk, he smiled. "Please, sit down. Can I offer you something to drink?"

The trio stopped about ten feet from the desk.

"That won't be necessary, Mister . . . Rhodes, is it? I didn't come here to drink or socialize, as you might imagine," said the man with the fedora, his voice surprisingly deep.

The cold, calculating vein with which he answered was no surprise. A man like him, who did what he did, had no reason to be sociable.

He nodded. "Mister Rhodes will do. And, no, I don't suppose you did. Let's get down to business then, Mister Smith."

"That suits me. I have another appointment tomorrow and would like to wrap this up."

Standing, Rhodes reached for the single manila folder on his desk and began to walk over to the three men. He was met five feet away by one of the guards.

The bodyguard reached out his wide hand and took the file from him, motioned for him to stay, and then turned and handed the file to his boss.

Smith opened it and studied the single sheet inside, then glanced up. "Again, are you positive this is what you want?"

Excitement coursed through his body like a wave of electricity. His thoughts shot directly toward his desire, his purpose.

Nothing, since the day he'd finally determined that he would rise like the proverbial Phoenix from the darkest pit of life, had truly prepared him for the accompanying emotion in reaching this point in his pilgrimage.

Was there anything sweeter than purpose accompanied by a sense of justice?

"Yes. That's what I require. Do you have what I need?"

"I do."

"Good."

Mister Smith shifted his feet without shifting his eyes. "I don't usually ask what a client wants with what I sell. But—"

"Then might I suggest that you don't ask now. You and I are businessmen. Let's conduct business and get on with our lives," Rhodes said.

The other guard began to reach into his jacket, but his boss stopped him.

"No need, Klaus. The man is correct. It really isn't any of our concern."

Smith lifted a thin finger in his direction. "Do you have the agreed-upon price in US dollars?"

"Yes."

Walking back to the desk, he pulled two silver hard-shell cases from underneath the desk and placed them on the table.

"Please count it."

"Yes, we will."

Five minutes later, Smith closed the cases, put them on the floor, and pulled out his phone. He typed a quick text and replaced the phone inside his blue jacket, then stood still.

"Now what?"

"My people will be here momentarily to deliver your order, and we will not see each other again. Clear?"

He nodded. "Clear. Very clear."

Three minutes later, two more tall, husky men, led by a dark-haired woman, entered the open double doors. She was carrying a metallic attaché case in her left hand, striding as if she owned the place.

Even in the fading light, he could see she was a striking, muscular woman, her long, dark hair framing her high cheekbones.

*Too bad.*

"This is my associate, Miss Jones, and her entourage." Smith then turned in her direction. "Please put the case on the desk and hand him the key so that he might inspect his purchase and we can be on our way."

"Gladly," she answered.

He detected a slight Middle-European accent as she spoke, his favorite.

With great caution, Miss Jones placed the attaché on the desk and handed him the key, their fingers touching.

She smiled. "You have warm hands. Are you nervous, my friend?"

He returned her smile. "Excited, Miss Jones, very excited, I would say."

Placing the key into the middle lock, he opened the case slowly, his anticipation off the charts.

The contents seemed to stare back at him like a long-lost friend. His smile grew. He could scarcely believe what was now his.

This was it, the final ingredient in his complex recipe. The journey had been arduous, but he'd done it. *They* had done it.

Closing the case, he locked it and put the key into his khaki slacks.

"Are you satisfied?" asked Smith.

"I am."

"Then we will make our way from you and this place. Per our normal exit protocol, you will wait fifteen minutes after we have left before you leave this building."

"I understand. It's been a pleasure."

Smith offered another curious look, a wordless question about what he was going to do with his new treasure. When there was no answer, Smith picked up the money, one case in each hand, and turned for the door.

Once all six people were directly in front of Rhodes, positioned correctly, he cleared his throat. "Mister Smith, there is one more thing."

Smith stopped in midstride. Rhodes swore Smith had read his mind, to no avail or consequence, however.

The small man dropped the cases, yelled at his guards to move.

But it was far too late.

Muffled shots rang from underneath the desk as Miss Jones and her two associates landed hard in successive thumps, bullet holes winking from each of their skulls, the floor around them already changing to a deep red.

Raising his customized Glock 9mm, Rhodes shot Smith and one of his guards before they could make another move, almost.

Klaus had managed to get his gun from his holster. Another shot from underneath the desk ended that intention.

Klaus's gun clattered against the wooden floor, after the right side of his face had disappeared, his remaining eye wide open with surprise before he tumbled to the floor next to his boss. The two of them lay still, face to face. He couldn't help but wonder if they were pondering, in death, the hell in which they found themselves.

Oddly enough, Smith's glasses were still on his face, albeit a bit crooked, supported by the one ear he still possessed. The cases of money flanking Smith were still standing erect, oblivious to what had happened.

The silence was tense and relaxing at the same time. All the while, he kept his gun trained on the six bodies some thirty feet away, even though he knew he need not worry. He never missed. Nor did she. Still, it never hurt to use appropriate precaution.

After another minute, he addressed his accomplice.

"Come on out. We have things to do and places to see," he said softly.

The slight woman crawled gracefully from underneath the desk, the silver suppressor on the end of her resized Beretta 92FS leading her from the floor to his side.

"That was different," she breathed, the excitement undisguised in her voice.

"It was. As always, you were superb."

She turned him in her direction with a gentle tug of his shirt, her bright-blue eyes alive. "And it's all for you."

Then she kissed him.

He returned her kiss, then held her at arm's length. "I thank you. Now, more gratitude to come. Shall we?"

"We shall."

Five minutes later, in possession of the two cases of money and the final ingredient required to fulfill his purpose, Rhodes drove the ten-year-old Chevy Impala out of the neighborhood and headed for one of the hidden gems offered to locals in the French Quarter. There was nothing like the reward of a celebratory dinner.

He couldn't remember feeling any better since the beginning of his new life.

# CHAPTER-2

The sun reflected off the pink finish of the shuriken throwing star. Milliseconds later, it thudded dead center into the heart of the adult-sized target in Manny Williams's backyard.

Before Manny could say an encouraging word, another star danced so close to the first that it was hard to tell there were two.

Then a third.

"Nice aim."

Sophie Lee, his close friend and ex-partner with the Lansing Police Department—and now the FBI, maybe—glanced at him, perspiration crawling down both sides of her pretty face. She nodded.

"Watch and learn, white boy. That's what we're doing here, right? Teaching you how to throw these babies. Besides, that's what Chinese folks do. We toss shit and make it stick to whatever we want."

"Yep, that's why you're here—I'm learning. But what does that other part mean, exactly?" He moved closer to her, already sensing what was about to happen.

"I can throw stars or I can throw dog dung. Either way, I'll get them to stick to something, especially me. It's part of who I am."

Manny ignored the last statement, far more in tune to the second.

"Explain sticking to you."

"Damn, you're thick for a hotshot profiler. Blond hair and blue eyes and all the rest of you."

Sophie took two steps toward him. Manny wasn't sure she realized she had. Then he was positive she hadn't.

"Let me explain, Williams."

She shuffled two steps nearer, her bare feet gliding through the grass.

"It's like the way I'm prone to having the shitty stuff from this life stick to me. I'm the target. Targets get damaged. Pretty soon they're destroyed, or worse, they aren't worth a tinker's damn or the time it would take to fix them. But that's okay. That's the purpose of a target, so the beat goes on. It's karma or some mystical crap like that. Get it? Or do I have to make it simpler for you?"

"Sort of. Keep talking."

Her beautiful brown eyes searched his.

They were now only a foot apart, but Sophie's glare bore right through him, demanding an answer he didn't have. Good God, she was a tough woman. But . . .

Gradually, like a slow-motion video, the tears welled and, within a few seconds, mingled with the glowing perspiration on her face.

"Are you going to make me ask?"

"Ask what?"

She turned away from him, staring at the target, then whirled around, emotion changing the very contours of her face.

"Sometimes I hate the freaking way you think. I ain't in no damned mood for a confession."

"That makes two of us; and maybe you are."

She swayed a little, then leaned in. "Why Dean, Manny? Why him?" Her voice was a ghostly whisper.

He reached for her, folding his arms around her, drawing her close to him. She gave in, not fighting him this time. He still had the bruises from the last instance when he'd tried to console her, some four weeks prior, right after her husband Dean Mikus's funeral.

Grief had no friends, but touched everyone. There was no escaping it.

Thank God she was finally taking this next step in her heartache, willingly or not.

His friend, as far as he knew, hadn't spent one tear before or after the funeral. Not one scream of frustration. Not one rage-filled outburst. Well, except for beating his arm. Not even a drunken escapade. Since the funeral, she'd not given a single indication that she was in mourning or grieving—other than not talking to anyone, except him sparingly, for these past weeks. Maybe she was hoping it all just might go away and she would awaken from the nightmare.

He knew how she felt. He also knew the answer to her heart-wrenching question would never fully reveal itself, at least not in this life.

She nestled closer to him while he contemplated the not-knowing for the millionth time.

"I don't know, Sophie. People make choices. The asshole sicko in Miami made one. Dean made another. That's all I know."

"That ain't much for a smart guy," she said quietly. "But maybe I can't handle more than that."

"You mean destiny or fate or God's will?"

Sophie released another pent-up sob, then quickly recovered. "Yeah, one of those. But I can only be pissed at one of them. If God is really there, then I'm pissed at him. If it's fate or some other mystical, undefinable hocus-pocus shit, then what am I supposed to think? That none of us has a chance to change destiny?"

He didn't answer but waited for her.

Her body heaved, then she continued. "There was never a gentler soul in this screwed-up universe. He didn't deserve this. Not in any concept of the word 'justice.' On top of that, I don't deserve this either. I've paid my damned dues already. Now I'm alone and left behind in this freaking mess of a world."

The face of Manny's murdered wife, Louise, journeyed into his mind, again.

After her death, he'd done his fair share of questioning, screaming, and shaking his finger too, but later understood that his knee-jerk reactions hadn't served a purpose, other to make him feel better—and that was temporary at best. Louise wasn't coming back from the dead. That had only happened a couple of times in history.

It was impossible to have a bigger frustration in life than to never again be able to touch or talk with the love of your life. The feeling was close to utter desolation and pure abandonment.

He stroked her long hair. "I hear you. Neither of you deserved what happened. I'm still not sure what God has to do with anything like this. I do know that no one's immune to heartache. It rains on all of us."

She pulled away from him, her hands still on his arms, and smiled a tired smile.

"Man, you suck at that philosophy crap, but you get an A for effort."

"Thanks, I think."

Her voice grew even softer. "I know you want to help, but it hurts like a bitch, Manny. What am I going to do without him?"

Stepping back into his embrace, she began to shake as the cascade of tears let loose, and this time with a vengeance. He felt his own eyes moisten as he plummeted into her despair. No one should go there alone. No one.

After a few minutes, Sophie's body stopped shaking, her sobs reduced to faint whispers, which were somehow even more haunting. He recognized that phase too. He thought he'd never get control of his emotions, his heart, his pain, after Louise's funeral. Hell, sometimes his wandering thoughts still embodied merciless torments.

Sophie stepped away again, her face more relaxed, if not tear-stained.

"Better?" he asked.

"Yeah, for now. But I'm not sure I'll ever be the same."

"No, but it will become bearable, I promise."

"Hey, don't promise shit you can't deliver."

He started to answer, but just then, the door at the back porch opened, and three men and a woman stepped into the yard, followed by his wife, Chloe. The redheaded, Irish bombshell, who had captured his heart and helped him heal, was carrying his young son, Ian.

Alex Downs, the balding, paunchy forensics expert who doubled as his good friend dating back to their days at the Lansing Police Department, was leading the other two men, his arm still in a sling for another few days. He'd undergone an intricate operation to attach a highly developed hand prosthesis and was still in the throes of healing. But he was already using it a little.

Josh Corner, his former boss at the FBI's Behavioral Analysis Unit, was right behind Alex, his blue eyes visible even from twenty feet.

Manny frowned. He understood Alex and Josh showing up—they both had something to say to Sophie—but why . . . *him*?

There was no mistaking the third man in the group. Mountains rarely moved with that much grace.

Braxton Smythe was the very definition of a musclebound, ebony giant, right down to his shaved head and Caribbean shirt. He was smiling that wide grin that was always so engaging . . . and hid his not-always-pure intent, like trying to have Manny killed a couple of years prior.

Manny had understood why and trusted Josh when he said it had been a misunderstanding orchestrated by Smythe's boss, but that did little to invoke a steady trust regarding the big man.

"I sort of heard that last remark," said Alex, making as quick a beeline for Sophie as his situation would allow.

"You got rabbit ears?" said Sophie, her voice cracking slightly.

Alex grabbed her with his right arm and hugged her the way people do when they mean it.

"I wasn't married to him, but I'm missing the heck out him too. He was a great friend, the most awesome geek, and a hell of a CSI. If you'll help me get through this, I'll do my best to do the same for you," said Alex quietly.

Sophie fought the next wave of tears, choosing to nod rather than answer Alex.

"I'm sorry I missed the funeral because of this damned surgery," said Alex, still hanging on tightly.

"I know," whispered Sophie. "I got all forty texts even after we talked. It's okay. I understand, Dough Boy."

Alex grinned through his own tears and held her away from him. "Glad to hear that, and you can call me Dough Boy for another few days; then it's on. Got it?"

Sophie nodded, her own smile on display.

Josh stepped in and embraced Sophie next. "I'll be here if you need me, okay?"

"Yeah, just remember that. I might need a man soon."

Josh laughed.

Sophie's grin grew.

Manny knew that sometimes healing started when the one who needed to heal gave permission. Sophie had. The road would be long, but she'd given at least partial permission.

It was a damn good start.

In turn, Barb, Alex's model-like wife, Chloe, and even Ian, who seemed to sense the gravity of the moment, gave Sophie hugs. The big man came last. She hadn't been keen on Braxton after he'd tried to have Manny killed. Nevertheless,

Braxton moved toward her and engulfed her in a true bear hug. He whispered something to her, she whispered back, then he stepped away.

Manny turned toward Josh, his instincts on full alert.

"Why is he here? In fact, why are all of you here?"

Josh raised his eyebrows, releasing a sigh. "Because we wanted to see Sophie. And bad shit never stops coming."

"What does that mean?" asked Manny.

"I'd like to hear what that means too," said Sophie, crossing her arms. "How can we have any more bad crap than we've just had?"

Looking from Manny to Sophie, then back to Manny, his bright eyes never wavering, Josh answered them.

"It means I need your help."

"We're done. We quit after Miami," said Manny.

"I know. I know. Just hear me out."

"No," said Manny, feeling his anger rise. Not just at the idea of Josh being here and asking for help, but also because it seemed disrespectful to Dean, one of Josh's own.

"I'm out. I told you. Sophie will do what she wants, but I'm done. No more psycho bastards for me."

"I'm with him," said Sophie. "I love you, Josh. But kiss my ass on that request."

Josh shifted his feet, his voice rising higher. "Even if that psycho bastard wants to destroy your family and your way of life?"

# CHAPTER-3

"What does that mean?" asked Manny, trying to smack down the dread that wouldn't quite take the beating and rose again.

"Come inside. Let's talk, okay? This situation needs to be discussed around a table," answered Josh.

"This is fine. It won't take long to tell you 'no' again," Manny said, slowly shaking his head. "I'm not doing this anymore. I have higher priorities than chasing down serial killers, watching the body count rise, and then having those dead people talk to me in my sleep. Let someone else do it."

"I get that, but what I said is true. This situation affects all of us, everywhere. Besides, who understands insane minds like you?"

Manny glanced at Sophie, who was watching him closely, then to Alex, who was holding his new arm with the other hand, staring at his black loafers.

"True? Damn, Josh. We've been friends for a while, and we've seen junk as a team that most people shouldn't. But I don't feel a lot of trust right now, no matter how dramatic your statements are. You didn't tell Sophie why you didn't make Dean's funeral until it was almost over. You wouldn't say where Alex was after we contacted the hospital to find out he'd been moved."

The more he spoke, the more the heat rose from his gut to his neck. He fought and got control of his emotion, if only to stay civil.

Josh rubbed his face with both hands. "Manny. I-I couldn't tell you everything. Not at that time. But—"

"That's not what I want to hear. If you couldn't tell me everything then, why should I believe you will in the future?"

"Because it's me, Josh Corner, your friend. And teammate. I've never lied to you. Never," answered Josh, getting pissy in his own right.

*Good, now we're getting somewhere.*

"How do I know that? The thing about lies is that you don't always find out about them. Isn't that right?"

"You know what your problem is, Williams? You think the world revolves around you. You think you're the only one with issues or pain or friends who hurt. I've got a few of my own. You think Connie and the boys are in love with what I do?

"Hell, you even think you've got the damned answers for everything. But you don't. You're smart but pretty damned self-centered sometimes, especially now, and that clouds your judgment."

"My judgment? You're the one who didn't tell us everything, did you?" Manny moved closer to Josh. "There's only one reason to keep secrets. You didn't trust us. You're just another freaking bureaucrat."

Josh's face evolved into a nice shade of red as he clenched his fists.

"Really? That's what you think of me? Fine. This has been coming for a long time. This bureaucrat is going to kick your ass."

With that, Josh began his rush toward Manny, fist drawn and spitting fire.

Manny felt Sophie move close and then waited, hoping he'd guessed right.

He had.

His former boss never made it to him.

Braxton had moved away from Chloe and Barb, reached out a long arm that looked more like a telephone pole, and grasped the neck of Josh's shirt.

"That's enough, mon. Do ya not see what's goin' on here?"

"Yeah, but I'm still going to kick his ass."

Josh's body rose, his feet dangling just above the ground.

"Naw, you ain't. You just might get hurt. Take it easy. Be happy."

It took a few seconds, but Josh regained his composure and then motioned for Braxton to set him down, his eyes still fixed on Manny.

After Braxton released him, Josh settled his feet on the grass, but the tense silence swirled around the yard like a cold Michigan breeze for minutes before anyone spoke.

"Are you two done? Or are you going to take out your weenies and compare them too?" asked Chloe, still holding a drowsy Ian.

"He'd get his ass kicked there too," said Josh.

The booming, infectious laugh of Braxton Smythe chased away the last bit of stress and made it impossible not to join him. Manny, and the rest of his extended family, laughed out loud. Even Sophie let loose some.

"Okay. Okay. Now come and sit down on the deck and talk with us. I'll explain everything, like I said I would," said Josh, taking charge and using that gift to its utmost.

"Fair enough. But no guarantees," said Manny, exhaling.

"I'm putting Ian to bed. So don't start without me," said Chloe.

"I won't let them," said Barb.

"Wait a second," Manny said before Chloe headed inside. He looked at Barb then Chloe. "Do you two know what this is about?"

"Let's just say I have a clue. Profiler here, remember?" said Chloe.

She was right. Sometimes he forgot where his wife had come from in her professional life and how good at profiling she'd been.

"I'm sorry. You're right."

"As usual. But it makes me hot when you apologize."

Then she disappeared into the house.

"She's got you down pat, Williams," said Sophie.

Barb nodded. "I'd say that's right."

"Yeah, well, it seems everyone does these days," Manny answered.

"Transparency is good," said Alex.

"Sometimes." Manny walked to the deck, trying to keep what was coming next at bay. Only that was like stopping waves from rushing to a Carolina shore. Especially for men like him.

He reached the deck and began to put chairs around the large glass table.

The part of him who was the Guardian of the Universe, as his daughter Jen had put it those years ago, wanted to know what Josh was about to say. It had been so ingrained in him to serve and help others that there was no denying the part of him that wanted to help.

Yet another part of him didn't want to know and couldn't care less about what people were doing to one another. People could be good to one another, but mostly, they weren't.

He ran his hand through his hair.

Yet, who could ignore something that could affect one's family as drastically as Josh had implied? There was also another factor, the one that caused him the most unease. He'd never known Josh to be a drama queen. That fact alone meant he had little choice but to at least listen to his former boss.

Five minutes after Chloe had returned, the seven of them sat around the deck table, each with a tall, frosty glass of iced tea.

Josh exhaled. "Here we go."

"Wait," said Sophie.

She got up, pulled an eighth chair up to the table, between Manny and her, and placed her cell phone gently on the seat. Dean's picture, smiling through his thick beard while wearing a red paisley cap, pointed in her direction.

Chloe's hand closed on top of Manny's. Like the rest of them, she was fighting hard to keep her eyes dry.

Sophie's steady gaze moved around the table, finally resting with Manny.

"I don't care much what you think of this, and I'm not nuts. I'm just not ready to give him up. If you can't handle Dean Mikus being at the table, now's the time to move your ass. Any questions?"

"Just one," said Josh softly.

Sophie tilted her head. "And?"

"Can we finally get him to dress so that his clothes don't hurt my eyes?"

She snickered, regained her composure, and then sighed. "That train has left the station, but I'll see what I can do."

Alex, sitting on her right, reached out his hand. Sophie took it. Manny reached across Dean's chair and took her other, squeezed it, and pulled away, turning toward Josh and Braxton.

"Let's hear what you have to say before I say no. I need to get on with my throwing-star lessons."

"Fair enough," said Josh, glancing in Braxton's direction, then over to Alex and Barb before focusing on Manny.

Manny noticed the interaction between the three of them, again.

"Why do you keep looking at Alex and Barb? And Alex, why do you keep looking like a puppy who just got his butt chewed for eating a pair of slippers?"

"I'll answer both questions. Alex knows what's going on and still can't quite believe it," said Josh.

"Thanks, Josh," said Alex. "But neither I nor Barb need anyone to speak for us. I'm already involved in this situation almost by proxy, you might say. And I'm feeling a little weird that I couldn't say anything until now."

"What situation?"

"Let Josh finish, Manny. You need to hear him out," said Barb, brushing her platinum-blond hair from her face.

Manny gazed at Barb. On the surface, and to most people, her body language gave away nothing more than a concerned wife. But there was more going on with her. Much more.

She'd always been sharp and had been in and around their cases more and more over the years. This time she seemed to almost, well, be involved, and she carried herself as if she were.

"All right, Barb. I'll hear him out. Then I have a couple of questions for you."

Her white smile didn't reflect humor as much as expectancy. "Of course you do. And I'll answer them."

"Deal."

He leaned in Josh's direction. "Okay, Josh, let's hear it."

Josh nodded. "Manny, I know why you left the BAU. I know you've hit the wall with psychos who do what they do for some godforsaken motivation that makes no sense to anyone but them, and maybe people like you. I get that. Profilers like you see them for what they are. People like me don't always. We just help fix it."

Several faces of serial killers they'd caught, and some of their victims, passed though Manny's mind's eye. He wondered if the silent, internal shivers might have given him away. Just in case, he blocked any more trips down memory lane and answered Josh. "True so far. And have I mentioned that I'm done with that?"

Josh folded his hands on the table. "You have. But what if I told you we could have an impact on saving lives that makes the BAU look like a session of *Romper Room*?"

"You know what *Romper Room* is?" asked Sophie.

Manny noticed that she'd leaned forward, elbows on the table. He'd subconsciously done the same.

"I do. My boys like it, or did," said Josh. "We liked being called good doobies."

"We can talk about sixties kids' shows later. Explain yourself," said Manny.

"I, we, want you both to join us—Braxton, myself, Alex, and two others—to form a very special unit. We've finally got the money we needed from a Congressional subcommittee that's bent on stopping some very bad people from doing what they live to do. Terrorists, to be exact. We need you to help get that done. Both of you."

*We need your help.*

Were there words that carried more of a dichotomy for him? Especially after Dean's death.

His thoughts moved a mile a second as the full intent of Josh's plea came into vivid focus.

Josh, his good friend, wanted Manny and Sophie to go from the frying pan into the fire then all of the way into hell itself. Doing what he'd swore not to do again and breaking the self-imposed vow he'd tattooed on his heart.

He reached for his hair, but Sophie caught his hand. "You have to answer this without the hand-through-the-hair crutch."

"Do I now?" he said, taking in the sparkle in her eyes.

"Yep."

"Okay then."

He pointed toward Josh then dropped his hand. "For the record, and just to get this right, you want Sophie and me to help profile terrorists?"

"This unit is and will be much more than that, but that's a good start. We'll be information gatherers and sifters too. We'll have access to assets and resources you only read about. You can impact thousands more lives than ever working as a cop or FBI special agent in the BAU. This will have deep meaning on a whole different scale."

Manny frowned, the conflict rising in him. "Oh, that's better. Not just the everyday, run-of-the-mill nutcase with a self-appointed agenda. But you want us to profile and catch the psychos with a delusional mission to destroy the United States and commit high-profile crimes against whomever they choose?"

"That's oversimplifying, but yes."

Manny laughed. Then shook his head in disbelief. "Are you out of your damned mind? Why would I want to do that?"

Braxton shifted in his chair; the joints and hinges groaned.

"Manny. Do you remember da first time you and me met?" asked Braxton.

"Of course. I should have listened to my instincts and shot your ass then."

The big man laughed loudly. "I taut you were gonna try, even wit dat Desert Eagle staring you in da face. But ya saw something on dis pretty face that stopped any shooting. Ya told me it was about da micro expressions dat I couldn't control so well. Ya knew me and what I was in a few seconds. No one does dat stuff better den you, Williams. Ya have da gift and dis new unit needs dat. Sophie's instincts makes us just dat much better. Dat's why you want to do dis."

"Great speech, but I have a family that needs the old man to stay alive and sane, I might add. No thanks."

Sophie stood, picking up her phone. She held it tightly in her hand, searching the others before she spoke.

"I totally get why he wants to stay out. Hell, he's got more to lose than most of us. And I don't have any death wish or some shit like that. But what else am I going to do? Sit around Lansing or go back to San Francisco and pretend what I've seen over the years doesn't exist? Particularly knowing that the ramifications of terrorism is far worse? I can't do that. So, I'm in."

She then bent over and kissed Manny on the cheek. "I'm going to take Dean out for a walk so we can talk. I'll be back in a while so we can get in some more practice time."

She left the deck and headed for the front of the house via the side yard. Sampson, Manny's huge black Lab, who had been sleeping in the shade, got up and walked beside her, touching her leg with every step until they both disappeared around the corner. Manny knew the dog sensed she needed him to walk with her and was willing to do what he could to help her lose the pain. People would do well to be like dogs, at least in that area.

Smart boy.

Looking at Chloe, he thought about Jen and Ian, and how he'd been looking forward to being a dad, a stay-at-home dad, before he went into something else. Something far calmer and less dangerous, like teaching or writing. Maybe cut that CD he'd always wanted to make.

Chasing down terrorists, as noble as that sounded to his Guardian of the Universe persona, wasn't what he had in mind. It wasn't even in the top one hundred choices of things to do. Not for him. Not for Chloe and especially not for Jen and Ian.

Josh was sincere. Braxton was aboard. Sophie and Alex had said yes. Somehow—he wasn't sure quite how it worked yet—but he suspected Barb was involved as well. That was a fine team.

Running a million scenarios through his mind, he focused on the pros and cons, and there were plenty of them. And part of him wanted to help . . . but, in the end, a man has to take care of his family.

"I'm sorry, but no. I'm out. Getting into the heads of psychopaths is one thing, but psychopath terrorists isn't my idea of fun. I want to have a normal family life. As much as possible at least."

Braxton began to speak, but Chloe raised her hand. She then turned toward her husband.

"Manny. I love that you want to stay home with us. I really do. But you can do so much to make this world a better place."

Her green eyes bore into his very soul, reading his every thought. Damn, he loved this woman. But she was making him uneasy.

"Let someone else do it, Chloe. Belle Simmons has talent. She'd do a fine job."

"True, but it's more complicated than that."

He frowned. "How so?"

Then his pulse quickened as he guessed the answer.

She took his hand, her eyes as alive as he could ever recall.

"Because, darlin', I'm already on the team."

# CHAPTER-4

"I'm tired of this shit. Get me?" she said.

"Yeah well, who isn't? You ain't the Lone Ranger when it comes to this assignment."

Detective Amy Brooks shook her head, absently wishing she would have cut her dark hair shorter last week. Sometimes, like now, it stuck to her forehead and face in the sweltering, humid weather offered by the fine state of Louisiana.

Her husband said she looked better, "hotter," with her hair a little longer. That was nice, and what girl didn't want to hear that from her husband? Besides, it had been a small concession to make in light of the other problems they were having. It was one less thing to build on a budding tension in their marriage.

No one had told her how hard it was to kcep a six-year marriage together, especially for cops. Cops who married ex-cons.

"I get that Phil," she said. "But this is the third one this week."

Phillip Fuqua, her three-year partner with the New Orleans Police Department, was a smallish man with graying, wavy hair and deep-brown eyes that accented his thin face. The deep voice that was all his didn't speak to his size and, at times, still made her smile at its dichotomy to his physical appearance.

"Hey, this is part of what we signed up for, you know that, right?" he answered, just a tinge of his Southern accent noticeable.

"Of course, I do. We all do. But knocking on a family's door to tell them that their kid is down in the morgue waiting to be identified wasn't supposed to happen this often."

Phil got out of the passenger side of the car and waited for Amy as she exited and walked over to his side of the unmarked Ford sedan. They leaned against the door beside one another.

"I know you saw a thing or two in Detroit that must have been worse than this. You told me about a few of them," he said.

"Yeah, I did."

"Then what's the problem?"

The young man's face emerged in her mind's eye, covered in blood and staring into a world she could only imagine existed, just after he'd died begging her to help him. Another damnable image contributing to her unceasing cycle of insomnia.

"The problem is that this boy was still breathing when we got there, and we couldn't do a damn thing to help him," she said quietly.

Phil stared at his well-polished shoes, adjusted his checkered tie, and then stood straight, still looking down as he spoke to her.

"I'm hearin' you. But that saying about 'the past is the past' applies here. We just need to do our job, okay?"

She could tell he didn't like this anymore than she did, but he was right.

"Okay, let's go," she said.

They walked up to the rundown duplex on Dumaine Street and stepped up on the cement stoop together. She knocked on the door. After a few seconds, an older black woman dressed in a worn, flowered smock answered the door, a toddler cradled in her left arm. She glanced at Phil, then rested her expectant gaze on Amy.

"What did dat boy do dis time?" she asked in a tired voice.

"Is this the home of Ronald Parrish?"

"It is. I asked y'all a question."

"Ma'am, he didn't do anything. We're here to ask you to come with us."

"Do what? Why?"

Truth dawned on her face as she shifted the child to her other arm.

People responded in dozens of ways to the news of a loved one's death. Shock. Anger.

Disbelief, and even expectancy, like Amy was seeing now.

"Oh God in Heaven. He's dead, ain't he?"

"There was a young man found near Canal early this morning and—"

"Y'all leave me alone."

The door slammed, leaving both of them staring at dirty, red wood.

Amy knocked three more times with no response. Her frustration welled up from somewhere deep. She just wanted to be done with this, to get on with the day. To be a damn detective instead of part of a death-notice squad.

She raised her fist one more time. Phil grabbed it.

"C'mon, Amy. We did our job. We've seen this here thing before. She'll call the morgue when she's ready," he said, more of his Creole upbringing seeping into his words.

"Okay. But I'm driving."

After placing her card and the number to the New Orleans Coroner's Office inside the doorjamb, she and Phil moved back to the car.

Once back in the vehicle, she started the engine, turned up the air conditioner, then reached for the gearshift. She stopped and then slammed the steering wheel three times.

"Just once I'd like someone to explain, with some kind of rational logic, why these young people are offing each other like this. Just once."

Then she shifted into gear, heading south toward I-10.

They drove in silence for a time, which Amy appreciated. He understood her question was rhetorical, but it didn't mean she didn't want an answer, even if it would never make sense completely.

She stopped for the traffic light and sighed.

"Are you better? I thought those green eyes were going to burst out your head," said Phil.

"Not really, but that helped. And my eyes aren't going anywhere."

"Good. We've got—"

Her cell phone rang, interrupting Phil.

She glanced at the screen mounted on her dash and frowned, sharing that frown with Phil with a quick side glance.

"What the hell does she want?"

"Who?"

"The captain."

Phil shrugged. "Maybe she wants to take you out for gumbo and biscuits being that y'all are so tight and everything," he deadpanned.

"Smartass. That woman we left probably just called to complain about something we did or didn't do."

"Answer it, and we'll find out."

Her stomach clenched ever so slightly at the prospect of speaking with Captain Rebecca Ellis. Just what she needed after leaving that house.

The gray-haired witch had a reputation for being a hard-ass, but that statement only broke the surface. Amy had never met a more miserable, angry woman who needed a man, at least for a night, than the captain.

"Okay. I'll do it."

She fingered the Bluetooth button on her steering wheel.

"Detective Brooks."

"About damn time, Brooks. Don't let that phone ring when I'm calling you; answer it."

"Yes, Captain. What can I do for you?"

"You can't do shit for me, Brooks. It's what I can, or have, to do for you."

Amy's angst rose. "Are you going to suspend me for that incident in the Quarter? I was just doing my job. That asshole grabbed my ass and . . ."

"Stop, Brooks. It ain't about your grab-ass complaint or anything to do with your average performance as a detective. Although I'd bust your ass on principle if there was anyone better to do your job."

"Thanks for the encouragement, Captain. Why are you calling?"

"I'll ask the questions."

"Okay, Captain. Then ask them. I've got work to do."

There was brief silence, and when Captain Ellis spoke again, much of the harshness had left her demeanor.

"Brooks, when was the last time you talked to your husband?"

Amy's mind raced as her instincts banged into high gear.

"Why?"

"Just answer the question."

"I talked to him yesterday afternoon. He had a double-shift all-nighter to work at the club where he bounces. I'm going to ask again. Why?"

She swore she heard Ellis exhale. "You know about the homicides last night in the warehouse on the south side?"

*Shit. Where is this going?*

"Of course. It was a drug or gang thing, right?"

"We're not sure. It might have been much more."

"What does that have to do with my Daryl?" Amy asked.

"That's a great question that you can help me to answer."

"I don't get it."

*But you are getting it, aren't you?*

"Damn, Detective. I'm trying to be tactful here, but you ain't making it easy."

"Suppose you explain what I'm not getting," she said softly.

The light turned green. Amy ignored it, fighting to catch her breath. The wait for Captain Ellis's answer seemed like an eternity.

"Okay. That works for me. I need you to come in and explain to me why we found your husband's body in that warehouse."

# CHAPTER-5

Haley Rose Franson watched her daughter lean in closer to her husband, closer than she probably realized.

Love was most certainly blind, and Chloe was deeply in love. Gone, as they say. She had found the kind of love that would take her to hell and back if it became necessary.

Despite her own bout with melancholy over the last few weeks, Haley Rose smiled. She understood how that heart condition worked, for she'd felt it herself once upon a time. There was nothing like it.

Folding her arms over her ample chest, she wondered if the world would be a better place if everyone could share in that feeling, could know that deep pool of passion.

Heartbreak would come to some, but the chance to love and be loved so true remained pure, powerful, and, in the end, incorruptible.

Chloe had found that true love, and not only in Manny, but in her son Ian.

Haley Rose understood that as well. Ian had become the most important man in *her* life, at least for now.

She focused on her daughter and son-in-law as the conversation among the seven people seated on the wooden deck intensified.

A moment later, Chloe touched Manny's hand and then said something that made Manny's handsome face go from calm to quizzical.

He wasn't angry or shocked, as if he'd already processed those emotions, but went right to why. She'd seen a few people like him in her fifty-six years, especially guests at the inn in Galway, but none who could process information and then read someone like a fortune-teller in a gypsy circus as Manny did.

Leaning closer to Chloe, he appeared to ask her a question, those blue eyes of his looking deep into her soul, it seemed to Haley Rose. Manny Williams could be unnerving at times. Now was one of those occasions.

If he really put his mind to it, he could almost feel someone's thoughts. Alex had always told Manny that his ability to do that came from a subconscious ability to notice detail—nothing more. She wasn't so sure.

Her stomach twisted at the thought of not being able to hide her deepest thoughts from him. She hadn't minded at first; her life and intentions had mostly been an open book. But lately . . . lately her thoughts needed to be hers alone.

Movement on the deck brought her out of her own world and into the present.

Manny had risen from his chair, kissed Chloe, then Sophie, nodded to Josh and the others, then turned on his heels and walked directly toward the house, toward Haley Rose. She seemed to be the intense object of his attention.

But why her? Did he know something? Had he seen her secret place? Or was she just paranoid?

Before she could think another anxious thought, the sliding glass door opened, the late spring air and Manny entering at the same time.

He moved close beside her, watching her. She held her ground, fighting the urge to step back from him.

No doubt he noticed her almost-flinch, of course, and responded by standing still, glancing at her, then his hands, then back to her. They sized each other up a moment longer, then he gave her a small taste of that magical smile.

Her heart was moved by that expression. It caused her uncertainty to depart as quickly as it had come. How could anyone fear a man with his nature, except maybe those on the wrong end of his abject sense of justice? She'd seen that up close regarding Doctor Fredrick Argyle. Yet this time it wasn't about profiling another person. Somehow she knew this moment wasn't about her, but about him. Manny Williams wanted to talk to her.

Maybe Chloe came by some of that profiling thing naturally.

"Haley Rose. Do you have a minute to talk?"

"Aye, I do. Ya look like ya need one, man."

"Is it that obvious?" he asked, tilting his head.

"Yeah, even to an old woman like myself. At least as obvious as ya get."

"Old woman, huh? I think you've got a few years before we go the old-woman route."

"Ahh. As kind as ever, you are."

Manny leaned against the inside wall. "I need some advice."

"If this is about this new unit Chloe told me about, I don't know what wisdom I could impart to ya, lad, but I'll try."

"It is, and you'll do just fine," he said, sighing. "All of my adult life I've tried to do the right thing. To be a good husband. To be a good father. To be the cop I should be and try to protect the people that come across my path."

"And not many have done it better. Good men are a rare thing, Manny Williams. Too bad Chloe saw ya before her mum had the chance at ya," she said.

He laughed, then grew serious. "Thank you for that. But I just don't feel like that man. I've seen too many people I love die to think I'm a good cop. I lost Lexi and Liz on that damned cruise ship. I lost Louise to a psycho in my own home. My daughter watched her die in our arms. I almost lost Alex in San Juan. We lost Max Tucker in North Carolina."

She started to speak, but he raised his hand and stopped her. "Let me finish."

She nodded.

He bowed his head, his voice growing softer. "I couldn't protect Gavin Crosby, his wife Stella, and his son from one another. There were like family to me."

His voice was now a little more than a whisper. "Then I let Sophie down by letting that sick punk in Miami take out the only real love she's ever had. That doesn't add up to a résumé the Guardian of the Universe would be proud to own."

"I'm stopping ya right there. Your thoughts ain't on the right track here. What of the hundreds of people you've saved, Manny? What would have happened if ya had not used that gift of yours? Are those others not as important as the loves in your life?"

"They are. And I've considered what you're saying a thousand times or more. Yet in the end, I'm as selfish as the next person who simply wants to live a life that watches my family grow and my friends laugh, and to take joy in all of it. I want to be here every Christmas morning. I want to walk Jen down the aisle. I want to take Ian to his first Tigers baseball game."

His eyes had once again focused on her face.

"I want to grow old with Chloe and breathe my last with her holding my hand. All of those things I want to experience, and it needs to be free from the haunting minds of the evil men and women who seem to dominate this screwed-up planet."

"So ya think stayin' out of the game, like you're fond of sayin', will accomplish that? Ya think ya can hide under a basket and none of that evil will ever get in?"

"I—"

She touched his mouth with her finger. "My turn to finish, Manny Williams. The answer is no. Because if most of the world can't ignore it, how will the likes of *you*? You hate the injustice of what's wrong in the world like no one man I've met."

She reached for his hand. "We get to decide who we are, mostly, but no one gets to truly pick *what* they are, Manny. Ya told me once that a person's passion, no matter what that is, can't land far from their soul's heart. That we're wired the way we are for a purpose. God's purpose, if ya want to go down that road. Was that a lie, lad?"

Reaching for her, he gave her a hug that most women would die for. It was the kind that said "thank you" with an emotion that was difficult to put into words. The meaning wasn't diminished, however.

He released her and moved toward the door, his hand resting on the handle.

"Yeah, I said that and I meant it."

"So?"

"So I've already decided what I need to do."

"And?"

He laughed out loud. "Now I know where Chloe, and Jen, for that matter, get their got-to-know attitudes."

"We stick together, don't ya know."

"Glad to hear that. Because I'm going to need you to help me."

"If I can."

"You can. I'm in. I have to be. Not just because my beautiful wife is involved, but because it's the right thing to do, no matter what I feel from time to time. Helping to save lives, if I can, is why I'm on this rock."

"Of course ya are, and it's the right call. Even this old Irish lass can see that one."

"Wise is a better word than old. Far better, especially for you."

"Thank ya, Manny."

She watched him run his free hand through his blond hair and waited.

"Haley Rose. This new unit will take Chloe and me away from time to time, and at some inopportune moments, I suspect. I need to know that Ian and Jen are taken care of."

"What does that mean?"

"It means I'm asking you to stay here and watch them. And if, God forbid, the worst thing happens, and Chloe and I don't come home, that Ian will have someone he can count on. That Jen will have her Granny, no matter what else goes on."

Haley Rose exhaled. She'd been ready to go back to Ireland, to find a life that was hers, to shake off the last couple of years that had been filled with new joys and incredible disappointments and heartbreaks.

She'd wanted to rid herself of the deceased Gavin Crosby's rugged face when she opened her eyes each morning and leave behind the thoughts of "could have been." She wanted to abolish the image of her insane ex-lover dying at the hands of Jen Williams when she pulled that trigger that saved her, and Ian, and Haley Rose from the murder Preston had in his heart, and the guilt that went with putting them in that situation.

To find the answers that were hers to locate and actually possess the peace that would finally rule her life. And, yes, to reconcile her bizarre relationship with Fredrick Argyle, whose words and actions still haunted her in more ways than she wanted to admit. But was that her destiny now, if there was such a damned thing?

"Haley Rose?" asked Manny, searching her face.

"Yeah, I'm here, boy. I was just thinking how I had to follow my own advice if I expected ya to listen to me."

"Life can slap you around that way."

Manny bent down and kissed her on the forehead.

"Listen. I know you've been through your own version of hell lately. You wanted to go back to Ireland after Jen's prom, but hung around for another damned funeral, which I imagine brought another issue or two closer to the surface," he said, his voice as smooth as an Irish whistle.

"I also know what it's like to blame yourself, or at least to be confused regarding someone else's actions. I'm here to tell you that you can't control anyone's actions but your own. No guilt, no what-could-have-beens, no condemnation. Life is life, and even though I'm struggling with *my own* advice, I know what I'm saying is true."

"Knowing is one thing," she answered.

"Yep, it is. But it's ninety percent of the battle." His smile broke loose again. "So are ya in with the rest of us broken folk, lass?" he asked in his best Irish lilt.

She had no choice but to grin back at him. "Yeah, I suppose I am, pieces and all. For a while anyway."

"Fair enough."

The door slid open, and Josh hurried inside.

"I'm sorry if I'm interrupting, but two things have come up rather quickly."

"What would those be?" asked Manny, more at peace than Haley Rose had seen him in a few weeks.

"Well, I have to pee. So that takes immediate precedence," said Josh. His cobalt-blue eyes twinkling.

"The other?"

"Well, it seems there's a problem in New Orleans, and this unit is heading there in the morning."

"So?" asked Manny.

"So. Are you coming?"

"I'll answer that," said Haley Rose, stopping Manny's response with a hand to his arm.

Josh frowned, looked at Manny then at her, and waited for her to speak.

Running the conversation with Manny through her mind one last time, as if the idea of it gave her more strength, Haley Rose Franson then took her hand from Manny's arm and placed it on Josh's,

*Right is right, is it not?*

"Well, Josh Corner, where else would the Guardian of the Universe be?"

Then, after kissing Manny on the cheek, she sauntered down the hall to check on Ian, feeling better than she had in months.

# CHAPTER-6

Manny stood near the metal door leading to the tarmac at Lansing's Capital City Airport, holding his overnight bag in one hand, coffee in the other.

It was only seven thirty a.m., but the Michigan sun was already struggling to add its special brand of light to the day. Fine by him. He loved the old saying that light overcame the darkness so that people could see what fear had hidden.

He smiled. Maybe that was his old saying. At any rate, working in the light made for a better day if for no other reason than because people could see what and who they were up against.

He sipped his coffee, taking in the aroma of vanilla bean and coffee.

The funny thing about people who embraced their twisted, evil side, if that was a truism, is that they preferred the dark. He could write a book on how that psychology had played out in his life and with his line of work.

Two books.

"What the hell are you doing here so early?"

He didn't turn around. He didn't have to. "Me? What are *you* doing here at this time of the day? You should have stayed in bed longer. You may not get much beauty sleep for a while."

Sophie looped her arm through his and nudged him with her shoulder.

"Yeah? Well, maybe I don't need as much as some of us."

He laughed, dropping his bag and putting his hand on hers. She wasn't anywhere near her old self, but there were small fissures breaking through her immense grief.

"What are you saying?"

"I think she's saying you aren't getting any younger and need more rest than you used to."

Josh circled his right side followed by Alex and Barb. Braxton Smythe was a few paces behind them.

It seemed like they had just left each other after a five-hour briefing session last night. They had put the final pieces together for forming the new Alpha Counter Terrorism Unit, of which he was now a card-carrying member.

While the work would be intense and could be far more dangerous than working with the BAU, it was good to be part of a team that could make a difference on a far larger scale. Despite how quickly and even crazily this whole thing had come together, he felt he was ready.

There wouldn't be any Argyle types, per se. He suspected the people they would try to stop would be far worse. That sent a mental chill down his spine. But, because of that truth, he was in.

The new ID in his pocket and the upgraded 9mm Glock 34 in his shoulder holster helped to seal the deal, but nothing galvanized his commitment like the people around him. Even the almost-unknowable Braxton Smythe had passed his profiling scrutiny.

During their prep and briefing get-together the evening before, Manny had gotten the rest of his concerns off his chest regarding trusting the big man. The conversation and emotion had grown tense, more than once, but when the dust had cleared, Manny's mind and intuition were in a better place regarding Braxton. Still.

"Hey, I heard when you get older you don't need that much sleep, so I'm good to go," answered Manny, gesturing toward Josh.

"That's a good thing, because you won't be getting as much either," said Barb.

"I was just going to say that," said Sophie.

"Great. Wisdom from you this early in the morning," said Alex.

Sophie stepped away from Manny, looped two fingers beneath the leather strap on the sling holding Alex's left arm, and brought his face close to hers.

"Listen, Dough Boy, if I want anything out of your helpless ass, I'll let you know, capisce?"

"Is that Chinese-speaking-Italian thing supposed to scare me, wench? And what do you mean helpless? You'll thank me when I find something in these databases that will save you and your fake rack. And don't call me Dough Boy. Capisce that?"

"Yeah, you'll be a ton of help with one hand. Hell, you couldn't work a keyboard with two."

"I don't need a keyboard. Voice-command software is through the roof these days. I'll be talking, and the databases will be listening. Besides, this sling comes off in a day or two. Now let go of me before I have to kick your ass."

Slowly, the smile spread across her pretty face. Then she kissed Alex on the cheek. "Good to have you back," she whispered.

Alex moved his mouth then turned his head, trying to hide the sudden attack of emotion. The forensic expert then cleared his throat. "Ditto, girl, ditto," he said gently. "Now get away from me before somebody thinks I really care what you think."

"Yes sir, Dough Boy."

"I see you two are going to be just fine," said Josh. He then glanced around the terminal area. "Where's Chloe?"

"She'll be here in a minute. She wanted a muffin and to make one more call to her mom," said Manny.

"Understandable," said Barb as she moved closer to her husband.

Manny watched Barb, revisiting her part in all of this. He hadn't really wondered why, over the years, Alex's wife was gone to visit relatives so often, especially given that Alex was busy working cases with him. But to be a member of the CIA doing undercover work hadn't even remotely entered his thought process. Never mind how deeply she'd been involved in a couple of covert operations with Braxton that bordered on Jason Bourne territory.

"Why, Agent Williams, you seem to be staring," said Barb, grinning.

"Sorry about that, Barb. I've had enough time to process the information about your other life, and I'm still trying to reconcile that with my ego."

"Join the club with that one," said Alex.

"Well, it's out there now, and I'm personally glad. Like I shared last night, at times it's been a rough road. I wanted to tell Alex a thousand times, and God knows, I was always on guard that you would see something in me that would give away my secret," said Barb, with a nod toward Manny.

"I saw nothing, so you did your job," he said.

"I did my best. But that phase of this operation is over. Getting necessary things done will be much easier being part of a team. And a team I trust."

"I think you're right," said Manny, hoping the team environment was going to be what it should. People like Braxton and Barb, who had worked on their own for years, sometimes had difficulty assimilating into a group.

Just then, Chloe walked up beside Manny, rolling her suitcase.

"What did I miss?"

"Nothing. Is everything all right? I mean, you left home a whole hour ago," said Josh.

"Things are fine, don't ya know, smartass. And for the record, I'll be callin' home any damn time I feel like it," said Chloe, a glint in her eye.

"That's the spirit," said Josh. "And I know you will. Okay. Now that we're here, I want to go over a couple of things again before the jet arrives. We need to understand each other's roles so we have each other's butts."

The feeling was noticeable and a bit odd, even with his experience, but Manny could swear the six others of the ACTU moved closer together in that one moment in time. Not just physically— that was obvious—but inexplicably more in tune mentally.

Maybe there was some truth in what Alex had claimed. Maybe he did process micro expressions along with body language like a computer, but there was no denying what he felt, whether that was scientifically measurable or something else entirely.

"Alex and Chloe will set up the data center. Chloe helping with the profiling as needed. Barb will help them with the hardware configurations and then help with accessing our Counter Terrorism Division and the National Strategy for Counterterrorism databases. Most of what we need is already on the jet, but there isn't anything we can't get if we need it, so don't be shy."

"Damn. Nothing like carte blanche for a geek in techno land," said Sophie.

"Oh hell yes," answered Alex.

"You won't get to use rubber gloves though."

"Some things are more important than others," he said. "Dean would have loved this."

There was an ever-so-slightly awkward silence as, in sync, the team glanced at Sophie. She abolished that demon before it took hold.

"Yes, he would have, even without the gloves. I'll tell him about it tonight when we talk," said Sophie, her voice steady.

Josh nodded to her. "He'll appreciate that." He turned back to the huddle. "Remember what I said about having a bit of expertise within each sub-team. Chloe will help with insight to domestic terrorist profiles on that end, and Barb will provide and research information on particular methods of finance and less-than-ethical sources of materials these creeps might need."

Josh made the organization of the new unit sound so complete. And for all intents and purposes it was, but there was something . . .

Manny then dismissed the thought. What could be missing at this juncture?

The FBI's new Gulfstream G650 then hit the runway behind them, speeding past the window like a white bullet as it headed to the west end of the runway.

"Dat belongs to us?" asked Braxton.

"We'll get to use it," said Josh.

"It's pretty dang shiny," said Alex, grinning.

"I like shiny," said Manny.

"Me too," said Chloe.

"Yeah? Wait until you see the inside," said Josh. "Soon. But let's stay on task for a few more minutes. The next part of the organizational setup is this: Manny, Sophie, and Braxton will be involved in profiling. We'll need to start piecing together the reasons why New Orleans is the place where . . . this incident occurred."

Manny watched as Josh finished. "We don't really know what that means, Josh. You keep saying all of the right things, but you're not really telling us anything about what happened in New Orleans, other than a husband of a New Orleans detective was killed in questionable circumstances with five other people in a warehouse."

"That's all true," said Josh.

"I know this must be a case for us, but tell me why?"

"I think you know why. But I'll make it easy for you. It's because of the circumstances surrounding the killing. Six people killed in an off-the-beaten-path warehouse is a spike on our radar."

"I get that. Why aren't we getting files on what happened?"

"I told them to keep their information until we get there. I don't want to taint any of your thought progressions when you're doing what you do—that goes for everyone, but especially you, Manny. When we get all of the names and background checks in, we'll discuss the particulars. Trust me on this one, Manny. I know what I'm doing."

Manny started to speak, but Braxton interrupted him. "Let me say someting here."

Josh raised his eyebrows and gestured for him to go ahead.

"If dese people were dealing in illegal shit, and it looks like it to me, den we have to figure out what. We don't know dat part for sure, so we need to be clean wit what we see from da beginning."

"So if we have a preconceived idea of what's going on, we won't be looking at everything equally? Is that it?" asked Manny.

"Yeah, dat covers it. Sometimes ya have to make sure ya don't miss nuttin, so start from da beginning. Dis profiling be a bit different dan da psychos you tracked down wit da BAU. Dey be better at dere trade. Dey have to be."

"That part is true," said Chloe. "They are unpredictable at best."

"We won't miss anything," said Manny, glancing around the circle of agents and friends. He felt his pulse step up at the confidence he heard in his own voice.

Any doubts about accepting the next chapter in his life were now gone. Maybe everything that he'd gone through over the last four years was a base for this. *Destiny doesn't give itself away until it's time to do it.* Manny knew that one.

"We can't afford to," said Josh. "Remember what I said. New Orleans may be nothing, or it could be everything. That's why we're going there first."

"Crime scenes are crime scenes, right?" said Sophie.

"They are," said Josh.

Together, they watched the jet taxi to the section of tarmac in front of the window in silence. A few seconds later, the airport's runway crew moved the mobile stairway to the gleaming hatch of the jet.

Josh looked at the group. "Are we ready?"

"Hell yes. Let's get this show on the road. I took my motion-sickness pill, so I'm right as rain," said Sophie. "And they better have good food. I'm hungry."

She picked up her bag and headed for the terminal door, each of the others following suit, Manny and Josh bringing up the rear.

"Are we, Josh? Are we ready?" Manny asked.

"We'd better be. I keep saying it, but we have to get it into their heads. If New Orleans is a precursor for something else, we'd better find out in a hurry. This stuff, this next part of our professional lives, isn't like the last."

"Argyle was nothing?"

"He was a baby compared to what these people are capable of doing." Then Josh walked ahead of Manny and entered the jet.

Baby, huh? He felt the confidence he'd claimed a few minutes before waver. People like Argyle were a far cry from harmless. Just ask the families of his victims. He boarded the jet, praying it wasn't true, but deep down he knew Josh was right.

# CHAPTER-7

Belle Simmons leaned back in her leather chair, hand rubbing her knee, staring out the window of her office in Quantico, wondering what the hell she'd got herself into.

She had always been good at what she did. Profiling, analyzing, and the rest of detective procedures had come easy for her. That was a huge reason why Josh Corner had hired her to work with the new BAU. And so far, that had been a heck of an experience. Especially getting the opportunity to see how Manny Williams did what he did, up close.

That old saying that nothing teaches like experience was invaluable regarding Manny's methods.

None of that experience, however, qualified her, at least in her way of thinking, to lead a BAU. Sure, she'd run a department of detectives in DC and understood the politics of leadership. But the BAU?

"Oh, and you had to say yes, didn't you, Belle Simmons?" she whispered. Now that the moment of excitement had died down, she realized what was ahead of her.

Turning back to her desk, she found the mirror in her top drawer and gazed at the ebony face that many said reminded them of Whitney Houston. "Damn, if I could sing like that, I'd be out of here," she said out loud.

Or would she? As overwhelming as her overall situation was, she wouldn't give up the triumphant feeling that electrified her from head to toe when they caught the bad guys. There couldn't be *anything* like that, ever.

Her phone began playing a Motown hit by Stevie Wonder, and she immediately knew it was Josh.

*About time, boy.*

"Hey."

"Hey yourself, Belle. How's it going?"

"I can't believe you asked that. It's total chaos. I have so many questions about re-staffing, payroll, benefits, and how to get new music piped into this place."

He laughed. "That's good. And I'll answer as many as I can. You'll have to get together with IT for the music thing. They'll like your choices, I'm sure."

There was a brief pause as she realized the pleasantries were over. Just like that.

"Belle, right now, there's only one thing I need you to do for me."

"Just one? You sure about that?"

"Yes, well . . . no, two things. You have to get your staff hired. You can't do anything without that being done. And you can't wait."

"Yeah, you told me that before. I heard you then too. I'm working on it," she answered, glancing at the stack of application files on the corner of her desk.

"Good. The load is easier to handle when you have help and share it."

She sighed. "That's true. I've interviewed six."

"Any luck?"

"Well, there hasn't been any Mannys in the group, but I like a few of them."

"There's not a lot of those out there."

"I'll take someone in the same ballpark."

Belle waited for Josh to answer. He didn't. Then she knew why.

"What's up, Josh? What do you need?"

She envisioned him smiling when he said, "That's why you were the right person to lead the BAU, Belle. I'll get to it. I'm going to send you two names, and I want you to do deep background checks."

"All phone records. All financial information, including deposits, withdrawals, paychecks, investments, and retirement accounts. All passport records, and domestic travel info as well. Any public records, right down to parking tickets and favorite restaurants. Hell, I want to know the size of their underwear and where they bought them."

"Why don't you have your new people do—" She stopped then switched the phone to other hand. "Oh. You don't want them to know that you're digging into these people, do you?"

"That's correct. I don't. You have all of the clearance levels you need. I want to particularly know what the NSA and CIA databases might show, including the secret and top-secret email servers too. There should also be information from the Sensitive Compartmental Information servers."

Belle exhaled. "I have access to the SCI?"

"You do. It's on the last few pages of the manual I gave you."

"I haven't gotten that far. I've been busy."

"I know. But before you do any more interviews, I'd like files on these two."

"C'mon, Josh. I've got a shitload of stuff to do here. We may already have our first case brewing in Los Angeles."

"I get it. I do. But this is more important."

"To who?"

"To all of us."

She raised her hand in surrender. "Okay. Okay. Who are they?"

Her phone pinged. Josh had sent her an email.

"There they are. Let me know when you get what I need. And remember. This is between us."

"Got it."

He hung up.

She then thumbed open the email attachment.

Her eyes grew wide, and she almost dropped her phone while she read the two names on the screen.

Re-gripping her phone, she looked again, then began to shake her head. "What the hell is this?" she whispered. "Why them?"

Five minutes later, Belle rose from her chair, went to the safe, and pulled out the thick, heavy procedural manual Josh had given her and sat down at her desk.

He'd said this job wouldn't be easy and she would do some things that didn't exactly fit inside her moral compass, but in the end, they had to protect the people of this country.

Any and all that they did and would do was to protect the greater good of all Americans. This task didn't seem to fall in line with that exactly. She also knew that not everything done behind a closed door was necessarily wrong.

Belle rolled her leather chair closer to her desk, logged into the first top-secret database on Josh's list, and went to work.

# CHAPTER-8

Manny stepped into the main cabin of the 650, did a slow half-turn and whistled. The jet was more than he expected. The craftsmanship and coordinated modern décor was beautiful, yet it rang of professionalism. There was also no doubt that the cabin was filled with all of the tools Josh had mentioned, and more.

On the far left of the compartment, a bank of four computers with twenty-five-inch screens were positioned for use individually or in networked tandem with each other, depending on the purpose of the operators. That arrangement gave a unique view of multitasking at its finest. Alex was going to be in heaven.

As was his usual mindset, Manny himself didn't care all that much for technology, though he realized the usefulness of it. Yet, even he could envision a little fun playing with this display of new-world investigations.

That wasn't all the jet offered.

On the back wall of the first passenger compartment was a sixty-inch, interactive, voice-activated LED screen system that would be used for posting questions and thoughts regarding any current case without the cumbersome process of writing on a dry-erase board. Perfect for brainstorming.

According to Josh, all anyone with proper clearance had to do was speak to the computer and it would post what was said, driven by the most advanced voice-recognition software on the planet. The clearance was set up before they took to the skies, allowing each member of the ACTU to use that feature right away.

He stepped in farther and shook his head slowly. This machine wasn't done showing off.

The ten separate foldout bunks were strategically spaced around the cabin, and as far as he could tell, were situated with the finest mattresses known to mankind. There was also a full kitchen armed with two Keurigs, a regular coffee brewer, a double microwave, and a fully stocked refrigerator. He wondered if the fine taxpayers of this nation realized they had financed something resembling the Bat plane.

"Damn, Corner. You outdid yourself this time. This even has that new-car smell," said Sophie as she sat in one of the beige leather seats around the conference table, wiggling for effect.

"Spared no expense, like I said. They want us sharp and rested when we do what we do," answered Josh.

"Mission accomplished," said Alex.

Manny took Chloe's bag and tossed both his and hers in the spacious locker area at the far end of the cabin. As he worked his way back, he hesitated and listened.

The excitement in each voice was obvious, but he felt it went far deeper than enthusiasm regarding the jet. It wasn't just the prospect of the new flying machine that would make any billionaire green with envy. There was something pulsating between all of them that flowed with a more subtle feel, especially in Josh's tone.

Manny understood.

No matter what the dark side of human nature had shown them over the years, and that had been plenty, the prospect of kicking psycho ass and taking names later held a draw that defied explanation for people like them. Like him.

Recalling part of the conversation he and Haley Rose had shared, he was reminded again that sometimes it was a good thing to embrace how God made you and use it. That seemed right, for now, for him.

"Before we take off, I want everyone to get settled around the table for a few minutes," said Josh. "We didn't really talk about all of the data sources and specifics last night."

"I thought you were pretty comprehensive," said Chloe, settling in beside Manny. "I think thirteen searchable federal and private databases is far better than the six we had five years ago."

"That's true. I was biased on what I had time to share. But there's always more. We've got some new feeds that include imaging and some hot-spot websites that send quick notifications to our alert analysts at HQ when those sites are accessed."

"You mean like who accesses the FBI or CIA sites, for instance?" asked Manny.

"Yes. But I want to concentrate on the six people we found in the warehouse first and any known associates, and yes, even Detective Brooks. Like I said, we'll get that info when we need it. The other thing this unit can't ignore is the general public, when people access info on how to make a nuke or some kind of dirty bomb or even chemical warfare. Hell, we even have to pay attention to who becomes interested in infamous domestic terrorists."

"Really? There's a site for that stuff?" asked Alex.

"Damn boy. Get with the program. There's a site for everything," said Sophie.

"No denying that," said Josh.

Josh turned back to Manny. "I know you didn't go straight to sleep last night after we left your house. You never do."

Chloe reached over and kissed Manny. "No, I can vouch that he didn't, don't you know."

The group's loud laugh was led by Braxton and good to hear, even though it was at Manny's expense, sort of.

"Ahh. We can leave that part out, Chloe," said Manny.

"I see. Is it because it makes those cheeks blush a wee bit?" she teased, that electric look in her green eyes as bright as ever.

He shrugged. "Maybe. But I doubt that's what we all want to discuss right now."

"True, but maybe over a girls-only lunch," said Barb.

"I have to admit, I'd like to be invited to that one," said Josh, grinning. "But let's see if I was right regarding our job and what Manny did, ahh, later in the night."

"Deal. I'm guilty as charged. I just wanted to become familiar with what domestic terrorism is and who does it and why and how access to some of those databases will help us."

"Keep it going, Williams," said Sophie.

"How about you keep it going? Like you said, we did talk a few times last night," said Manny.

"Yeah well, I'm not sleeping a ton these days. Okay, I will. When we met as a group yesterday, Josh said, about fifty times, that we need to find out if the murders in Louisiana really mean something is going down soon against our government or if this was some kind of revenge shooting or some other dumb-shit thing."

"Dumb-shit thing? Good terminology," said Alex.

"You know what I mean, heifer. Anyway, I decided to profile shootings like this in a few of the criminal databases that Josh mentioned. Including the CIA's, especially their Information Operations Center Intel, the FBI's, and even the Office of Homeland Security's."

Manny smiled on the inside as Sophie took another long draw from her coffee. The death of her husband was on the back burner for the moment. Her concentration on the beginning of this new unit was a suitable diversion. More than suitable. Negative emotion, any negative emotion, reaches a critical limit before it begins to exact its toll on one's sanity. Sophie was getting a reprieve from those late-night thoughts and tears. He'd walked that mile and knew how good it was to move away from them.

"What did you find?" asked Barb.

"Just what Josh has said and the reason Manny has his underwear in a little bit of a bunch. Circumstances like those usually meant a product deal gone south. Like drugs or arms deals. A couple of times, they were gang related."

"She did better in matching those up than I did. She's way ahead of me in the cyber arena," said Manny.

"Don't forget it either," said Sophie.

"Like you'd let him," said Alex. "But keep going, Manny. The fog is starting to lift for me."

"I ain't going to touch that one," said Sophie.

"Bite me."

"Oh, that's never going to happen, so let Manny finish. Then you can get your doughy ass to work."

Alex bit his lip and then pointed to Manny. "Do continue. I'll straighten this wench out later."

"Thank you both. Not much to finish, in my mind. The murders dictate an unusual set of circumstances and fit into what we should be checking into. But I still don't like the idea of not having files to read on our victims."

Just then, the co-pilot, a tall woman with bright, brown eyes and an angular face emerged from the cockpit.

"We'll be taking off in about six minutes, so please get yourselves ready," she said.

"Will do," said Josh.

She nodded and then returned to the front of the jet.

"You heard the woman, Williams," said Josh, turning in his direction.

"Shouldn't take that long."

"Sophie and I ransacked the FBI's Investigative Data Warehouse, and the CIA's IOC, for more history. Whether or not this is a case for us, I wanted to understand more on how our targets communicate."

"That makes sense," said Josh. "Please share."

Manny scanned the group slowly, capturing everyone's undivided attention.

*Time to do what we do.*

"Here's the question: if you wanted to keep what you were planning to do away from anyone except your own people, how would you communicate?"

"Obviously not cell phones or email. Too easily traced and hacked," said Josh.

"Not even the burner phones are immune to that kind of search," said Sophie.

"True. Particularly given the FBI's software development. So for the sake of this conversation, let's eliminate those two possibilities," said Manny.

"Snail mail. But that's slow and not effective for immediate communication, specifically when the shite begins to hit the fan," said Chloe.

Manny nodded. "I wouldn't use that as a primary source either."

"What about go-betweens?" asked Barb "It would be safe, and only the people involved in any plan would have knowledge of what's going to happen. Maybe a bit slow, but a plane can get from one end of this country to the other in four to five hours. Not totally efficient, but it would work. I've seen it."

"The trouble with that is airport security checkpoints and cameras. If I were trying to stay invisible and my profile low, that could be an issue. I wouldn't risk it."

"Good point," said Barb.

The others had looks of concentration on their faces. All except Braxton, who had remained silent for most of the last fifteen minutes. He was wearing that cockeyed smile that reminded Manny of the first time they'd met in Puerto Rico.

"Braxton? Do you have a thought?"

"We tried all of dis stuff when I worked for dat drug lord, Fogerty. None of dat was foolproof, so we didn't really try to fight it, mon."

"What does that mean?"

Then, in the blink of an eye, he understood where Braxton was going.

"Wait. You hid in plain sight."

"We did dat."

"How in the hell did you do that?" asked Sophie.

"I tink Agent Williams can explain it."

"I'll try. I read a DEA report on how they brought down one of the Columbian cartels."

"Good God, I can't believe some of the crap you read," said Sophie, shaking her head.

"Oh it's true," said Chloe. "I'd be snoring in five."

"Hey, you never know what might come in handy," he said. "At any rate, the cartels were feeling the pressure from every Caribbean government as well as the United States on their backs. But the folks feeling the most pressure were the government officials and high-ranking cops on the take. As investigations grew more intense, those people knew they were in deep."

"Dat is good so far, Agent. Keep after it," said Braxton, his smile wider than before.

"The problem was that no one could find a communication method between the officials suspected of being dirty and the cartel contacts. It wasn't like they were talking via email. No evidence means no case."

"That would have been stupid. It would have only taken a few hours to bust their asses doing that," said Alex.

"True. But as the suspect list grew, there was an increased communication pattern among those thought to be on the take."

"Okay, but those suspects still weren't talking about drug trafficking, right?" asked Sophie.

"They weren't. The emails looked innocent enough, especially if they were asking about budgets or tourism, or if they were condemning the drug trade," said Manny.

"Code?" asked Josh looking at Braxton.

"Let da good mon finish. He be hittin' a homer so far."

"Yes. It was code. Each time one official on the bribe would mention a certain cartel by name, the other official knew there was a shipment coming in or in the process of being planned, or even that the heat was coming and to lie low for a while," said Manny. "The system was complex, but they all had it down pat."

"What brought them down?" asked Barb.

"What usually does. The investigation got closer and led to one of the high-ranking Mexican officials wanting to make a deal with his government and our own DEA."

"Bravo, Agent. Dat's exactly what Fogerty relied on, right till de end," said Braxton.

"How does that work here?" asked Alex.

"That's why we're talking. That's the sixty-four-thousand-dollar question. We first have to find out what's going on in New Orleans. If this is something designed to go to the next step as a terrorist act, we need to know how that communication was handled," said Manny.

"People do things differently, but in the end, they have to talk," said Sophie. "We've figured that out."

He ran his hand through his hair, staring at the table. Sophie was right about people doing things differently.

His thoughts leaped from one terrorist extreme to another. People doing, at least on the outside, what they think is right, supposedly. Idealism to the point of violence was never what it seemed. He didn't buy the "doing right" thing so much. These people were all driven by one purpose. If he'd learned anything as a profiler, he knew that.

"Listen. Part of the profile of anyone wanting to hurt another in anyway is driven by some internalized ideal. But in the end, the emotional reason for inflicting pain is to be able to feel better about themselves and balance out the universe and some preconceived wrong."

"You're talking revenge, right?" said Sophie.

"As always. We've seen it. In the end, the reason for acting out is not some pie-in-the-sky ideal to make the world a better place or some crap like that, but a need to feel vindicated. That's true with psychopaths like Argyle all the way to people like Timothy McVeigh. Revenge. Period."

"Where are you going with this?" asked Josh.

Manny leaned both hands on the table. "Listen, if you want to make a statement, don't you want to do something no one else has done?"

"Damn. So you think that's the key? Finding a lead that points to some awful thing that's never been done before?" asked Josh.

"I do. You can't ignore the other intel we have regarding other possible attacks on our soil, and I think we'll know more when we get to the crime scene, but, yeah, that fits."

"That could be a thousand things," said Sophie.

"It could. The profiling in this situation is not so different though. We have to think like these people think," answered Manny.

"Where do we start?" asked Barb.

"I know that one. We have to get in touch with our dark side, right?" asked Sophie.

"I'm afraid so. You have to dig deep and put yourself in the shoes of these people. What motivates them. The 'how' and the 'where' that best satisfies their revenge. Who they talk to and associate with. Whatever else we can come up with."

Barb tapped a pen on the table. "You mean what setting?"

"Yes. That too. Think. What kind of person wants so badly to kill and exact revenge that they would do almost anything to pull it off?" Manny leaned back in his chair. "Josh asked me to pull together some basic stuff on who that looks like, so I did."

"Let me guess; you've done your first terrorism profile," said Alex.

"I'll answer that one," said Josh.

The new boss of the ACTU reached into his briefcase and pulled out a stack of blue folders stamped TOP SECRET ACTU.

"*You* were a busy man last night, darlin'," said Chloe.

Manny smiled. "I can multitask."

"Aye, ya can."

"Remember, these are guesses and, in my case, feelings too. I had to guard against what I would do and stay neutral with my input. That was difficult."

"Just no escaping *your* dark side, huh?" said Sophie.

"No, but I've always known that. Read what I wrote and let's see what we can see."

At that moment, the jet's engines revved and buckle-up signs illuminated. Manny walked around the table, sat beside Chloe, and buckled his seatbelt.

The jet raced down the asphalt runway, and then they were airborne, banking west before straightening toward the south.

As they settled into their flight pattern, Manny couldn't keep the sense of urgency away from his thoughts.

Deep down, he realized New Orleans and the murders in the warehouse were only a beginning, but of what?

# CHAPTER-9

He watched with more than a casual interest as the woman stepped out on the front stoop of her small, modest ranch on the west side of the city. She looked down in apparent reflection, then raised her head to look toward the rising sun to the east of the New Orleans skyline. She folded her arms over her chest, her right hand slowly moving over her upper arm. There wasn't a sign of joy in any of the woman's body language. Why would there be?

Stepping down, she hesitated and then leaned toward the red azaleas, seeming to inhale their sweet scent.

"She's trying to figure out if she is upset or relieved. Then she's working at sorting out the guilt that pulls at her for even contemplating any relief at all," he said, turning toward the woman seated in the passenger seat.

"Who can blame her? She thought she married a good man. Most women live in that illusion. But truth is a freeing bewilderment to many. It was to us."

Her pale-blue eyes sparkled as she shifted to face him more directly.

The woman beside him believed deeply in her ideals. On how life should be, and her devotion to that core belief was remarkable. It lived in her luminous gaze.

Naïve. Idyllic. And perhaps outright nonsensical at times, but her dedication was what indeed had brought them together.

The two had met through that secret-of-secrets Internet arena, and the subsequent joining had been most opportune, there was no denying that. Her ability to accurately fire almost any handheld weapon, and with a complete willingness to do it at any time and toward anyone, all in the name of justice, was almost surreal. Her gift had been enormously beneficial to *him* and *his* cause. Never mind her extraordinary lack of inhibition in the sack.

Bonuses come in all forms.

"You are correct, my dear Lucretia, as usual. Any truth that rips away the chains of limitation is worth embracing."

He patted her on the leg.

She smiled.

"I don't think I can stand it if you touch me again. You'll start something I'll have to finish right here in the morning light. Right here in this car."

"Well, that would be a first since high school. But I believe we should stay on task and take that tantalizing suggestion to the hotel."

She shrugged. "You are right, lover, but the possibilities in here are, well, endless."

"They are always endless with a beautiful lady such as yourself." He looked back at the woman standing in front of her home. "Staying on task, what should we do? I abhor senseless violence, as you well know, but is she a loose end that could lead to our discovery?" he asked.

"Well, *mon ami,* looking at her body language, I would say she is far more concerned with her own state of mind than anything else," said Lucretia.

"I would agree. I don't see fear, only some emotional confusion. Yet, Amy Brooks is a cop, a New Orleans detective. She and her late husband will be the subject of a very intensive investigation and interrogation, particularly when our deceased friends in the warehouse are fully identified.

"Her finances, her work habits and routine, and most importantly, her cyber world will be of great interest to the authorities. Depending how careful her husband was or wasn't, we might be in danger of having our true mission discovered," he said.

As was her style, she said nothing while processing what he'd said. Her mind worked toward a problem-solving solution as quickly as anyone he'd met. Fortunately for him, her sociopathic personality usually led to the same identical conclusion each time. He'd never told her to kill anyone, only led her down the path.

"We can't risk them cruising into that area of her husband's life. It will not take but a moment, lover. I shall return shortly."

She bent close to him, kissed him on the cheek while grabbing his manhood, squeezing.

Laughing, she then opened the car door. "Better pull around the corner."

She then began a leisurely walk toward the New Orleans detective.

# CHAPTER-10

"Alex? Are you getting this?" asked Manny.

There was a momentary silence then the slight buzz in his ear transformed.

"Yes sir. Don't you just love these multidirectional cameras? I push a joy stick and they respond like a Rolls Royce on steroids."

"You like playing with sticks, right?" said Sophie.

"What? I thought we muted your mic and turned your Asian ass off."

"Nope. Just keep playing with your stick. We're going to need all of this on video."

"Don't worry about me. Just earn your paycheck. I've got this video and imaging thing down to a tee. Even from the comfort of my leather chair in the jet."

"We needed a hack job in there, so, hey, we found something you could do. Now stop bothering me. I have to talk to Manny."

"What about? Another boob job? Alex out for now."

Sophie's voice rose a tad. "What? These babies are big enough, and don't forget about paybacks, Dough Boy. Just keep working on those names and database info with your little stick. I gotta go."

"Manny? Oh wait, I see you."

Manny turned, grinning despite their circumstances. To see Sophie high-stepping in his direction, the dust on the dank warehouse floor swirling in tiny puffs at her heels, was a welcomed sight.

She was in a hurry, making a beeline of sorts in his direction, but careful not to step across the yellow plastic tape displaying the New Orleans Police notification that they were near the crime scene and not to enter.

He looked again at the tape and the outline of the bodies.

It had been a while since he'd seen this much blood in one small area, even as a member of the BAU. Come to think of it, he wasn't sure he'd ever seen this much in one place.

The white chalk designating the six body positions hadn't been able to contain the deep-burgundy stains that had a mind of their own and crawled away from the victims in eccentric, desperate patterns. Throw in a scattering of body and brain tissue, their eclectic locations specifically numbered with red placards, and this site looked more like a setup for a Halloween horror house than anything spawned from the real world.

"Well, we're back in the saddle," said Sophie, stopping by his side.

"That's one's way to put it. I don't recall this kind of ranch before though."

"Me either, but that's why we do this, just to see something new. Anyway, I need to have your blond butt come with me for a minute."

"Lead on."

Sophie turned away from him and walked the thirty feet or so to the old, wooden desk, he on her heels. She stopped on the left side and pointed for him to go to the right side of the desk. "Okay, I know we finally saw the reports and pictures and some of the forensic stuff before we got here, including that little area under the desk, but there ain't nothing like being here."

"That's why we made the trip, remember?"

"Yeah. Anyway, you always talk about starting from the beginning, so let's do it."

He nodded. "I'm listening."

"You've probably already figured most of this out, but let us short-bus kids catch up. I have to tell you that the people who killed those six, and I think there at least two, never intended to let them walk out of here."

*Good girl.*

"Why do you think that?"

"First, there was only one true entrance and exit to this part of the warehouse. The two side doors were nailed shut with new nails. That could be just for security for whatever shit was going down, but I don't think so."

"What else?"

"See how this desk is slanted toward the front entrance on about a thirty-degree angle? It gives a great view of the double doors and gave the shooter or shooters a perfect angle to shoot from."

"Could that have just been for protection? Whatever deal went down here, and there was a deal, that's certainly obvious now that we're here, may have had a need for some form of protection if things went south," said Manny.

"Yeah, I thought about that, but let me show you something else," said Sophie, stepping to the back side of the desk and getting down on her knees. She was careful to keep her hand off the fingerprint dust scattered on the desktop as she moved a foot under the desk.

Manny circled the desk and squatted behind her.

Sophie pointed to two small squares cut into the wood that had been fitted with the ability to slide open from the inside, at the front of the desk. "If you wanted to keep an eye on the people you were dealing with, I get it. By why two openings? One was enough. That wouldn't have been necessary unless you knew you were going to need them to get better angles with your weapon."

"Maybe, but maybe these people were just cautious and covering their bases."

She shook her head. "I don't buy that. Why hide anyone at all then? Why not just show them strength and make sure nothing happens? I think whoever killed these people wanted to surprise them and then take them out."

"Good thinking. I think so too. Come on out. There's a couple more things that might make us about ninety-nine-percent right on that theory."

Sophie scrambled out from the desk and stood by him just as Josh, Barb, and Braxton entered through the door. The three walked in their direction almost stride for stride.

Manny wasn't sure what was going on now, but knew he was about to find out.

"What do you think?" asked Josh.

"We were just about to put the finishing touch on the first part of our theory," said Manny, scrutinizing Josh's face.

Braxton laughed out loud. A big belly laugh that had almost become his trademark.

"What was that for?" asked Barb.

"Because da man knows dere be something else going on here besides dese murders."

"Why would you say that?" asked Josh.

"Because there *is* something, and you're going to tell us," said Manny.

Sighing, Josh gave a wry grin. "Still can't hide much from you. I do have something, but let's hear what you've found."

"Deal on both parts."

Manny explained what Sophie had surmised and that he agreed. "But there's more. Come with us to where the bodies are outlined, then we need to go back to the desk."

The group reached the place where the killings had taken place and fanned out in a semi-circle, anticipation written on their faces. Stepping a foot inside the group, he then looked at Sophie.

"Pull your weapon like you mean it and target someone standing on the other side of the desk."

"Do I shoot?" she said, eyes sparkling.

"We'll save the bullets, but pretend you're at the OK Corral and Doc Holliday is about to meet his maker." Then he stared at his watch.

"Awesome."

She reached inside her jacket and did what Manny had asked, whipping out her Glock as fast as she could.

"By my calculations, that took about one and a half seconds. Sophie is fast, so I say it would take most people in the neighborhood of two to three seconds to pull their weapon and aim it from here. Throw in how hard it can be to hit a target in a stressful situation, I'd say the killers had about five seconds to do what they did."

"How many killers?" asked Josh.

"Two."

"The NOPD thinks it was at least three, maybe four."

"No. Just two. Let me finish, and I'll prove it."

Josh raised his hands in surrender. "By all means."

Manny nodded. "The crime-scene photos showed, and the reports verified, that the victims had each been shot only once. That means six shots that hit home.

"Since there were no bullets lodged in the wall by the door or bullet holes leading through the wall, we have to assume that there were only six shots fired in this direction. We already know, based on the NOPD's report, that the victims all had weapons on them, with the exception of one. The big man right over there didn't have one on his person," he said, pointing at one of the outlines on the floor.

"The Smith and Wesson .45 found on the floor near his body probably belonged to him, indicating he was at least trying to fire his weapon before he was killed. But the fact that none of the victims' guns had been discharged means they weren't expecting or weren't ready for what happened to them."

"So you tink dat means dey were surprised," said Braxton.

"I do. If there had been a shootout, so to speak, we'd see physical evidence on both walls and the bodies, or at least some of them would probably have had more than one wound."

"The fact that there were only two types of slugs found on the victims strengthens Manny's theory," said Sophie.

"Our theory," said Manny.

"Yeah, I guess ours. Anyway, the fact that only six shots were fired and, none at close range because of the lack of GSR on any of the victims, also says something for the type of shooters involved here."

"You mean dey be damn good shots?" asked Braxton.

"That's what I mean," said Sophie. "Anyone who hits someone at thirty feet away square in the noggin with one round is good. Anyone who hits multiple targets at that distance is someone you don't want to piss off. They've got their shit together, with their guns at least."

"Ex-military?" asked Josh.

Manny shrugged. "Maybe. But there are plenty of good shooters who never had formal training. There are a couple of other things that might zero in on that possibility, however."

"Like what?" asked Barb.

Sophie pointed to the desk. "Underneath the desk, located on the wide panel facing where we're standing, are two small panels that can only be opened from behind and underneath the desk. It's crude, but I think it worked as a form of camouflage designed to keep one of the shooters concealed until the time was right and also a way to shoot from more than one angle."

"Or maybe even if it was necessary to start shooting. Sort of a security measure," said Manny. "But I get the impression that these two meant to kill this group from the beginning."

"Why?" asked Josh.

"I think whatever was going on here, whatever deal was being made, the killers wanted no loose ends. Whoever these victims really were, including the cop's husband, I'm betting they weren't here selling Girl Scout cookies. The fewer people who knew what was going on, the better. The perps who shot these people were damn good with a gun, a handgun to boot, and loaded with reasons not to let anyone leave with knowledge of what went down."

Braxton released a long exhale. "Dis is feelin' worse all da time. Someting is shitty here. We need to know dese people and why dey came to dis place."

Alex's voice rattled through their earpieces. "I can answer the 'who' for five of these people, including the cop's husband, so far. That is if Josh thinks it's time. We're still working on the last one, the woman. I gotta tell you, based on their profiles and arrest records, they weren't going to get any presents from Santa this year or until hell freezes over."

"Fire away," said Josh. "It can only help now that I've heard the latest theory."

"I will. The three big men had a history of working as hired muscle for various people and organizations. Two were from Germany originally, Klaus Richter and David Feighner. They became American citizens when they were children after their families relocated to Baton Rouge.

"Amy Brooks's husband, Daryl, and the other one, Robert Donald, were American born and raised. None of them were military, but each of them, except Daryl, had some association with organized crime on their records, at least on local levels. Three of the four were arrested for assault at least twice and did time for it more than once. Daryl Brooks was the exception, only going to the pen a single time."

There was a pause, then Alex continued. "Nothing really new there for these kinds of people, and I won't bore you with the other particulars. Here's what I want to tell you though.

"They were all at the Louisiana State Penitentiary in Angola at the same time and were released within months of each other. That was about six years ago. But what's *really* interesting is that all of them sort of dropped off the grid after their release, except Brooks. He married the New Orleans cop a year later and, by all appearances, tried to lead a normal life."

Manny's mind was running a mile a minute with the new info. But he kept the festival of questions at bay for the moment because he *really* needed what was coming next.

"Who's the other man?" he asked.

"Yeah, this guy is a piece of work. His name is Gerhardt Wanger, also German born. We don't have any DNA or anything in IFAIS for him but the facial recognition brought him up at ninety-six percent likely. This kind of thing fits his profile to a tee, to boot."

"He's had several aliases, but Wanger's his real name. Like the other two German nationals, he and his family, eight strong, came to the US when he was a kid and settled in the New Orleans area.

"Average kid with average life, though his IQ was high. His dad worked the boats and apparently his mother stayed home and took care of the kids. Not much on him after he graduated from high school, but over the last ten years, his list of suspected activities is long, yet he had no convictions. He's been as slippery as a snake."

"Like what activities?" asked Manny.

"Glad you asked. He's been involved in illegal interests since he was hatched, it seems. His biggest and most profitable mode of business is, er, was, weapons dealing. INTERPOL, DEA, ATF, and our own terrorist units knew of him but could never quite put him away."

"Damn, I hate guys like that," said Sophie.

"And there's more of them out there than you think," said Barb, shifting her feet.

"Then about five years ago, he fell completely off the map until today. Weird. These people don't just retire. But they do reinvent themselves from time to time."

Scanning the warehouse room, Manny was struck with something that this whole scene reeked of but wasn't evident until he looked back toward the desk and began moving that way.

"Alex. What sort of weapons? Does the file say anything about that?"

There was a brief silence then the earphone came alive.

"Not really. He was thought to have sold a shipment of around a hundred AKs stolen from a gun dealer in Kentucky and there are . . . whoa!"

"What?" said Manny.

"Here's one report that he was suspected of trying to move some modified mustard gas to a radical supremacist group in Wisconsin, but the ATF could never put a finger on him or the intended customers or the meeting place. Another one having to do with liquid explosives. Then the really scary report that says he was a suspect in a stolen cache of sarin from the CDC. But—"

"The nerve gas? Damn. Let me guess, they couldn't pin it on him," said Sophie.

"That's right. They couldn't even find him alone talk to him, until yesterday, that is."

"So this guy might have been dealing in some kind of chemical weapon?" asked Josh, his voice growing low.

Reaching the desk without responding, Manny studied the surface for a few seconds, then stepped back, running his hand through his hair. His pulse began to race as the whole reason for this meeting came to him in a heated rush; the telltale movie that his gift revealed inside his head was almost as vivid as the floor on which he stood.

"What are you staring at, Manny?" asked Sophie.

Manny looked back down at the desk and motioned for the others to come to him.

Once they'd gathered, he showed them the vague outline of a wide side of a ribbed metal briefcase nestled in the thin layer of dust on the desk's surface.

"Dat impression looks like da design of those metal cases we used to transport drugs and udder bad shit wit. And it ain't big enough for a box of AKs," said Braxton in a near whisper.

"No, it's not. Not at all. It could be that six bodies are the least of our worries," Manny said quietly.

# CHAPTER-11

Amy Brooks frowned, the way people do when they are trying to sort out the implacable facts from the unfathomable emotions to the real-life circumstances that, for the very near future, rule their lives. Not even the beautiful New Orleans sunrise could mitigate her anxiety.

Daryl was dead.

Her husband of five years, her friend, her lover, and her confidant was now on to the great mystery beyond this life, leaving her heart in an emotional lurch.

While it was true they hadn't exactly been on the same page over the last month or so, the situation was a far cry from divorce and an ocean away from wanting him dead.

Two oceans.

The fragrance of the red azaleas drew her down from the stoop; and she inhaled it gratefully. Stealing beauty from the realm of nature was always an appreciated reprieve, no matter how short the duration.

And there was more of that damned dread coming, wasn't there?

She'd known about Daryl's time in Angola. Of course. He'd been totally upfront on their first date. He'd explained how he ended up there in that shithole of a prison.

How the bar fight hadn't been his fault. How he'd been on the wagon and only came in to the bar and grill for its famous Southern-fried chicken dinner. He'd told her how the drunk cop had hit his own wife after blaming her for him falling on his ass. How Daryl had stood up to protect her and had been attacked. That he'd hit the cop, and the blue boy had bounced his ugly face off the floor, leaving blood and tissue in a large, scarlet pool.

Unfortunately for Darryl, the judge saw it the cop's way, and since Daryl had been arrested some ten years prior for a different kind of fight outside the Aloft hotel in downtown New Orleans, the justice saw fit to teach Daryl a lesson. A year later he was out of the Louisiana State Pen. All for being a good boy. But his visit had changed how he looked at life, mostly in a good way. Mostly.

She wouldn't have bothered checking out his story if he hadn't been, well, so damn charming, good looking, bright, and built like Hercules.

Amy crossed her arms again.

He'd told the truth, and she'd allowed herself to fall hopelessly in love with Daryl Brooks. They were married about six months after that and had been relatively happy. Until now.

The tears wanted to make another grand entrance but they stayed away this time. She didn't know how many she had left after soaking her pillow in a sleepless night.

The stay of relief from tears was good for now. Phil was on the way to pick her up and take her to headquarters for meetings with Internal Affairs, her captain, and whoever else wanted to take a shot at her, and Daryl.

Not to mention, the CSU would be out to the house when she was away to do what they do, including the complete implementation of new cyber procedures designed to catch child-porn scum, illegal financial hacking, and terrorists in the act of communicating via computer.

Good God. She'd never dreamed any of those situations might affect her or her husband. Yet here it was.

It was hard to ignore the fact that he had been found shot dead with five others in a warehouse, where she was pretty sure they weren't up to anything legal. She didn't know details yet, but she was a detective, for crying out loud. Besides, obvious was obvious.

But why? Why had Daryl been there? Why had he been with those people? Who were they?

Important questions, but not as important as the one burning in her soul.

Why had he risked it, taken the chance on not growing old together? What was she going to do?

Love was still love no matter what temporary bump in the road people were navigating.

She shook her head again, positive that dying hadn't been on *his* agenda either.

*Yeah, but your pain is over; mine isn't.*

Pondering that truth, she wondered if the Bible was right and that everyone had a chance to have Jesus wipe their tears away. She found some comfort in that idea and hoped so, because those rivulets of saline were going to do a return tour.

Not now, maybe not tomorrow, but they would return, as sure as Louisiana was hot.

Exhaling, she tried to clear her mind and prepare for the long day ahead. Cop-mode wasn't always a bad place to retreat to, and that precarious sanctuary was where she wanted to go. Now. Thinking about the logistics of any crime was always better than dwelling on the victims, especially this one.

Reaching up with both hands, she placed her hair behind her ears and walked toward the street in anticipation of Phil's arrival. As she did, she noticed a smallish woman with long, blond hair walking in her direction. She'd appeared out of nowhere.

Amy watched the blonde as she strode up the street directly at her. She wasn't walking on the sidewalk, like most people do, but on the road itself, hugging the curb, her eyes riveted on Amy.

Grief and pain can dull the senses—she knew that—but she was a cop. It only took her a split second to realize this woman was a predator, a dedicated hunter, and for some unknown reason, Amy was the prey.

She reached for her service weapon at her right hip, feeling her fingers wrap around the warm grip.

She was a fraction too late. The imp of a woman had already raised her own weapon, leveling it at her with an eerie quickness.

Diving to the ground, Amy heard the first shot come so close to her head that she swore she felt the heat of the bullet. She had no time to dwell on how good a shot the woman must be, almost hitting a moving target like that.

The second shot convinced her of the woman's ability. The bullet slammed into her shoulder, creating the blinding pain she'd only heard about.

She screamed.

The sudden sensation of warm blood running underneath her blouse was an unexpected and sobering rush; pain be damned, she hated how it felt rushing down her shoulder.

And the damn blouse was brand new.

*What the hell is going on here? Why is this woman shooting at me?*

In her semi-shocked state, she found herself oddly thinking how rude it was to take shots at someone on such a pretty morning.

The temporary shock gave way to the moment. The mingling of painful and fearful sensations cleared her head. That and the desire to survive sent waves of adrenaline surging through her body.

Somehow, she raised her Sig Sauer 226 and fired in the direction of her assailant. She fired again. She fired a third time, not really seeing, but counting on her heightened sense of direction . . . or her desperation. She thought she heard a moan, but it could have been her after she'd bit her lip.

Another round slammed into the ground close to her face. The gritty Louisiana dirt sprayed into her eyes like it had come from a desert sandstorm, causing her to yelp in agony.

The next one soared over her head. Barely. Amy tried to raise her weapon a second time, but the pain in her shoulder revealed a mote of stars. The gun dropped to the ground, a foot from her hand.

*This is it, woman. It's been fun. I'll see Daryl sooner than I thought I would.*

She steeled herself for the inevitable.

The sudden roar of an engine and the subsequent squeal of rubber skidding along the concrete to her left invaded her senses. It might have been the most wonderful thing her ears had ever heard.

Phil.

The car door slammed open, and she heard her partner yell for the woman to stop. He repeated himself, this time with more conviction. There came a quick report of gunfire from Phil's direction, followed quickly by a second. Then came a quick two-shot answer from the woman's direction and the sound of bullets hitting metal. Phil swore. Then silence.

Gathering all of her strength, doing her best to ignore the pain in her shoulder, she managed to struggle to a sitting position, expecting to see the woman hovering over her with a gun pointed at her head. But that wasn't what she saw. Instead, she caught a glimpse of her attacker running toward the corner and then onto the next cross street, before disappearing.

Relief flooded her emotions. She wasn't going to die this morning after all.

"Amy! Amy! Shit. You be all right, girl?"

Phil was down on one knee, his hand on her back, his other holding her arm.

"I-I think so. Other than having a hole in my shoulder."

"What the hell was that?" he asked.

"I don't rightly know."

Amy Brooks's world swirled from light to gray to black, and she felt herself fall into Phil's arms, embracing that darkness.

# CHAPTER-12

"Do you really think that a possible imprint of a briefcase on the desk means this Wanger asshole sold his buyer chemical agents?" asked Barb, her arms folded in what was now becoming a familiar pose. "I mean, that's a hell of a leap, Manny. Even for you."

Tilting his head toward Barb, he ran his deductions through his mind for about the millionth time, then answered her. "Yes, I do. Especially in light of the two imprints in the dust of cases showing up near Wanger's body. I'd bet those were money cases, or maybe even diamonds."

"Okay. That makes some sense. But tell me how, because this could be as simple as a drug deal gone south or some other illegal contraband worth a few dollars."

"That's a fair statement. Let me explain."

Sophie laughed, looking at Barb. "Just remember, you asked for it."

"I'll make it quick," said Manny.

"You'd better. If you're right, this could get ugly fast," said Josh.

"Listen. If it had been a gun deal or a drug deal or even something less serious than contraband, three things would have been different about this scene, besides the fact that there were three bags carrying something here."

He exhaled, sending the musty air away from him.

"One. There wouldn't have been six people here for something like that. I believe Wanger and his people had kept as low a profile as possible. Like Alex said, nothing for around five years on him. If anyone had spotted six people, far more visible than one or two, leaving a deserted warehouse, that may have led to a phone call to the police or, at the very minimum, cause the six to be remembered. That part is risky."

"I'll buy dat," said Braxton.

"Secondly. I've never seen drug dealers, gun buyers, or any part of an organized-crime group shoot like this. Never. Those scenes are typically riddled with bullet holes and shot damage that end up nowhere near the intended target. The expert marksmanship alone forces us to think in a different direction."

"You're making good points as usual," said Josh, "but don't you think there's at least a chance these killings were 'wrong place at the right time'? I mean, come on, Manny, these people were glorified thugs."

Manny shook his head. "No, I don't. These killers have a pointed logic. A very specific purpose. They are extremely specialized in their approach to, I'd say, everything. Details. Details. Details. The car they drive, the clothes they wear, maybe even the way they look, to an extent, is very normal and ordinary. I absolutely believe there was never going to be any chance of a loose tongue or unraveled end with these people.

"The minute Wanger said yes to this deal, he and his minions were going to die. That tells me the people who killed the six are careful and aggressive, willing to do whatever it takes to protect their one mission."

Manny felt his pulse rise a bit more, fed by the uneasy silence while his crew absorbed his logic. Verbalizing his profile convinced him about how right he was. And there was more to come.

Chloe's voice rose through his earpiece. "Manny, you said three things. Braxton and I have seen some of what you're talking about. What else?"

"It's simple. The killer and the partner, given the lack of mistakes, right down to leaving no traceable evidence, leads me to believe they are mission driven. That's obvious by their patterns and what drives them to be more than meticulous."

"That doesn't sound so simple," said Josh.

"Like I said, they are bright to accomplish what they did here and their planning for the situation proves it. Again, based on what we can see here, and my research of these kinds of people, I think they're very mission minded and would rather die than get caught.

Taking a step closer to his team, he paused before speaking again, making sure he was ready to say what he had to say.

*But I'm right about this last detail.*

"Listen, what clinches it for me is the fact that they showed up here, I believe, with what looks like a large sum of money or gems or whatever, that they never really were going to relinquish."

"Shit," said Sophie. "The trifecta you always talk about."

"Yes. These people have all of the components necessary to make a splash that can put this country on notice, if that's what they're up to. They are extremely motivated to control an outcome, whatever the reason. Plus, they are smart and have money," said Manny.

"I get your line of tinkin'," said Braxton.

"Good. There's one more thing that should scare the hell out of us."

"I'm already thinking about a change of underwear, so . . . what else?" asked Sophie.

"We don't have a clue, yet, as to who they are or what they want," said Manny.

Josh nodded. "Sophie's right about being afraid of what might be next. I'm there too. I also hate like hell what you just said. We really don't know these people. That fact leads me to the other thing we have to discuss."

"What would that be?" asked Manny.

"Well, I've already told Barb and Braxton and Chloe and Alex and they are aboard."

"Oh yeah, the last to know. Great," said Sophie.

"Get to it, Josh. We've got to get back to the jet and see what Alex has for us," said Manny.

His boss and friend raised his hands, palms up. "I hate to do this, but we're doing what we have to do. I'm splitting the ACTU into two teams."

# CHAPTER-13

Lucretia reached for the chrome handle of the Chevy, flinched in pain as she grabbed her side, then gingerly piled into the front seat.

"Is it done?" he asked. "I wasn't able to see after she went down."

"No. We need to leave, now."

She saw the mild surprise in his face. It reeked of disapproval. God in heaven, she hated that look and what it meant. She, for one, had endured enough of that scathing glower as a child growing up with an asshole father and overbearing mother. She didn't need it from him. Especially him.

For one brief, almost undetectable moment, she wanted to shoot him directly between those lovely dark eyes. Exactly as she had her own daddy dearest those years ago. Then her mother.

What would she do then? Whatever she wanted, she supposed, but in her own way, she loved this man, this Rhodes, and not having him near her would cause her more pain than the temporary satisfaction of blowing that infuriating expression from his face.

Another sharp pain ran up and down her side, returning her to the reality of the moment.

"We can talk about this now and be interrogated by the police or get the hell out of here and discuss what transpired while you take me to a hospital to see how badly I'm shot. Your choice," she said.

His eyes darted to her side, then back to her face, giving rise to an enchanting smile. "I see you didn't care for my reaction to the fact that the woman cop is still breathing. I think you are angry. Angry enough to hurt me?"

"Of course I am. You know me inside and out. The fact that you are still breathing means I love you more than myself. Do we stay or go?"

"I think we'll pursue the latter," he said.

Shifting the car into drive, he sped up the street, banked hard to the left, and a moment later entered the ramp leading to I-10 west toward the airport.

She watched as he glanced into the rearview mirror. He repeated that action a moment later.

"It appears we made it out of the neighborhood without a police escort."

"Good," she said.

Her voice sounded far away, even to her. She raised her hand to her face, fresh blood covering her hand, the coppery scent thick in the air.

"Does it hurt?"

She nodded. As she did, her eyes lost focus.

"What happened back there? Obviously you were shot, but how?"

Drawing in a fresh breath helped to clear her head. "She saw me coming, but that wouldn't have mattered if I hadn't stepped into a rut on the street. She dove, and I missed her with the first shot. I hit her with the second one, the shoulder I think, then she fired three at me. I was hit with the second one. I started after her, but what must have been her partner showed up, and I decided I didn't have enough focus to kill them both."

"So he saw you too?"

"I don't think so. I turned and ran first. Maybe, though."

She reached up with her other hand and pulled off the blond wig. "Even if he had, they saw a different shade of hair, not my true hair color."

"I see. Great thinking on your part, as always."

There was another rush of searing pain as she swore she felt the bullet move deeper into her side, touching her rib. She leaned her head back against the headrest, fighting the nausea and lightheadedness.

"I need a doctor, Mister Rhodes. I'm losing blood faster than that time in Miami," she whispered.

"I can see that. Fortunately, we have a friend in Luling who could patch you up."

"Good. Let's get there."

She leaned back into the seat, grateful for the man who looked out for her as she did for him.

They were a perfect team.

The intent for each of them, the true purpose for why they were alive, had only cemented the bond they had formed. New Orleans, and then the rest of world, would soon discover how true that bond was. It didn't hurt that their relationship was fulfilling in so many other ways. She even loved the sound of his smooth, deep voice. It gave her comfort and—

*"Fortunately, we have a friend in Luling who could patch you up."*

*Could* patch her up?

Her eyes flew open as she reached for the Beretta in her pocket.

*** 

Poor Lucretia. She'd made one mistake too many.

Despite his affection for her, no one could be allowed to endanger his true mission. Not to mention, her wound had taken away her sharpness. In fact, he might conclude, she wasn't sharp to get herself shot in the first place.

He watched her as he reached into his shirt pocket.

In a normal state of mind, she would have had her weapon resting uncomfortably in his right ear by now. But she wasn't herself. Throw in the murderous look she had tossed his way when she got into the car, and he could no longer assume the best from her. That fact, more than any other, would cost her.

Pity.

His companion's eyes flew open while her left hand searched her jacket pocket.

With the speed his previous training had honed, he thrust the blade deep into her neck and twisted.

Her eyes grew wider, then unhurriedly rolled up into her head. Her body convulsed twice before slumping into her seat.

"Goodbye, my love. You'll not be forgotten," he whispered.

# CHAPTER-14

Manny settled into the front passenger seat of the black SUV, getting his mind around the last few minutes and Josh's new twist on what was coming next for the ACTU. He couldn't help reflecting on an old idea that a house divided was doomed to fall. Then again, another one said to play the hand you were dealt. Something he understood all too well.

A moment later, Sophie threw open the driver's door and hopped in, her face contorted, reflecting the way Manny's guts were feeling.

"What the hell does that actually mean for us?" she said.

"Good question. Just hang tight while I think it through a little more. I will say that splitting us up into two teams allows us to cover more leads."

Sophie started the vehicle, the air conditioning going to work immediately to help alleviate the heat inside the vehicle and, to an extent, the heat building inside Manny.

"I get that. We've been around a couple of blocks ourselves, but this terrorism take is a little different than playing games with some of the sick bastards we've dealt with in the past," she answered.

"It is. It'll help to have Alex still doing the data analysis for us, plus Josh said he's bringing in Belle Simmons to help. She should be here in a couple of hours."

"I don't know how he pulled that off, but we'll take it."

"He said she's got no real caseload yet for the BAU, so she's coming here," said Manny. "But if she gets a case, she's gone. This isn't her deal."

"So Braxton and Barb and Chloe go with Josh. That's okay. He's right in keeping you and Chloe away from each other, like Barb and Alex, in case something happens," said Sophie.

She hesitated, no doubt recalling how awful the inference that "something happens" could mean. Another reminder of Dean's absence. His strong friend regained her composure.

"Still, I'd like to have someone with experience on this team dealing with these terrorist psychos," she said, her hand tightening on the steering wheel.

Sophie had two good points. No need to leave Ian and Jen alone in this world if both Chloe and he were killed. And as far as splitting the unit, Josh's idea was sort of *six of one and a half dozen of the other.*

Josh had said that one team shouldn't be hampered by old methods and ideas used in fighting domestic terrorism. A fresh look and untainted analysis might bring better results in finding these two killers, if there were only two. Something Josh had been preaching since before they'd left Lansing. Manny agreed with that; thus, by adding Belle, for however long that was, three of them would be more likely to do a better job profiling and following unconventional leads. And who wouldn't want Alex sifting through the immense data available to them?

That form of logic made sense, if nothing else applied in Josh's decisions regarding each team's make-up. Yet, rookies might be prone to rookie mistakes.

"We'll manage, Sophie. We'll just have to get Alex's butt more involved."

She looked at him and offered a wry smile. "He'll hate that. Less time to eat and all."

"You know, the one thing I like about these communication earpieces is that I can almost hear you think. Both of you," said Alex, his voice as clear as the proverbial bell in Manny's head.

"Hey, Alex," said Manny.

"Oh, we forgot you were there, Dough Boy," Sophie said. "So, what am I thinking now?"

"You're wondering how a man like me, who was born with so many talents to go along with his rugged good looks, would put up with your crap. My own general thoughts here on top of this new development? I think you're both a little nuts."

"What? Us? Did you pass the last part of the annual psych exam? The part about having hallucinations and delusions? You're messed up."

"Could be. But it's not me. You do know I can turn whomever I want on and off this communication system with just a little flick of a switch? If I don't want people to hear the crap coming from your lips. And yes, by the way, I passed with flying colors. I did hear you had trouble passing the drug test though, right?"

"Damn right. I got the tech to overlook it though. He likes Asians with big knockers."

Alex sighed. "I didn't chime in to talk about your knockers."

Had Alex smiled through that sigh? Manny thought so. Alex would continue to do what he could, in his own way, to help keep Sophie's mind from focusing on losing Dean. He suspected she knew that.

True friends were always friends, no matter what came out of their mouths.

"You know about the team split, obviously," said Manny.

"I do. I think Josh has a good idea, and I wouldn't sweat the lack-of-experience thing. They don't have what we have, so it will be a good balance. And it's not like the eight of us will be out of reach if we truly need something done."

"All true. Okay, enough about that. Let's get to work. We were on the way to see what you've come up with, but the fact that you're talking to us means you've got some more info."

"See, that's why you make all of that money. You're right, sort of. I don't have any real hits on any of the people in the warehouse. Some general Google references, but nothing that puts us ahead of this game. Still nothing on the woman."

"That's unusual about the woman, right?" asked Sophie.

"It is. With the search we're doing, she should have had some sort of facial recognition or imaging system pop up from public security cameras or traffic videos somewhere in this shrinking world. We'll keep trying. If nothing else, I suspect we'll have something from CODIS or AIFAS with her DNA and fingerprints. Still, it's odd."

"Have we gotten in touch with the NOPD about interviewing Detective Brooks? She's probably clean, but we need to talk to her about her husband," said Manny.

"I left a message for her captain a few minutes ago, so we should have that set up soon."

"Good. What else?" asked Manny.

"We've got a boatload of financial information compiled into separate categories that will help us figure out where these folks banked and how they deposited money to go along with credit-card transactions. But I'll admit, I suspect those will probably be unhelpful. People like these don't use credit cards unless they think they can mask the transactions. Again, the exception will probably be Daryl Brooks. So far, he doesn't seem to have anything to hide, from what I can see."

"All good points. That line of thinking should help us see who they dealt with online and via the public, but what about private cash transactions?" asked Manny.

"I'd need a crystal ball for that, buddy. But we *can* trace withdrawals and deposits to locations around the country and cross-reference them to see if there are any criminal events within a day or two of those transactions. Who knows? We might hit something. Again, I'm concentrating on these five and Detective Brooks."

"That's as good a start as any. I have a couple ideas myself. We'll talk about those when we get back to the jet. I don't want to get too deep though until Belle gets here. She'll have some thoughts we won't want to ignore."

"Got it. But we won't be using the jet for a control center. That's changed. It seems they might need the plane for other things, like flying to other crime sites, something like that. So, to let you know, this data and info center, computers and all, will be moving to a private room at the New Orleans field office. I've sent you the address. I should be there in thirty minutes or so."

"Makes sense. See you soon," said Manny.

Sophie looked at Manny. "About time I got to drive down here. It's on."

She reached for the shift lever just as the rear door swung open. Josh leaned inside the SUV, excitement radiating from his face.

"I need you to go to Tulane Medical Center. We might have caught a break in this thing."

"What? How?" asked Manny.

"Amy Brooks was shot this morning. She's okay, but she got a look at her attacker."

"Get out," said Sophie.

"What?" asked Josh, a puzzled look on his face.

"Get out of Dodge, and then get the hell out of this vehicle. We got shit to do."

The door barely thumped shut before she slammed the vehicle into drive, the smell of burning rubber wafting through the warm Louisiana air.

# CHAPTER-15

The cold ambience of the cell extended far past the lifeless steel, tiled floor, and accompanying off-white walls and ceiling. That cold dove deep inside Anna Ruiz's heart and captured what remained of the biggest single thing that gave her a reason for getting out of bed each morning.

Hope.

Hope that, one day, all of this would be behind her. What she'd done for most of her adult life would somehow dissolve into some abyss and never return.

Hope that her previous actions wouldn't rise up and dance through her mind as she ate, wouldn't invade her very soul while she did something as simple as read.

Never mind the unspeakable haunting as she slept, tossing and turning until the nightmares caused her another life-sucking, sleepless night.

Hell, she wasn't safe while she sat on the john. There was no escape from her past. Despite it all, she held tight to the notion that she might have an opportunity at redemption, knowing full well how slim those opportunities might be. Still, she held on.

Violent killers, even those who had gone through the wondrous epiphany she had, as rare as that was, would always remain untrusted. Always. She got that. She understood. Monsters of any ilk were nonetheless monsters.

She moved from her bed and walked over to the six-inch-thick, bulletproof glass that escorted the sunlight into her cell. Not everyone in the Florence ADMAX Super Prison got access to this light. Only those who behaved well, whatever that criteria embodied. She was pretty sure it wasn't formally written that she have sex with a few of the guards for favors, but sometimes a girl had to do what she had to do in order to get what she wanted.

Pressing her face against the warm glass, she closed her eyes and smiled. It felt wonderful, in deep contrast to the cold cell.

Inhaling deeply, she hoped against hope that her mind would trick her lungs into thinking the air was clean and fresh and filled with the scent of pine directly from the Colorado wild.

It had almost worked.

*One day. One day.*

After one more deep breath, she returned to her bed, fitted tightly against the steel wall of the twelve-by-seven room that had become her home. She glanced at the bright-green door, then back to the open book beside her, *Do Androids Dream of Electric Sheep?*

With the care of a mother toward her child, she reached out and touched the spine of Philip Dick's creation. He had created a fantasy world, yet deep within that place in his imagination, he'd captured an interaction between the living and the artificial that caused the latter to seek something better. A life worth living. A dream, if you will.

She caressed the book. There was that concept again. Even machines in this book's futuristic world dared to hope.

And wasn't that what he'd told her to do? To have faith, to anticipate, to believe in something better. To trust him if she couldn't trust God. To know that he was fighting for her, and someday, just maybe, she would be out of this world and into the one in which she'd never really learned to function. The real world.

His words rang in her head as if he were right beside her. She thought she could even smell his scent, the one that was his and only his.

"Hurry up, my friend. I'm dying here," she whispered.

Reaching for her book, she pictured an image of her noble hope deftly displayed in her mind, needing one final reassuring look from him before she would journey to Dick's realm of fantasy.

She swore she could see him, her hope, smiling back at her, his blue eyes encouraging her to hang tight. She'd try.

# CHAPTER-16

Amy Brooks cringed in painful anticipation as she raised her arm, but she was surprised at the absence of agony despite the bullet that had torn through her shoulder. She felt the ravage of flesh, no question, yet there were no waves of nauseating pain matching the kind she'd experienced in the ambulance.

The elderly ER doctor's stare scanned her face. He then smiled.

"Good. I'm glad it's better. I've seen this kind of gunshot before. Too often, I'm afraid. That one could have been a life changer. However, it wasn't. You were luckier than a dog in a butcher shop."

Amy grinned. It had been a couple of days since her last smile. Maybe longer. God knew she didn't feel so lucky, but the vision of a dog in the butcher shop made her think of her old beagle, Chester. She had loved him the way kids love dogs and dogs loved kids, unconditionally.

The old mutt had found ways to make her laugh that she'd forgotten about until the doctor used his analogy. She'd especially enjoyed the way Chester used to eat. He'd turn his tan butt sideways to protect whatever was in the bowl and growl at anyone who came near, except her.

The little angel in devil's clothing would even occasionally bring her a piece of the scraps that had been tossed in his beat-up, old bowl, all the while looking at her with those rich brown eyes. She swore he had been smiling.

"Thank you, doctor. It feels much better."

"Yep. Now don't get crazy, it'll be a few weeks before it heals completely, and the bruising will be there a while too. That bullet passed clean through the soft tissue about three millimeters on the outside of your shoulder. You've experienced the prototypical flesh wound, albeit a larger caliber load than I'm used to seeing."

She looked away from the doctor as her partner, Phil, strolled into the room, one uniformed officer on each side of him. They took up residence on the inside of the door, hands folded in front of them. It was impossible for her not to feel uneasy.

"Better?"

"Better. It's a hardcore flesh wound, and I'll be pumping iron in no time."

Phil grinned. "Yeah, since you do that all the time."

She tilted her head at her partner. He mimicked her, but couldn't hide the concern in his eyes. More tracks for the uneasy train.

"Phil, what the hell's going on here? I keep thinking this woman had a hard-on for me over something in my past, God knows that would cover a few hundred folks. But I can't think of anyone who fits her description or even a family member of someone, you know? Now you bring in two blues to stand watch?"

"Don't jump to conclusions, Amy. The captain and I want to make sure there's nothing else going on here. I mean a random attack is one thing, but—"

Her infamous temper crawled up her throat from somewhere deep. She saw only red. Enough was enough. Her husband was dead in bizarre circumstances, the captain thought she was a mess, and now she'd been shot.

More red. She exploded.

"Stop the bullshit, Phil. I've had enough the last two days. My husband was killed in that warehouse, and no one can figure out what the hell's going on with that yet? Now I'm to be protected or watched for more than one reason, right?"

"Come on, Amy."

"No. You all come on. Don't give me that shit. Let's get real here. The captain thinks I have something to do with what happened. Then throw in the Feds and whatever shit they have to say, and I'm a suspect for something I don't even understand. Well, to hell with all of you. I'm a good cop, and I don't deserve this. I quit."

Amy rose from the edge of the bed, danced a few steps with dizziness and nausea, then took a few unsteady strides toward the door, regaining most of her equilibrium.

"Detective Brooks. Wait. You're right; you don't deserve this, not yet anyway."

Her eyes darted in the direction of the voice, the really nice voice, that had spoken to her.

The good-looking man stood just inside the entrance to the room, a pretty Asian woman at his side. She had no idea who he was, then it came to her.

Feds.

She caught his stare with one of her own. She couldn't look away if she'd wanted to do so. His blue eyes were riveting, like he could see through her, yet there was an air of complete honesty about him. She didn't know how she knew, but she thought she could trust him. She immediately felt her pulse slowing.

"Feds?" she asked.

"I'll tell you, if you don't quit your job for another hour," he said, smiling.

"I bet you think that smile works with all of the women, don't you?"

"Naw, just the ones that are still breathing," said his partner.

Sighing, she realized the woman was probably right.

The two stepped forward, both reaching out their hands.

"I'm Special Agent Manny Williams, and this is Double Special Agent Sophie Lee."

Despite the emotional roller coaster over the last few minutes, she had no choice but to smile at that. She shook both of their hands.

"Detective Amy Brooks, as you know."

"We do," said Agent Williams.

"I thought Feds were stuffy-ass and all business. You two don't seem to fit that mold."

"Oh, we can be, but hey, you've had a tough couple of days, so we're going to do the good cop/good cop thing and see what's going on with you," said Agent Lee.

"Not that we think you've done anything wrong, Detective. We just want to talk for a while, okay?" asked Agent Williams.

"I suppose I don't have a choice, but I'd like to sit down first," she said, fighting another wave of nausea. Amy turned back to the bed and sat down, feeling better after getting off her feet, her throbbing shoulder still talking to her.

Agent Lee sat on the bed at an angle so Amy could see them both without twisting. Agent Williams pulled up a green padded chair and sat a few feet in front of her. He then motioned for Phil and the blues to leave.

Phil hesitated, looking at her then back to the agents. "Are you okay with that?"

"Yeah. Don't worry. I guess I'm in good hands. "

"Okay, I'll be outside the door if you need me, okay?"

She nodded. "Talk to you soon. And Phil, I'm sorry for snapping at you. I've had better weeks. Thanks again for saving my ass."

"I know, Amy, I know. That's what partners do."

Her partner walked out of the room and closed the door.

She then turned her attention to Agent Williams. "So this is what an interrogation is like, agents?"

"First thing. This isn't an interrogation. It's an information-gathering session. Second thing. Call me Manny."

"And call me Sophie. Never did care for that agent stuff," said Agent Lee.

"First names it is."

The momentary silence should have been unnerving, but it wasn't. Instead, it was almost soothing. These people were here to do a job, yet they were far more than that. She was no profiler, like Manny obviously was, that much she knew. It was also obvious that Sophie complemented him in ways she could only imagine, making them a true team.

"You two have been working together for years, haven't you?" she asked quietly.

"You could say that," said Sophie. "I've had to put up with his workaholic tendencies, lack of tech skills, and profiling everyone on the damned planet, but we make it work."

"I bet you do." She looked at Manny. "Have I been profiled already?"

"Not intentionally, but I suppose so. That's part of the reason we're here and not at HQ with your captain and Internal Affairs standing over our shoulders."

"Thank God for that. What do you see?"

Manny tilted his head, a tiny smile tugging at the corners of his mouth.

"Enough to know that you're honest, caring, can be hard-assed, and that you have some anger issues probably stemming from the job more than your childhood."

He leaned closer. "That's the obvious stuff. I also know you have a sense of justice, despite the pain of losing your husband in that warehouse and someone trying to kill you this morning. Your sense of duty and the desire to figure out what the hell is going on lets you compartmentalize your emotions, for the most part, so you can get to work.

"Your tenacity, I suspect, is your most helpful tool and why you made detective as quickly as you did." Leaning back, he ran his hand through his hair. "How am I doing so far?"

"So far? There's more? If you get any deeper into her head, you'll know her favorite color and what she fantasizes about," said Sophie, rolling her eyes.

Amy shrugged. "Well, it's a little unnerving to be an open book like that, but I'm glad you're a Fed rather than someone local. And you probably have an idea about both of the things Sophie said."

"True," said Manny.

The agent gathered his thoughts. She could tell that much, never taking his eyes from her face.

"Listen, we have to talk about a couple of things in terms of recollection of what happened this morning," he said.

"I've answered every question Phil had. And over the phone, whatever Captain Ellis wanted to know, and Internal Affairs, until I get to go face to face with them. I don't know what else to say."

"We weren't part of those sessions. While I can guess what went on, we still have to do this, okay?"

"I get that. Like I said, fire away."

"Do you have any idea why you were attacked?" asked Manny.

"None whatsoever. I now understand that it probably has to do with the shooting death of my husband, but that's all I've got."

It was still odd to say that out loud, that her husband was dead. The tears welled up again. Shit.

Daryl Brooks would no longer come home late, slide into bed, his large body warm and inviting, hold her in his arms, and make love to her. It had been rough the last few weeks, but once you have those moments with someone, they never disappear, never.

Sophie's hand reached out for her arm. "I get what you're thinking. What's going on in your brain. He was your husband. That won't change, ever. And you'll find things down the road that make you wish you were drunk or stoned so you don't have to think about him. But right now, let's figure out what's going on, okay?"

It didn't take a mind reader to see that Sophie was speaking from experience.

"When did you lose your husband?" Amy asked softly.

The agent exhaled and smiled a sad smile. "Let's just say it's still very real. Maybe we can talk later. Right now, let's stay on task. There will be plenty of time for mourning, trust me."

"I think that's a good idea. We believe more lives are at stake," said Manny.

She nodded. "I'll do my best."

"Do you know why your husband was at the warehouse?"

She shook her head. "No, for the tenth time, no."

"Did you know any of the people he was with when he was killed?"

"No. I studied the mug shots last night and again this morning. I've never seen any of them. Not even at the club where he worked as a bouncer."

"Did you go there often?"

"Two or three times. I'm not a big party girl."

"What about social-media accounts? The cyber unit will go over your phones and computers, but was he active there?"

"You know, he wasn't. He was a bit of a throwback regarding tech. He finally got an email account last year. Three months ago, he got a smartphone so we could text. It took him days to get the hang of it. He preferred being around people. He actually hated it when we'd go out for a meal and people were staring at their damned phones instead of talking to each other."

Manny smiled that mesmerizing smile. "Sophie thinks I'm the only one like that. I use the tech stuff, but I'd rather be in the crowd."

"True dat," said Sophie.

"What about people to your house? Did you entertain much?"

"No. I'm a cop; he worked weird hours. I don't remember the last real visitor we had. He didn't have much family, and mine is mostly out of state. I don't have a lot of friends. He had even less, at least that I knew about."

"If our assumption is right, that you were attacked was because of how and where he was killed, why come after you?"

"I answered that. I don't know."

"The person, probably people, behind shooting at you, think differently. They think you might know or have something that will lead to discovering who they are. So you can't think of one reason why this woman wanted you dead?"

"I can't. She might be someone's friend or relative from a case I was involved in, and maybe her showing up this morning was a coincidence. Either way, I've never seen her before. I have no idea what she wanted with me, other than to end my life."

Leaning back in the chair again, Manny looked at his hands, then over to Sophie. "Got anything else?"

"Naw. I think we can come back and talk later, but I believe her."

"Yeah, me too. I think you're telling the truth as you see and remember it, so we'll move on to the next step."

"As I remember it?"

"You're a cop. You know that sometimes when people are in stressful situations, their minds aren't geared for this type of questioning."

"And they might think of something later? Okay, I can buy that. But I don't have anything for you."

"Fair enough. The next step is to take you back to this morning and put you in a situation where you can recall more details. The fresher the experience, the more likely we are to make this work. Are you up for another session?"

She rolled her eyes. "Again, do I have a choice?"

"Of course, but I think I can help you retrieve a few more details to assist the investigation."

"Okay, I'll do my best."

"Great. Let's get started. I want to work backward, because I think the near past unlocks the earlier past."

"Whatever you say. Are you going to hypnotize me?"

"No, it's not like that. I think people just need to be put into the right frame of reference. I just need you to relax and concentrate."

He leaned closer.

"Take us to five minutes before you were attacked this morning. I want to know everything. What you felt. What you heard and saw. Even what you smelled. What you were thinking, truly thinking? There is nothing too unimportant here."

"Is this kind of like getting into repressed memory?" Amy asked.

"Sort of, but more like a visualization of a past experience. It's like the drill you did in the police academy to help you remember a crime scene, only far deeper. Sophie and I won't suggest anything; we'll just listen to you talk. You'd be surprised what we see without realizing that we did."

"Got it."

"And don't worry; this is between us chickens," said Sophie.

"That's good to know. Okay, let's get this show on the road."

Manny nodded. He then scooted the chair so close she could smell his aftershave. He began to talk softly. "Like I said, close your eyes, relax, clear your thoughts, and picture walking out of your home."

It took a few seconds to get Daryl's face from her mind, but she eventually did what he asked.

The sound of his voice was as quieting as anything she heard, especially in light of the last two days. The tension began to run out of her body and ultimately, it seemed, leave through her toes.

"What are you seeing? Sensing? What about the feel of the door when you opened it to go outside to wait for Phil? Warm? Cool?"

Amy began to talk about her morning just after she exited the front door of her ranch home. She verbalized every detail. It was as if she were watching an HD video.

At times she swore she felt the breeze or the warm sun on her face as she spoke. Manny had been right—she was sharing details that she hadn't really taken much stock in. Buzzing bees and car engines on the street behind her. The sound of lawn sprinklers and even the street cleaner that had passed her home only minutes before she was attacked. Then the slight woman came into her mind's view.

"The woman is small, blond, but there's something about her hair that's not right. It doesn't bounce when she walks."

"What does that mean?" asked Manny.

"She's a high stepper. The kind that men like to see walk. Her hair would bounce with that kind of stride, but it doesn't.

"Her teal blouse is tucked into her jeans. She's right handed because I can see that she's holding something. It has to be her gun. I look back at her face, thinking that this is a problem because of where and how she's walking. Even though she's fifty or sixty feet away, I can see she's pretty. Small nose, big eyes, high cheekbones tapering to her pointed chin."

Amy felt herself swallow. *Damn, this is crazy.*

"She sees me staring and realizes I've made her and know she's not there for a social call. She raises that gun as I start to dive. I actually see her lose her balance for a second, then I lose sight of her."

The moment Amy heard the second shot, her eyes flew open as she reached for her shoulder, praying she wouldn't feel the heat of the bullet course through her shoulder again.

A strong hand caught hers before it reached her shoulder.

"Whoa. Not so hard, that might hurt a little."

He was right. It would have.

"Reflex. I could almost feel being shot again."

"That's what I suspected." He guided her hand away from her shoulder and held it. "You did a great job. I could see the woman, after the way you described her."

"Yeah, well, you led me there. I didn't really think I could do that."

"Oh, he excels at that stuff . . . you know, leading where we don't really want to go," said Sophie. "At least he's on our side."

Amy turned back to Manny and held back the remark that she was ready to voice. The man was frowning, forcing him to look years older than he was. It sent a chill down her spine.

"What? What's wrong?" Amy asked.

Manny rose from his chair and glanced at Sophie than back to her.

"I want you to get with your departmental artist. A composite sketch should go out to every cop in New Orleans."

"That's a given, but you didn't answer my question."

"I know that look, Williams. Spill it," said Sophie, standing and moving to face him.

Manny exhaled, but that act didn't erase the troubled expression from his handsome face. "I know this sounds crazy, but I think I know who this woman might be."

# CHAPTER-17

"Did you get the background checks I asked for?"

Belle Simmons shifted the cell phone away from her ear, listening to the soft sound of the wings of the jet cutting through the air, all the while rubbing her knee. Her own version of a nervous tic that had haunted her since that incident long ago in the Caribbean.

*Why these two?*

The question had been haunting her since Josh Corner's request had sent her to the databases, ones the public could only imagine existed.

She was new at FBI procedure—official procedure, that is—but not to police work. She was intimately familiar with what this kind of information was designed to discover or, in some cases, verify. Belle put the phone back to her ear.

"Yes, Josh, I've got them. They're sealed, just like you asked. I have them in a locked briefcase."

"Great work. Thank you, Belle."

She waited for him to continue. He didn't.

"So?

"So what?"

"Don't play coy, Josh. You know damn well what I mean. But I'll state the obvious in the event you might misunderstand my meaning."

"Belle—"

"Just tell me why you're digging into their lives. I sort of get why for one of them, but the second one? Really?"

More silence from her friend. The kind that forced her, for one taunting moment, to reevaluate what the word "friend" truly meant. Josh had always been upfront with her, but at this juncture, she wasn't so sure exactly what that denoted.

"Listen. I know you have questions, and although I'm not a profiler, I'd guess you're wondering as much about me as you are my actions."

"I'd say that's accurate," answered Belle.

"Would you also agree that there are simply some things that are on a need-to-know basis?"

Belle's angst rose. "Are you saying there could be secrets in this new unit of yours?"

"I'm saying I've probably said too much already. Just know that the nation's security is more important to me, especially given what we're running into in New Orleans, than it's ever been.

I'm only scratching the surface of what that entails."

"You think one or both of them threaten national security? Come on, Josh. You've known these people for years."

"I have. That's why I need to make sure of a couple things."

"Tell me—"

Josh interrupted her, irritation in his voice. "Enough, Agent Simmons. Just get me the files when you land, then you need to team up with Manny, Sophie, and Alex. That's the end of your concern and our conversation regarding this subject. Are we clear?"

Exhaling, Belle shifted the phone to her other hand. "Yeah, it's clear. And I'll do my job and keep this to myself. But you're a fool if you think this is the end of this subject."

"I'm no fool, Belle."

The phone went dead, his words echoing through her head.

Belle placed the phone in her lap. "No, you're not. And just what in the name of God did you get me into?" she whispered.

# CHAPTER-18

Rhodes finished wrapping Lucretia's body in a thin layer of plastic. He stood, wiping the perspiration from his brow, swearing under his breath. He enjoyed the warmth of the sun as much as any man, but the godforsaken humidity in this part of Louisiana still wasn't to his liking. Not at all.

Yet, in the grand scheme of things, and the vital role that New Orleans would play on that stage, the weather was a minor inconvenience. Certainly not in league with getting rid of poor Lucretia's body.

The memory of her face pinned itself on his mind. He could see the conviction of the mission they shared in the sharp recesses of her eyes. The expression drawn over her face in intimate detail as they discussed what would come next in perfect harmony and accordance with the grand scheme. How the law enforcement fish had swallowed the bait—hook, line, and sinker, as the saying went.

Looking toward the end of the dirt road that ended at this secluded section of North Shore Beach, making sure he had no company, Rhodes turned back toward Lake Pontchartrain, then glanced down at Lucretia, blood spatter still visible on her distorted neck and face.

Squatting on one knee, he put his hand on her forehead one final time. "You were clueless, were you not, my love? You thought you were into something noble, but you never realized just how far I can be from that concept."

He stood. "In the end, all roads lead to the same destination; they are forever self-serving. Mine is no different. Perhaps you've figured that out, if there is a life after this one and you can still think. If not, you'll not be concerned with the depth of my deception and your role as a loose end. Goodbye, my love."

Five minutes later, after dumping her body into the lake, a fitting feast for the gator contingency, he drove the old Chevy back to McLane City and entered I-10, in the direction of New Orleans proper.

He'd have to finally get rid of his dependable ride, despite feeling a measure of affection for the old girl. But nothing could be excluded as a potential complication. The bloodstain on the seat was just one more example.

A fire on an abandoned street after dark should handle both problems. He'd already removed the vehicle's VIN numbers, so tracing the car back to him through the previous owners would be next to impossible, especially since he really had nothing on this planet in his real name. Almost nothing. Besides, by the time any investigation occurred regarding the car, his plan would be completed.

Reaching into his pocket as he passed Irish Bayou Lagoon, he fingered the old photograph without looking. He didn't need to. It had been etched in his mind years ago. For an unnumbered time, he fought the storm accompanying that simple action. Again, his controlled rage swallowed another miniscule piece of his heart. He wondered how much of that heart remained.

*Not much, I suspect.*

He brought the faded photo to his lips and kissed it gently.

"In another day, everything will be made right. Everything. I promise," he whispered.

# CHAPTER-19

"What the hell does that mean? You might know her?" asked Sophie.

"Just that. I've seen pieces of this physical profile before, and her psychopathic actions would verify the twisted mental profile as well," said Manny.

He turned to Detective Brooks. "I'm not sure what your department wants you to do next, but we'll be in touch with your captain soon. Right now, we have to go. Thank you for your help. Let's go, Sophie."

"Wait. You aren't going to tell me what's going on?" asked the detective.

"Not yet. Like I said, we'll be in touch. Take care of yourself."

Manny spun on his heel and rushed out the door, Sophie right behind him. They reached the front entrance of the hospital, and he began to jog toward the SUV, his mind running a different race now. One that required Alex's help searching the

Feds's databases and, he suspected, another source.

Sophie reached out and grabbed his arm halfway before they made it to the SUV.

"Whoa, big boy. You might be in great shape, but I've been slacking in the exercise department for the last few weeks. That, and I want to hear what you're thinking."

He patted her hand and nodded toward the vehicle. "I'll tell you on the way. We have to get to Alex. We've been jumbled up with lack of real leads and only conjecture so far. I think this could be important."

"If you say so, then let's get our asses in motion."

Two minutes later they entered I-10 and were speeding toward the local FBI building near the southern shore of Lake Pontchartrain.

Sophie stepped on the gas then gave him a curious side glance, complemented with a momentary narrowing of her pretty eyes.

"Ask. You've never been shy before," he said, smiling.

"I need to ask?"

"No, you don't. There are two things going on here. First, whatever we have, at this point, I'm reluctant to share with any of the locals. I have a feeling that that's not wise."

"You think Brooks knows something about these killings and what's coming next?"

"Maybe not Brooks. I get the sense that she's being upfront. But whatever we would have discussed with her is going to get around the department."

"Dude. You don't trust the cops? You think someone on the force could be a terrorist? Really?"

Manny thought about what Sophie had said out loud. The very nature of the statement seemed absurd. Yet . . .

"I'm not saying that, exactly. I'm saying information has a way of getting around. We need to control that."

"I understand. But NOPD, really?" She flipped the blinker to exit the Interstate.

"Being cautious. Wait. Go straight." He then handed her his phone, his GPS flashing a large red dot. "We're not going to the FBI's office. We've got another location that's more private and secure."

"Damn. When were you going to tell me about this change?"

"It slipped my mind."

"What? Nothing slips your mind."

"Okay, I just wanted to make sure we weren't being followed."

Sophie glanced out her side mirror then the rearview. "I don't see anything strange."

"Nope, me either. Just making sure. And no smartass comments about being paranoid."

"I'll control myself."

Sophie glanced at Manny's phone sitting on the seat, the sun hitting her face, then she pulled back into the middle lane.

Manny realized that his partner was looking better, more alive.

After Dean was killed, she appeared to have aged twenty years, inside and out. He remembered wondering if he had looked the same way after Louise's death. He was sure he had. Maybe older.

"What?"

"Have I told you lately that there's no one on the planet that I'd rather work with?"

The sudden onset of emotion seemed to take her by surprise. She bit her lip, then took a deep breath. "Thank you, Manny. You'll always be my favorite man and cop. Always."

"Yeah, I know," he said, smiling.

"Don't get too full of yourself. The market for a big-boobed Asian partner is pretty strong right now."

"I'll remember that."

"Good. Okay, we have Brooks's situation handled for now. Tell me about this woman you think you might know."

Manny rolled down the window a few inches, allowing the warm, fresh air into the vehicle. "You know how much I read, right?"

"Yeah, makes me kind of sick to think about how much real fun you've missed."

"Thanks for your condolences. At any rate, three years ago, I was researching tendencies regarding different types of serial killers. Mission oriented, sexual, visionary, and control. We were knee deep into Argyle's game, so I was desperate to recognize more of his motivation."

"And?"

"And I ran into a series of cases, from Florida to Louisiana, over a four-year span. Five murders, to be exact. Each victim was male. Each one was overweight, and they were all shot in the back of the head within millimeters of the exact same location on their skulls. Not true execution-style either because there was no GSR indicating close-range shots on any of the victims' noggins. The estimated distance for each shot was between twenty-five and thirty-five feet away."

"That would suggest someone who considered themselves weaker than their victims. Maybe a women or someone with a physical issue, right?"

"Exactly. In this situation, given the victims, chances are high that the killer was female. To fuel that possibility—surprise—ballistics matched the rounds for all of the murders as coming from a modified Beretta 92."

"Like the one that was pulled from the warehouse victims?" asked Sophie.

"Almost, according to Alex. I sent him the old ballistics reports I had in my email from one of the investigators. They are different to a degree, but if she had re-bored the barrel, then that would explain the subtle differences."

"So she's a clever wench, sort of."

"I suppose she thinks so, and she must have been extremely careful because none of the local or federal investigators could find any other links to the victims in those five killings."

Wheeling down a tree-studded side street off of Saint Charles Avenue, Sophie looked at the GPS again, slowed down, then glanced at Manny. "Damn, this is getting into an old neighborhood."

"Old, but beautiful. Nothing like a well-cared-for Southern Victorian home. And Braxton did say it was out of the way."

"He wasn't lying. Back to your shooter case, that's not unusual . . . to not be able to find leads on cases like that."

"True, but with a pattern like the one the killer embraced, there had to be more facts than that they were white and needed a good diet. That's just too general, at least for my taste."

"Let me guess; you ordered the case files."

"Yep. The rest of them. Like I said, I had ballistics but wanted all the files. Just told the FBI's records department I was a big shot with the ACTU, and that was all it took. Alex will have them sometime today."

Sophie rolled to a stop in front of a smallish, two-story Victorian home framed with two huge, ancient oaks draped with Spanish moss.

Behind the impeccable wrought-iron fence running the length of the well-landscaped sidewalk rested a wraparound porch that extended toward an unseen area on the west side of the home.

On the second level of the house was a pillared veranda, accented with lace-design metalwork between each white pillar. The white accented the quiet seafoam-green that made up the color for the rest of the exterior of the home. The home was so immaculate that Manny felt like he'd gone back a century and a half in time.

"Well, shut my mouth," said Sophie in her best Southern drawl. "You sure this is it, big boy? This place is gorgeous."

"I'm sure, and you're right, it is," said Manny, still taking in the details of the FBI's safe house. "The thing is . . . every house on this side street is in the same condition, so it doesn't stand out as unusual. Good thinking."

"If you say so."

Scanning the residence, he turned to Sophie. "Tell me what you see."

She leaned forward and studied it with the concentration he'd seen her develop over the years. A minute later she leaned back, unbuckled her seatbelt and opened her door, allowing more Louisiana heat into the vehicle.

"Hang on to your ass, Williams. I've got this."

"Yeah? Stop talking and start walking."

"Oh real funny. Just stick with being a hot profiler. You'll starve as a comedian. Okay. I see nine domed, long-range, maybe three hundred feet, HD night-vision security cameras on the corners and roof of the house, two each in the big trees, each angled to detect horizontal as well as vertical movement. Spared no expense on those puppies.

"Since there's no garage, I have to assume parking is hidden from the street by the back of the house, which backs up to the dead end between this and the next neighborhood. That's smart because it makes it difficult to get to the back of the house, which I assume has the same type of cameras situated on the rear perimeter, so that every foot of the exterior of this house is under surveillance."

"Great. What else?"

His partner frowned. "Do you mean movement on the street? I did see a couple of sedans that blended in but were probably our people . . . well, the FBI's."

"Good. I think you're right about that. The tinted glass gives them away some."

He opened his door and exited the SUV as Sophie walked around to his left.

They began to make their way to the sidewalk. "There's one more thing here."

"Really? What did I miss?"

"The entrance doesn't appear to be guarded. Even from the inside. Unless these people think the security system is enough."

She shrugged. "Could be. Or your paranoia is working overtime again."

He sighed. She was probably right.

Sophie looped her arm through Manny's as he pulled open the gate and continued up the brick walk.

"Don't look now, but I think we're being followed," she said.

"We are. I heard the car doors shut when we got through the gate."

"They're our people, right?"

"I'd say so. But I'd get your hand next to your piece, just in case."

"Agents. Please stop where you are, hands where we can see them."

He and Sophie turned in unison.

In front of them, weapons at their sides, stood two people—special agents, Manny assumed. The one on the left was a short, burly man, his bald head glistening with perspiration. At his side was a much taller, ordinary-looking, dark-haired woman with black-framed glasses. It was hard for Manny not to think of assorted Mutt-and-Jeff analogies. He kept the smile to himself.

Sophie did not.

"Hello, Special Agents Lee and Williams. And yes, we get that look all the time," said the woman.

"Yeah, us too," said Sophie.

Both agents returned her grin.

"I'm Agent Grimes, and this is Agent Buford. We'll take you back to where Agent Downs is set up. He's expecting you. First we'll need your weapons and to see your IDs, of course, before you enter the house. You'll get them back when you pass the security scan."

Manny looked at Sophie and nodded. He pulled his Glock from his holster, still trying to shake the ringing in his brain. This kind of security was new to him, no doubt, yet . . .

"Sweet. An eye scan, I hope," said Sophie. "I always wanted to do that."

"Thank you. I assume Agent Simmons is with Agent Downs," said Manny, pretending that he was having trouble pulling his gun from his holster. Sophie had already handed hers to the woman.

There was a slight hesitation before Buford answered, "Yes. She arrived about thirty minutes ago," he said.

Manny stopped in his tracks. "How long?"

The two agents looked at each other in an almost orchestrated dance, both holding their weapons.

"I do apologize for this," said the woman. "Orders are orders. You both have to die."

# CHAPTER-20

Chloe hit the red button on her phone and then stuffed it into her vest pocket.

Her mum sounded great, and Haley Rose's report of how Ian, Jen, and even Sampson were doing was music to her ears. She'd almost forgotten how being in the field, away from her home, could affect the way she approached her job. Not worrying about her family, at least quite as much, helped her to relax and concentrate, unless of course, she threw in worrying about Manny. That was another conundrum altogether.

The fact that they were in separate units made sense, especially in this situation . . . but hadn't they worked together in dangerous situations before? And hadn't they been successful? Yet, one never knew.

Leaning over the oak table of the hotel's conference room, she exhaled and reached for the dark-blue, sealed file, branded with the TOP SECRET ACTU stamp. She pulled it closer.

Readying to open the file without Manny and Sophie being in the room drove the point home even further that Josh had made two teams from one.

She still wasn't sure his decision was wise, but she reminded herself that the logic was sound.

She tapped her finger on the file, thinking how the terrorist game had changed over the years. How sophisticated technology had allowed those with a despicable intention to pursue their warped sense of purpose. But it worked both ways. The FBI's jet bore witness to that.

Yet, there wasn't anything like thinking out loud and discussing possibilities within the team. The full team. She still liked strength in numbers to combat twisted thinking, but she'd known Josh a long time and trusted him. He was a consummate leader, always looking out for his people, even to a fault. The leader of the ACTU knew what he was doing, even if it didn't please everyone, including her and Manny.

But she also trusted her instincts as a profiler and her experience in the fight against terrorism. This Irish lass had seen a thing or two herself.

"We can't open those yet."

She glanced at Barb, sitting to her left, and offered a small grin. "Yeah, I know. We're supposed to wait for Josh and Braxton to get back. But I was never good at following orders, don't ya know."

Barb laughed out loud.

Chloe decided it was a good laugh. Genuine, like Barb's love for Alex. The two of them, especially Alex, had been through some mind-bending situations over the last few months, no question. She wondered how many men could handle the fact that the woman they'd been married to for over a decade was a covert agent for the CIA, the FBI, and the DEA.

Not many. It spoke to the quality of Alex's heart and Barb's persistent love for him. And she suspected, somewhere deep, Alex had always known something was different about her, and not just those Hollywood looks.

"They'll be here shortly. But I'm as curious as you," said Barb.

Shifting in her leather chair, Chloe faced Barb. "Did you have any idea that the team would be split?"

Barb nodded. "Let's say I've seen it before. You understand the importance in covering as much intel as possible regarding international threats to national security. But this domestic arena is a different animal."

"So I've gathered. I've seen some impressive databases in my time, but nothing like the toys Alex and I were playing with while you were at the warehouse. Plus, the response time for those searches is uncanny."

"It's only the beginning. While Manny, Alex, Sophie, and Belle are diving into that, we've got another whole line of, how should I say it, information gathering. Not related to what Manny and his crew are doing," said Barb.

Manny.

Suddenly, inexplicably, she missed her husband as an image of his face came to mind, bringing into focus the total package that had saved her life from the loneliness that had threatened to stalk her for the rest of her days.

The curve of his jaw, his hair, those blue eyes, his strong hands. The warmth of his hard body while they made love. There was nothing like being with him. He loved just like he did his job. When they were finished, it was just them, lying close and making small talk. No serial killers. No terrorists. No Guardian of the Universe persona. Only them.

"Chloe?"

Barb's question brought her back. "Sorry, I was thinking of something else."

"Career choices?" said Barb, laughing.

"You could say that. Anyway, what are you referring to? What form of information gathering?"

Barb uncrossed her legs and leaned closer. "Paid informants. High-priced, high-profile international criminals and terrorists on every INTERPOL, FBI, CIA, DEA, CTD, and MI6 priority list."

Chloe's anger flared. "What the hell would we do that for? I worked hunting these assholes down, don't ya know. One of them shot me. These people can't be trusted. They only have their own agenda, their own purpose. They're radicals who will bend sideways, or bend us over, to get what they want."

"We know what we're—"

The door opened. Braxton entered, followed by Josh. Chloe stood up and moved around the table, grabbing her boss by the tie.

"What in God's name is wrong with ya? Are ya crazy?"

"Whoa," said Josh, pulling his tie from her hand, almost.

She pulled him closer.

"Settle down, Chloe. I always wear red ties with blue suits."

"Not funny, asshole. You know what I mean."

He glanced at Barb. "I take it you told her what we're doing here."

She saluted, her blond hair shimmering as she did. "As instructed, sir."

There was no humor on her face.

"Do as da mon says, Chloe. Chill out. We can explain dis ting, okay?" said Braxton, his deep voice calm, almost reassuring.

Glancing at each of them in turn, she then pulled Josh close enough to smell his breath. "You have five minutes, and it better be good, or I'm out of here."

"I won't need that long," he said quietly.

"I hope not. You may have already painted a big red target on our backs, all of us."

# CHAPTER-21

Manny never thought twice. He suspected Sophie wouldn't either. She'd seen his reaction to the lie about Belle Simmons's arrival. There was no time to hesitate.

If today was the day they would die, then they'd do it on their terms.

Moving quickly, hoping to take the two would-be assassins off guard, he dove at Buford, reaching for his gun hand. He closed his eyes, waiting to hear the gun's explosion and feel the immediate pain of a searing bullet entering his flesh.

It didn't happen.

For a reason he'd probably never know, the gun didn't discharge. Instead, Buford went down in a heap, his breath exiting his lungs with a loud, painful grunt as the gun skittered across the cement sidewalk and rattled against the wrought-iron fence.

A muffled shot sounded to his right followed by a shrill scream, but Manny had no time to see what was happening. The shorter, very powerful Buford had recovered. He had somehow managed to climb on top of Manny and then locked his vise-like grip around Manny's throat, instantly blocking any air trying to get into his lungs.

Manny's eyes watered almost to the point of blindness. Life-giving air was suddenly scarce. He tore desperately at the man's hands, trying to loosen Buford's hold, but he may as well have been trying to crack steel with a noodle. He needed to do something else, and quickly.

Shifting his body under the man's considerable weight, he swung a solid left hand to the side of his attacker's jaw, getting his attention, but only for a moment.

Buford grunted, smiled one of those crazy bastard smiles, and pressed harder on Manny's windpipe. Manny's eyes were now blurred, and what air he had managed to keep all but disappeared. The previously bright world was now spinning in a kaleidoscope of colors, sounds, and superficial hazes that, oddly enough in this circumstance, proved to remind him that nothing was guaranteed. Not even one's next breath.

*Enough, Williams. Get this done, or you and Louise will be having dinner tonight.*

With all of his strength, he bent out his knee and brought it hard against Buford's spine. The accompanying thud led to an immediate cry of pain, but the death grip remained intact around his throat. Raising his hands to Buford's face, he then drove his thumbs deep into the shorter man's eyes. Even in his less-than-cognitive state, the scream was startling.

Buford released his grip and reached for Manny's hands. It was all the opening Manny needed. He drove his hips up and shoved him over to the side of the cement walk. The quick turn of events, and a deep draw of air, sent Manny into advantage mode. He was on Buford in a flash.

As he drew back his fist, there was a micro-moment of déjà vu as he recalled the petty thief who had pulled a knife on Ian and Chloe. He had wondered if he would kill that man then. There was no such question here, only the will to live.

Somehow, even in this moment, he drew some comfort in that.

Reaching back even farther, he sent his right hand crashing into Buford's square jaw, sending him to Sand Land, blood dripping from the man's eyes and mouth.

Checking to make sure Buford was out, he then fell to his side, gasping for air. After catching a couple more breaths, and realizing just how sweet that act could be, his mind switched to where he was and . . . Sophie.

Spinning to his right, he began to scramble on all fours in her direction, only to stop as quickly as he started. He should have known better.

His partner sat on top of the tall blonde's midsection, her hands folded over her knees. Her gaze was intense, but that old impish expression that he loved so much was clearly on display.

"What the hell took you so long, Williams? Good to see you finally got it done. I thought I was going to have to step in, but you made me proud. Not to mention, it might have been a little embarrassing to tell the group, especially your wife, I had to save your ass, ya know?"

"So you've been watching him try to strangle the life out of me?"

"Not really *watching*, per se. Just observing how you would get out of his death grip and kick his ass. You tell me to have a little faith, so I had faith you'd come out on top."

"Faith, huh?

"Yep. Faith."

"We'll be talking about that one later." He nodded toward the woman she was sitting on. "What did you do to her?"

Sophie stood and wiped at her make-believe mustache. "Let's just say, partner, that she'll be a-sleepin' for a right bit of time, y'all."

"You're not shot?"

"No, she missed when I kicked her. The scream you heard was when I twisted her boob. After that, I knocked her out. Really simple."

"Good for you."

The stocky man began to stir, moaning as he reached for his eyes.

She cringed. "Not as bad as you did to his eyes though. That looked like it hurt."

Manny shrugged. "It was him or me."

Then, stepping back to Buford, Manny hit him with another hard right, knocking him out again.

"We have to cuff these two and find Alex," he said, shaking his hand.

Sophie's eyes grew wide. "Shit. Alex. I forgot about him."

Jumping up, she pulled the woman's hands behind her and cuffed them together.

Manny pulled his cuffs from his back pocket and repeated the act on the man lying near him. As he stood, a deep voice boomed through the PA system from the outside of the building. "Put your hands over your head and lie face down."

"What?" said Sophie.

"I think we have a bigger problem," said Manny.

"Do it now," resonated through the speakers.

A moment later, the front door burst open, and no less than ten of the FBI's finest sprinted into the well-manicured yard, weapons readied.

The leader of the group pointed at Sophie and him.

"You've got five seconds to hit the ground, or you'll leave in body bags."

# CHAPTER-22

"Thomas! You best be gettin' out of dat water, or Momma is gonna wup yo ass when she gets home."

Benjamin Thibeaux shook his head and headed to where his younger, ten-year-old brother was splashing along the lake's northern shoreline.

It was always tough being the big brother. Especially when Momma told him to take care of his siblings while she went shopping or to do an extra job, even if he hadn't wanted to. That choice wasn't offered to sixteen-year-olds in this family. In fact, not in his friends' families either. That was just how it was in his neck of the woods.

He guessed he should be lucky he had only Thomas today and not his two little sisters as well. He'd be pulling his hair and saying things his Momma would wash his mouth out with soap for saying. Right after one of them turned tattletale.

He reached the tiny ridge of green grass that sloped to the stony beach, where Thomas continued to ignore him.

"I told you, boy, get yo ass out of da water. You damn deaf or what?"

"I heard ya, Ben. But I be hot and dis water is cool. 'Sides, I ain't gettin' nothin' wet but my skin."

Benjamin kept moving in Thomas's direction. The boy wasn't real bright yet, but he made a good point about the hot afternoon sun.

"I suppose you're right about dat hot thing. In fact, I think I'll join ya. But then after dat, we got to get ourselves home before Momma does."

"Whooee. Now yo talkin'."

Benjamin couldn't help laughing out loud. Thomas was still his brother, and brothers, no matter what else was going on in this crazy world, should be brothers, especially when it came to playing in cool water on hot days.

A moment later, Benjamin was stripped down to his walking shorts and wading into the inviting, cool waters of the lake. The hard stones under his calloused feet didn't bother him, not after all of those years going barefoot.

"Did ya look for gators? I sure don't want to wrestle one to get your butt out his mouth," said Benjamin, scanning the area.

"Nah, we don't see many on dis side anyway. Well, except maybe for the da one Billy Richards says he saw last week. He's a bull-shitter though.

He claims he saw 'bout a fourteen-footer bumping along da shore over in dat direction," said Thomas, pointing to the west.

Benjamin took one more cautious glance in that direction. After seeing nothing that would put fear in a Louisiana lake boy, he proceeded to splash his little brother with a well-aimed blast of lake water.

Thomas screamed with laughter, then returned the favor. Soon both boys were lost in the moment, water flying and laughter drifting through the sticky air.

Ten minutes later, Benjamin's internal clock sounded, and he knew they'd better get out of the water and get home. They had some time, but he just knew Momma was on the way.

"Okay, Thomas, this is da last throw, then we gots to get home, so climb on up my thigh and we'll do a big toss."

"I'm up for dat, don't ya—"

Benjamin glanced up at Thomas when he didn't finish his sentence. His heart almost stopped when he saw the look of pure terror on his brother's young face.

He whirled in the direction that Thomas was staring. Any doubt about his brother overreacting to anything or pulling his leg was dispelled in the time it took to blink.

Gator.

The fourteen-footer was leisurely swimming so close to them that Benjamin probably could have reached out and touched the creature's rough, brown hide.

But the reptile's intimate proximity wasn't what sent the two boys into a sudden, orchestrated screaming symphony. Benjamin and Thomas had seen gators close up and real before. But not like this.

Never like this.

It was the half-eaten head of the woman lodged in the corner of the gator's jaws that did that.

# CHAPTER-23

Josh Corner stood on the spotless wraparound porch of the Fed safe house, shaking his finger in the face of the agent in charge of perimeter security.

After another minute of animated gestures, he then tapped the thick-chested man to emphasize his last, but apparently not least, point of the one-sided conversation. Manny found himself feeling a little compassion for the agent, but then again, his lack of judgment and action had almost cost Sophie and him their lives. Almost.

"Now that's what I call an ass-chewing," said Sophie.

"Hard to argue with you on that one," answered Manny.

"Yep, wouldn't want to be on the end of that one," said Alex.

"Yeah, but you might lose a couple of pounds," said Sophie, shifting to look at Alex, who was on the other side of Manny.

"Maybe. Or I could just have surgery to take care of my physical deficiencies, like some wench I know."

"Deficiencies? What? I just enhanced what was nearly perfect. And I notice you looking at the girls from time to time, for the record. And why would you want big tatas? Your man boobs are doing just fine."

Manny put one hand on the arm of each of his friends. "As much as I'd like to hear this highly intellectual conversation play out, we'll wait until later, got it?"

"Whatever," said Sophie, crossing her arms, lifting her bosom higher.

"What she said," said Alex, shrugging.

"Ha, he looked when I crossed my arms. Did you see that, Williams?"

"What? I did no such thing."

"Agents. Are you deaf? Stop."

Just then, Josh turned on his heel and made the thirty-foot trip over to where the three of them stood. Manny saw the stress on his face. Maybe even more than should be there.

"I'm sorry about that little greeting snafu. Are you sure you're both all right?" Josh asked, hands on hips, breathing hard.

"We're fine," said Manny. "A better question is what happened? Who were those two?"

Exhaling, Josh motioned toward the agent he'd just verbally hammered. "The agents monitoring the exterior cameras apparently misread the situation. They thought those two were with you and set their attention to a sensor breech on the backside of the property. By the time anyone noticed the front monitors, you two were doing the mamba with those imposters. We'll ID them shortly.

"Good thing most of the people who live on this end of the street were away from their houses, otherwise this would be a real snafu."

Manny frowned. "A set up?"

"Looks like it. Combine that possibility with the fact that our people weren't sure, in all of the confusion, which two of you were the real agents. This place is supposed to be a mile under the radar. Their decisions didn't meet my expectations or agency protocol," said Josh.

"The confusion with your agents is understandable, but obviously we need to get to the bottom of who these two are, and whether the distraction to your agents on the backside of the property was truly a set up."

"We've locked those two in separate security cells on the lower level of the house. I figured you'd like to take a shot at them. Maybe we won't have to bring in the testicle presses and the Judas Chair if you can get something from them," said Josh.

"Oh man, I want to work those bad boys. I only saw them in a couple of those, like, thirteenth-century movies," said Sophie.

"Actually, we have people skilled in the operation of those tools, so you'll have to watch."

Sophie wiped at her twitching nose and then tilted her head. "You're not kidding, are you? You really would torture these people?"

"Let's simply say there is nothing more important than the safety of Americans. We have to be prepared to do whatever it takes to protect the fine citizens of the good old USA," said Josh, his gaze steady.

"Really? Torture?" asked Alex.

Leaning toward Alex, Josh put his hand on Alex's new bionic arm, now free from the sling he'd worn for four weeks. "I'm tired of the bad guys living by any rule that fits them, and we, the good guys, the protectors of freedom and justice, have to play by rules that our enemies only laugh at. I hate it that they walk free out of courtrooms because of some dumbass technicality or because their lawyers were more persuasive than ours."

He stepped back, taking off his jacket, sweat from his armpits seeping through his shirt. "No more. I took this job and formed this team to make sure we don't become distracted from the objective. We'll be nice first though."

Manny hadn't seen Josh this fired up about his vocation in sometime. His passion was obvious, but so was the almost-always hidden anger his boss kept under wraps. Maybe not anger so much. Frustration, for sure. Yet, if there was such a thing as righteous anger, maybe his boss's was justified.

To serve and protect was every cop's motto.

On top of what Josh was espousing, Manny understood how the confines of the American justice system could hinder the very thing it was designed to prevent: criminals getting away with unspeakable acts. But it was a slippery slope to fight evil with shades of evil.

He reached out and gently removed Josh's hand from Alex's arm, who remained staring at Josh.

"We get it, and we signed up for this gig knowing we could make a difference, remember?" said Manny. "But if you think borderline methods, especially torture, aren't going to be questioned, then you don't know all of us like I think you do. Besides, we all know there are a dozen ways to get the intel we need."

"What he said," chimed in Alex.

"Bet your ass," echoed Sophie.

Josh opened his mouth to speak, then caught Manny's expression. He exhaled, looked down to his wingtips, then back to them.

"Yeah, I get that part too. I do know you, and you all know me. We go back to that godforsaken cruise years ago. We've gone through a bunch of shit and a lot of sunshine. I just want this job, this responsibility, to be the best thing we've ever done. No delays. No obstacles, no distractions. I—"

"Wait. What did you say? Never mind, I heard you. Shit, that's it. That's what's going on here. Damn it," interrupted Manny.

The whirlwind of the last hour, combined with the attack on Detective Brooks and the breach of security at the safe house, came roaring home when Josh uttered his last statement. It was like the last piece of a complex puzzle had been found on the floor and was inserted to complete the picture.

"What's *it*?" asked Sophie, tilting her head to get a better look at Manny's face.

"This is all orchestrated," said Manny, standing taller.

"All of what?" asked Josh.

"The attack on us. Brooks's shooting, the house breach, the holdup with getting you over here, and leaving your half of this team to follow you here. Hell, even the protocol snafus were part of this thing."

"What in the name of God are you talking about?" said Alex, frowning. "Shit happens in this business."

"Think about it. Whoever sent these people after us, and I suspect I'm right on this, went after Brooks too, knew exactly what would happen here. That we would react the way we did. That it takes time to organize a proper investigation. And forget implementing agency conventions, etc. I'm betting these people weren't even here to actually kill us, only cause another delay."

"Delay in what? We're going full bore in every . . . oh shit," said Sophie. "You're talking about staying on task."

"I think I'm right, there. We're being pulled away from what we should be truly concentrating on to get to where we need to go."

"That means whoever was involved in the warehouse incident thinks there might be something out there that could expose them? Is that what you're thinking?" asked Sophie.

"I am. We have to go back to basics, at least for us."

Manny turned back to Josh. "I think you need to bring everyone here. Forget that other intel or whatever the hell you're doing. What we need to find isn't in those databases and websites, looking for people who hate the government or whatever."

"Great, what then? I've spent time on this stuff, and so have the rest of us," said Alex.

After running his hand through his hair a few times and measuring his words, Manny made eye contact with the group. "Josh, like I said. I think we have to discuss a different approach to a couple of things."

"Like what?"

"Like all hands on deck. Complete focus. We need all of the help we can get in a concentrated time frame. And we need to ID that woman who died at the warehouse. ASAP. There's something fishy with that."

"Okay, we can do that. But you didn't answer Alex's question. Where does he start?" asked Josh.

"That's easy. He needs to do what he does. We all do."

Just then, the rest of the ACTU arrived in another white SUV. After greeting them, Manny looked around his circle of agents and sighed.

"We have to narrow the search down to a few possibilities of attack. That means we all have to use the gifts God gave us."

"We've been busting ass to that end," said Josh.

"We have. But we're all experts in different fields than the one area we need to be. We need someone who is."

"Wit what? Spit it out, mon," said Braxton.

"Have you ever heard of the Darknet?"

# CHAPTER-24

Thirty minutes later, the mess outside the Victorian was a distant blot on the radar screen. The seven members of the ACTU were gathered around a wooden table in a large room on the south side of the house, set aside for just this type of meeting.

Manny noticed no direct sunlight reached the cool, dim room through any of the windows. The skylight directly above the entrance was unlike any he'd ever seen, consisting of thick glass—bulletproof, he guessed—and a smoky tint that diminished the effect of the Louisiana sun, yet added another level of light.

The room smelled almost like a sterile examination room in one of a million doctor's offices with the exception of the faint coffee aroma. He suspected there would be more of that java odor before this situation reached its pinnacle.

"Did you all ever think there was this many conference rooms on the planet? I feel like we've met in most of them," said Sophie.

"Yeah well, that's what cops do. We meet and discuss cases," said Josh, a tinge of irritation in his voice. He looked at Manny. "We're here and we're ready. This better be good. I feel like we wasted a day on research you say doesn't matter, so what's next?" asked Josh.

"I think we've been going about this the wrong way."

"As you said. But—"

"Let me finish, okay?"

Josh threw up his hands. "Fine."

"What if we did our searches on the Internet a different way? What if we take what we *know* and expand the search based on that, instead of trying to guess what might be going on?"

"I hear you, but the problem has to do with what we know," said Sophie. "It doesn't appear to be a whole hell of a lot."

Manny shook his head. "No. I don't think that's true. The reason Josh brought us all together was that we each have knowledge in different areas, right?"

"Go on, mon," said Braxton.

"I read people's tendencies and actions. Alex is a forensic scientist. Sophie uses her intuition and understands the physical art of confrontation. Chloe is a profiler with experience in terrorist motivations and plots.

"Barb and Braxton have done the double-life, undercover thing and understand what that takes to be successful. No one organizes and recognizes the need for a quick decision like Josh. Belle, when she gets here, brings that profiler gift with a police expert twist. She's seen more of the different genres of crime fighting because of where she has done her investigations."

Josh tilted his neck, his vertebrae cracking. "All true, but what does any of that have to do with what you said a few minutes ago? I'm a little confused by us being distracted from this case and then you throw in the reference to the Darknet."

"I get that. Listen, our sense of urgency has been continually interrupted, like I explained before. The best way—"

"—to alleviate that pattern is to get us back to basics, to what each of us do better than the rest."

The large oak door had opened, and Belle Simmons, framed by the elaborate woodwork, stood with hands on her hips, her ebony countenance bright and alive.

Leading the way, Manny and the others moved to her, arms open and smiles on their faces. After the greetings were completed, Braxton and Belle seemed to enjoy a longer-than-the-rest hug. He wasn't sure anyone else noticed, but Manny filed that one away for future reference.

"Well, young lady, you're right as usual. It's hard to distract single-minded purpose, especially for the type of personalities in this room."

"So what are you suggesting? That we don't have the right chemistry here?" asked Josh.

Manny shook his head. "Not at all. I'm saying we don't have the total package. We need to add one more element to this team, in my opinion."

"What would that be?" asked Alex.

Opening his mouth to answer, Manny felt Sophie's hand on his arm. "Hold on, cowboy. Let us figure this out."

"All right. You tell me."

The room grew quiet, yet Manny swore he could hear the wheels turning as what he had said filtered through the team.

It didn't take long.

"Damn it, mon, I should have taut of dat. We don't have one of dem hacker types, now do we?"

Josh frowned. "The hell we don't. We have five or six of the best hackers and IT specialists that money and training can buy. Some of these people were, how shall we say, on the other side of the law and have very unusual skills. Damn. We can and do dig into everything. There's nowhere on the Internet these people can't go. Who do you think put together these databases that we're sifting through?"

"Josh—"

Josh raised his hand while his voice became more animated, his blue eyes on fire displaying more of that frustration. "Wait, Manny. You're wrong here. These people are at our beck and call. Even though they aren't on this team, per se, they . . . and I'm missing something, aren't I?" He sighed.

"Ahh, I'd say so, by the look on Williams's puss. But I'm not sure any of the rest of us are where he is either," said Sophie.

"I'm not," said Alex. "Sounds like we have top-of-the-line geeks working this thing. And I can tell you, the databases are well done."

"I agree with that, Alex. And I've seen the stats on what the information has done in terms of crime prevention and arrests, great stuff. But I also noticed that there were two categories of criminals we aren't doing so well locating and prosecuting," said Manny.

Josh folded his arms, his expression one of pure fascination. "Really, Manny? You broke down our data and linked it to our arrest records in separate criminal categories?"

"Yes, I did it the night I said I'd join this unit. I wanted to see how well we Feds were doing. I was looking for two things. And we've not done well with either, despite special units dedicated to them. Our very own BAU, over the last seven years, has captured less than forty percent of serial killers, by strict definition, that is."

"And the other," asked Barb.

"Domestic terrorists, as explained according to Chapter 113B US Code. If you take the three-part delineation literally, we've only managed to stop about thirty-nine percent of the homegrown type of attacks that fall in that category."

"Hell, I didn't think it was that good," said Belle.

The urgency bell rang loud in Manny's mind as he realized he'd gotten off track. Knowledge is good, but not always practical.

He turned back to Josh. "The Darknet is a creepy haven for anyone seeking help—from contract killers to pedophile requests to slavery auctions to terrorist networks, including hidden cell communication, which I expect your people know well. But I want someone who thinks like these people do, even darker. Your people are good, but I'd guess they haven't reached a couple of places that maybe someone with almost-evil experience could, agreed?"

"Okay, maybe," said Josh.

"The bottom line is that we need a hacker or computer expert who understands the people we are looking for better than we do. Someone who knows the Darknet and the next step into the deep web and can see the subtle communication tendencies between some of this slime that we don't."

"So you want a serial-killer/terrorist who can hack and wants to help the ACTU bring down the people responsible for what happened in the warehouse and expose what they are planning? Does that cover it?" asked Josh.

"It does. And I know—"

Josh raised his hand and pulled out his phone. After a few seconds, he responded with a curt "Got it."

"What now?" asked Sophie, rolling her eyes.

"Apparently the APB we put out, based on the description Detective Brooks gave, may have a hit."

"What does that mean?" asked Manny.

"It means the NOPD located a body, what's left of it at least, near the north end of Lake Pontchartrain. It could fit Brooks's attacker. They're waiting for us."

"Let's go," said Sophie.

"Wait," said Manny.

Sophie was right, but it was time to change what and how they did what they were doing. Another distraction wasn't what this team needed; a concentrated, coordinated effort attacking all sides of the investigation was in order.

"We can't keep going away from our strengths and expect results. Whatever is going to happen is going to happen soon. We need to do more."

"Tell me what you want, Manny. I'm a little stumped here," said Josh.

"I will, since you asked. Chloe, Alex, and you need to head to the lake. The scene, if there is one, has to be processed, has to be done right with the three of you in charge. That's what you do."

Shifting, he faced Barb, Braxton, and Belle. "You three need to go to work on the two who tried to kill Sophie and me. You know how a good interrogation is done, and profiling that interrogation could help uncover who was behind that little dance. Hopefully that will lead to something."

"And what the hell are you and Sophie going to be doing?" demanded Josh.

"I started to tell you that I know someone who might fit our bill for a hacker-type. Sophie and I are going to take the jet and find out if I'm right. We'll be back in about four hours."

"Okay. It sounds like you've thought this through," said Josh. "I like this approach, and I think you just taught me something."

"I did, huh?"

"You did. I still have things to learn about seeing the big picture. By the way, where are you going?"

Sophie grinned. "I'd like to say he's taking me out for great Cajun shrimp. But I think we're headed for Colorado and the Florence ADMX Super Prison."

# CHAPTER-25

He'd anticipated this. It wouldn't be long before the Feds and their new super team put some pieces together and made a few educated guesses about what was to come. They had been easily manipulated to this point, but he suspected that was about to end. New teams take a while to gel—he knew that from experience.

No matter. He'd keep following what he knew to be the proper path toward the goal of balancing the scale of justice. His scale.

Lifting the old chrome handle, he exited the Chevy and stood in the ever-waning light of the late New Orleans afternoon. The heat of the day dissipated with the light.

"Ahh. What is life if not constant evolution and change?" he whispered.

Looking up and down the street for a fourth time, he saw only a couple of young kids riding their bikes away from where he stood. Other than that, he was alone.

Leaning back against the car, he resigned himself to wait a few more minutes to make sure his solitude wasn't an illusion. Caution eliminated mistakes. Cases in point were the people in the warehouse, dear Lucretia, and all of the others over the last four years.

While killing was still on the unsavory side for him, doing what was necessary was not.

Rhodes's thoughts shifted in another direction as he continued to wait for the right moment.

His final undertaking needed to be handled with effort and concentration, particularly with the advent of invasive technology over the last few years. He had to stay careful. Focused.

He hadn't enjoyed expending effort on diverting law enforcement. But it had to be done. The less they discovered, the less time they had to discover it.

Were they sometimes incompetent? Perhaps. Easily mislead? Yes. But fools? Certainly not. Especially Agent Manny Williams. He'd have to watch that one, at least for another day and a half.

The other members of the ACTU were talented in their own rights, including their leader, Agent Joshua Corner. Some were even dangerous, but Williams was the straw that stirred the drink. Yet, Williams had weaknesses that would lead to his downfall, his failure to catch a killer. He would finish his task, and the media would explode into their usual uninformed frenzy, telling the world what he'd done and the Feds would be left holding their dicks. Including Agent Williams.

The profile regarding the profiler extraordinaire was straight forward.

The man was tireless, a true workaholic when turned loose, and he was most certainly out of the cage now. According to the research dating back from his days as a detective, he had "the gift." Williams understood people, their motivations, and their anger. Which probably led to a few expressions of rage of his own.

All of that came in handy in Manny's line of work. However, for all of his assets, Williams also held two explosive intangibles. One made him dangerous; the other was his Achilles heel.

Manny believed in the existence of God, the afterlife, Heaven. This outlook could lead him to be a little lax in regards to his own personal safety—he was saved, after all.

Fair enough. There was a part of Rhodes that hoped God *did* exist. But how could that be true, given the lack of justice on this planet?

"Wrong there, I think," he whispered.

*Yet . . .*

The Achilles heel for this team was their regard for human life, especially true for Williams.

He laughed out loud. In a manner of speaking, he and Agent Williams were one in the same regarding that. He wondered just how far the Fed and his team would go to see that mission of justice and protection accomplished. It may come to that.

Reaching into his pocket, he dialed the number he'd been waiting to call his whole life.

"Yes?" answered the smooth voice.

"Are you ready?"

There came a small, amused giggle. "I was born ready. Tonight, then?"

"Yes. Tonight. At the time we agreed upon."

"Has the money been moved into my account?"

"You'll find that it has."

"That's appreciated. Good luck with your endeavor."

The phone then promptly went dead.

He stared at the throwaway, realizing there was now no turning back. Yet, had there ever been?

He tossed the phone through the open window of the Chevy. He then pulled the lighter from the pocket of his khakis, hesitated while scanning the area one last time, and then flicked his finger, the golden fire-starter coming to blue-tinted life.

"Goodbye, old friend. Onward and upward."

He threw the lighter inside the vehicle.

As the flames began to caress the seat and then rise to the dash, he walked the fifty feet to where the old Dodge pickup truck awaited him, his mind electrified with thoughts regarding the next morning.

# CHAPTER-26

Sophie felt her stomach clench, stronger than usual, as the FBI's jet banked west and then north. They'd just taken off from Louis Armstrong Airport.

Instinctively, she reached toward the seat beside her, anticipating Dean's large, strong hand would envelope her own and make this flying crap more bearable. In fact, Dean had made a couple of those trips almost enjoyable. On those occasions, she hadn't even experienced a tinge of nausea. Not so today.

When she had realized what she'd done, she pulled her hand back, shaking her head, hoping upon every hope that she wouldn't go *there* again.

Too late.

It had been a few hours since she'd really allowed the abyss, filled with guilt and pity, to drag her down deep, threatening to drive her insane with grief. Allowed? Like she could stop it.

His bearded face rose up and stayed where her mind's eye could see him. She wanted desperately to touch the tiny crow's feet at the base of his big eyes, to stroke his beard the way she did after they'd made love. To kiss his full lips once again would be akin to the heaven Manny spoke of.

She needed to breathe in his special scent that helped to make him wonderfully Dean.

*How much more of this can I take?*

Just when the heartbreak was about to bring about another teary-eyed shower of Biblical proportions, he was beside her, holding her hand, talking softly close to her ear. She looked up, her eyes wide with unnatural anticipation. Then she smiled, shaking her head.

"Damn, Williams, can't a girl go insane in peace every so often?"

"Well, you can go there if you want. I actually think I might remember the way down that road. I'll sit here and wait for you to get back, if you'd like."

Unbuckling her seatbelt, she rested her head on his thick chest, his heartbeat slow, steady, and strong. It seemed to almost blend with the sounds of cutting through the air at twenty-five-thousand feet. The effect was calming, if not hypnotic.

After a few minutes, the demons retreated and she sat up, kissing Manny on the cheek.

"Sometimes, Manny, just sometimes, I want to be where he is. If your God was as loving as you say, that place would boggle my mind. Just seeing Dean one more time would probably boggle it even more . . . I mean, to really see him."

She watched the quiet, intense cloud appear in Manny's eyes. It was only alive for a moment, then it disappeared—but some moments were lifetimes and that cloud had shown her that. Her best friend was still in pain.

He pulled a little closer.

"I know what you mean. I was afraid I'd not remember Louise's face or the touch of her hand or the color of those incredible eyes. Even the sound of her voice when she called my name. That her memory would run to some bottomless recess of my mind and that she would be an insignificant shadow. Especially after Chloe and I were married."

"And?"

"And nothing could be further from the truth. We had a connection that was one of a kind. Just like the one I have with you and Alex and Josh and, of course, with Jen and Ian and Chloe. I think we need those others to survive when a part of our heart is ripped away. They help us keep it together and give us a little resolve."

"You didn't always think that, right?"

"I didn't. Do you remember the day you and Alex came over dressed in your own special baseball outfits? You stepped out of the vehicle, and after a month of wondering what the hell I was going to do without her, I suddenly knew. I had to get to it again. Not for me so much, but for Jen and you two. You had always counted on me because you could. It was my turn to let you carry the load."

"Yeah. That was a sweet outfit too."

Sophie sat up, her stomach rumbling, and reached over to pick up the bottle of water resting in the cup holder. She didn't know how many men on the planet were like Manny. Probably not many. Maybe there was something to this guardian-angel stuff. He'd saved her from more desperate situations than she could count.

They were on that road again, but she felt her angst melt away.

"Thanks again, Manny. I'm good for now. Let's get our asses in motion here. We've got a killer or killers to find."

Manny got up and moved to the seat across from her. Trusting her words, she suspected, he had already gone back to cop mode.

"You're right. I hope splitting up like we have, and what we do next, works."

"That's where she comes in?"

He nodded, his hair moving as he did. "She'll give us more insight on what's going on here than we can ever glean on our own, I hope. It's at least worth a shot."

"So why do you think that? I know her complete mind shift has people curious on how a confessed serial killer can do that, but what's the real deal with her?"

"Still a good question. Do you remember when we took her into custody and we had a series of interviews with her?"

"Of course. I had a few nightmares because of what came from her mouth. Especially the animal-killing thing when she was younger."

"I did too. But the part of those interviews that has stuck with me, other than what I believe to be a complete reversal of her psychology regarding life, was the fact that she found ways to visit and interview dozens of serial killers. A couple of those names on her list had greater aspirations than following their perverted sexual desires to stack up bodies."

"You mean the two who wanted to make a bigger statement than watching someone die by their own hands or even by some dumbass suicide bomber?"

"I do. Even though she made good notes on the interview with those two, I think she knows more. I think, given their delusional narcissistic needs, they bragged and told her more than they think."

Sophie thought about what Manny was suggesting. She sighed. "You know, I think I like chasing down weird-ass serial killers better than this terrorist thing. They're straightforward with their purpose and almost always do their thing alone, you know?"

"I get that. But how different is what we're doing, really? We have to strip these people down to the simplest motivations and logic. Just like before, except on a deeper level. If possible. I think she gets that better than us," said Manny.

"So I agree these assholes are more complex in how they do what they do, and way more covert. Guys like Argyle wanted us to know who he was. It was a game, and he totally enjoyed the confrontations we had with him. And he wasn't the only one who did it that way."

"I know what you mean. But I think we are getting it, and what you say is true. These people would love to stay shadows, ghosts," said Manny.

"Great. We're freaking ghost hunters."

"We are. That's not all either. We're money hunters too. I suspect there is far more money at work here than even with the likes of Argyle. Those people who attacked us didn't do it as a community service to Criminals Anonymous. More available money means more folks involved, at least to help these people accomplish a step in their plan, then *boom*, erase that loose end and on to the next level. We find the money trail and we're on to something. I think Braxton and Barb might give us our best chance to figure that out."

Sophie rubbed her eyes, feeling a little more fatigue than she thought she should, but hell, what a day they'd had, and flying twice on the same day was more than draining to a person with her phobia.

"So where does she come in regarding all that?"

The plane veered a little left as the copilot told them they were beginning their descent into Colorado.

"I'm banking that Anna Ruiz has seen more than she knows."

Sophie hoped he was right. Even she could feel the hourglass draining.

# CHAPTER-27

Alex stood beside Chloe and Josh as they watched the long, sedated reptile rest leisurely on the narrow beach. It was some forty feet from where the three of them stood on the north side of the big lake. It could have been more, to suit him.

The vivid smells of fish and decaying weeds reminded him that this wasn't Michigan. That and the heat. Even in the late afternoon, Louisiana was still Louisiana.

He wiped at his brow with his right hand where even more sweat had accumulated, his forensic kit resting comfortably near his feet.

"Well, at least the Orleans Parrish Animal Control people were able to save the gator's life," said Chloe. "But they'll have to drop him off deep in the swamp; he now has the taste of human meat on his menu."

"That works for me. They wouldn't have had a choice if he'd eaten more of the body. I told them I can figure out what happened to her, I think, as long as most of the remains are here," answered Alex.

Josh cringed. "She's missing a leg, an arm, a part of her abdomen, and about half of her face . . . and you call that 'mostly there'?"

"Hey, I've dealt with worse. Luckily her body was still attached to her head. Hey, did I ever tell you about that decayed body I had to process on my first rodeo? We found it in a hot, steamy warehouse loft sitting in a bit of gasoline. Damn. I mean the smell alone was a killer, but all of that green slimy bio—"

"Okay, Downs. I get it," said Josh, raising his hand.

Alex smiled. "Crap. You just ruined a good story. But I suppose we'd better get to work."

Chloe moved beside Alex, wearing her own smile. Alex was suddenly struck by how beautiful she was, even in this situation, and what she'd meant to Manny over the last two years. Yep. He supposed he would lose another hand to protect either one of them.

"This woman fits the APB and description, minus the previously mentioned body parts. Alex, you're spot-on; we need to get rolling with this," said Josh.

"Right-o," said Alex and headed toward the picnic table where the body was laid out.

Chloe stepped up next to him. "I'm going to help you go over it while Josh leads the NOPD going door to door."

Alex stopped and turned to Josh. "What about the forensic team?"

"Awaiting your instruction."

After thinking about that for a moment, he nodded. "Okay, it's like we said on the way over. Tell their boss to start with tire tracks on any road or turn-out within two miles of this spot. Someone had to have dumped the body somewhere close."

"Will do."

"I also want them to check for footprints. I need casts of everything. I doubt seriously that we'll find any fibers on her or what's left of the plastic she was wrapped in, because the body was in the water, but I suspect she was transported in an inconspicuous manner. Check for anything . . . hell, even fresh paper byproducts from candy wrappers or cigarette packs. They'll know what you mean. They also might look for impressions in the dirt, maybe he laid her on the ground while he wrapped her up."

He rubbed his chin with his prosthetic, still getting used to it being out of the sling. "You know, there could be blood traces as well. Have them check each place they stop for that too. This isn't a sandy beach, at least not much of it, so there could be traces on the rocks."

"Anything else?"

"I'm still thinking. We've already sent DNA samples, along with strands of clothing and a piece of that plastic to the NOPD's lab, as well as fingerprints, so they can get started. They need to analyze that material in a hurry."

He refocused on Josh. "You know, we could use access to any tapes from surveillance cameras, private and public, installed anywhere around here. Then have it feed to our system. I know this location is off the beaten path, another reason whoever dumped her chose this area."

Josh saluted. It reminded Alex of his favorite wench, Sophie, and her reaction to instructions.

"Stay in contact with me," said Josh. "I'm waiting to hear from Barb's team on the interrogation progress, and Manny and Sophie will be landing near the ADX facility soon."

He put his hand on Alex's shoulder and smiled at Chloe. "I'm good with this change in direction. Manny had basically quoted that old saying: *there's nothing like good police work.* He was right. We were distracted and running in circles, it seemed with no traction, even though the database searches will help in the long run, I hope. At any rate, I feel at least like we've shifted gears. Good luck."

"Thanks, you too. We're going to need it," said Alex.

Alex watched him walk away, grabbed his case, and then turned toward the body, Chloe in tow. They stood over the end of the table where the remainder of the woman's head lay. He glanced at Chloe, expecting at minimum a hint of repulsion, but saw none. He'd almost forgotten how tough she'd had to be throughout her career.

After she pulled out her phone, she slid her finger and then showed him the screen.

"This composite profile picture that Brooks helped with is close. The hair is different, but the curve of what's left of her face and that chin line looks like a match, to the naked eye."

"It does," said Alex, squinting at the photo, which he already had memorized. "That's where proving it comes in. I'm going to leave the whys and what-fors to you, for now. If this is the same women, the science might help determine some of those questions."

"Agreed." Chloe bent closer to the body. "Where do we start?"

Reaching into his case, he took out his Nikon DSLR camera and began taking pictures, steadying it with his newly constructed left hand, pushing the button with the index finger on his right.

Stepping back, he then bent close, changed angles, all the while circling the body, careful to allow as much sunlight as necessary. He supposed if he hadn't fallen in love with forensic science, he might have tried his hand at photography. Taking pictures felt natural to him.

Changing directions, he took a step, then bumped into Chloe, not realizing she'd been following his path closely.

"Oops, sorry. Just trying to see what you see," she said.

He put the camera down on the faded wooden table. "Okay, Mrs. Williams, what do you see?"

Chloe raised her eyebrows, then smiled. "Okay. I'll try, don't you know."

Her Irish intonation always made him grin.

"I see too many teeth marks left by the gator in a couple of places to distinguish any trauma there. So let's look at the other places where she was covered and relatively clean."

"Great start, Agent."

Scanning the remains with an expert eye, Alex watched while she stopped at the woman's side, near her right breast, just above where a huge part of the victim's flesh and internal organs were missing.

Putting on her synthetic gloves, Chloe reached down and lightly touched a symmetrical hole that didn't appear gator related.

Good eye. It wasn't.

"Gunshot?" she asked.

"Yep. That'd be my guess. Let's find out for sure."

Reaching into the black leather kit, he removed a long, narrow, tweezer-like instrument, winked at Chloe, and then slowly, his hand as steady as a surgeon's, he lowered the tool into the hole.

There was a quiet sucking sound as water and tissue oozed from the wound. The accompanying aroma was far less than savory, but Alex ignored it, intent on his mission. After a few more seconds, he felt metal hit metal. Maneuvering the piece until he was satisfied he had it in the proper position, he withdrew it, the crinkled slug dangling from the tip of the tweezers as it left the woman's torso.

"Get me an evidence bag, please."

A breath later, the spent slug was sealed in polyurethane.

"Can you tell what caliber it is?" asked Chloe.

"It's not in bad shape, and we'll have to run it through ballistics, but I know Detective Brooks's service weapon is a Glock 22, forty caliber. This looks like it could be a match for that caliber."

"But we can't jump to conclusions, right?"

"Right. Follow the science, and it takes the guesswork out of it."

Leaning back, Chloe put her hand on her chin, Basil Rathbone-like. "Was that what killed her?"

Alex shrugged. Another good question.

"Again, we'll verify that in the coroner's lab, but no, I don't think so. Looking at the entry of the bullet and where it ended up, and I'm not a doctor, but I believe it must have hit a rib. That's why there's damage to the slug. I think she would have bled significantly, but it wouldn't have killed her right away."

"So we keep looking for something exterior?"

"Right again. If we don't find anything, we have two conclusions to sift through."

"Those are?" asked Chloe.

"She was either killed by something internal, like poison, or something else not so obvious. Or the gator snacked on the part of the body that would give us a clue as to what really happened."

He reached up and pulled open the victim's one remaining eye, then examined her neck and throat area.

"Okay, there are no ligature marks around her throat, and her eye doesn't show any petechial hemorrhaging, so I think we can rule out strangulation."

"Got it."

"Let's check the next possibility on the forensic list. She could have drowned."

"Water in the lungs?"

"You're a natural at this, Chloe. But that's not the only thing that determines death by drowning. She doesn't appear to have any wounds on her hands and arms from struggling against an attack. Particularly, injuries that might have led to being forcibly thrown or held in the water. The bruising around the gator bites looks postmortem to me, so I think we'll not assume she drowned."

He ran his hand along a small section of plastic still attached to part of the leather belt near her waist.

"Throw in the fact that she was probably completely wrapped in plastic like this, I'd say she was most certainly dead before she became a meal."

"Makes sense," said Chloe softly.

Glancing at her, he noticed she was looking at the left side of what remained of the woman's neck.

She pointed a finger at a small hole, purple and blue in color, below the woman's ear. It appeared to be too clean to be a bite or random injury caused by rocks on the lake bottom.

"What's that, Alex? It looks different."

"You're right. It could be a stab wound. Let's see."

Stepping back to his kit, he pulled a narrow flashlight from a bottom shelf, then grabbed a smaller pair of tweezers.

"Here," he said, handing Chloe the light. "Shine this right into the wound. Sometimes, every once in a while, depending on the angle of the thrust . . ."

His voice trailed off as he became lost in the idea that this could be something special. Manny would have been proud of the fact that he was riding high on a mere feeling, and not science.

At first, he saw nothing. He moved a small section of pale, shredded flesh, and there it was, reflecting against the steady rays of the light.

Gently, carefully, he latched on to the barely visible piece of metal. He then held it close to his eyes. He felt Chloe standing over his shoulder, her warm breath reminding him he wasn't alone.

"What is it?"

"That, Agent, is the miniscule tip of the knife that helped sever this woman's carotid artery."

# CHAPTER-28

"How do you want to do this?" asked Belle.

Barb pointed at the two-way mirror leading to the holding room of the safe house. The two attackers sat across the room from each other. Both showed pointed physical effects of losing their encounter with Sophie and Manny—bruises, a black eyepatch on the right eye of the man, and a bandage across the woman's arm where a hot bullet had left its mark.

"We do what we always do, Belle. First, we asked nicely. If that doesn't work, well, then . . ."

"Dat's right. It probably won't do any good, but we will try," said Braxton, his mammoth arms crossed against his thick chest.

"Okay, I understand that, and I know we don't have much time," said Belle, frustration seeping into her voice. "But we usually separate suspects into different rooms. It makes them uneasy, and they don't gather any strength or resolve from their cohorts."

"Ahh, dat's what ever'body does, but not dis time, not in dis circumstance."

Barb coughed lightly into her fist to clear her throat, then explained. "Sometimes in these high-pressure situations, the perps will show us something with their body language because of the increased tension of being together. You'd think they'd take a little comfort from each other. I haven't seen it work that way very often. No one wants to be the first to crack. Hell, sometimes they argue with each other. Either way, when the heat is turned up, you can almost see them get ready to turn on each other. They want to be the first one to make a deal, especially when you ask the right questions. You can profile. Tell me what you see."

Belle stepped toward the glass, her eyes riveted on the perps sitting a few feet from each other. She flinched slightly when the man raised his head, glanced at the woman, and shared a toothy, exaggerated grin.

Barb touched her arm. "And?"

"Okay, it's subtle, granted, but they are on the same page. I don't see any real fear in them. Anxiousness maybe, but no fear."

"I agree. But why aren't they afraid?" asked Barb.

"I don't know. Arrogance?" said Belle.

"Maybe, but that's why we need to get in there and get this thing rolling. We've let them stew long enough. We're under the gun here."

It was Belle's turn to cross her arms. The look on her face was becoming more troubled. Barb knew what was coming next. And it did.

"What about their rights? Their legal rights?" Belle asked.

Braxton's loud laugh almost made them both jump, then Barb smiled. His laugh was very infectious, even at inopportune times.

"Do ya tink dese people have rights? Or dat we give a shit about dem if dey did? Dey tried to kill two agents of the ACTU. Dey got nothing."

When Belle frowned, Barb waved her hand. "We can discuss this trip down morality lane another time. We've a terrorist problem, and these two are going to help us solve it."

The steel security door opened behind them, and another agent walked in holding two sheets of paper, which he gave to Barb. "We've identified these two, for what it's worth. It's a little bizarre."

"Why?"

He shrugged. "See for yourself. I've got to go. We have another issue to deal with in Metairie." He then spun and abruptly left the room.

Glancing down at the first page, featuring details of the tall woman, Barb read quickly. She then shuffled to the second page and read the man's information. It was almost identical, except for the name and gender.

The "oh shit" feeling inside her stomach swelled to storm proportions, chasing her as she ran to the door.

"We have to get in there now," she yelled, reaching for the ashtray on the solitary metal table.

"Why? What's wrong?" asked Belle.

"These two are members of God's Hand."

"Shit," said Braxton, falling in right behind Barb.

"Who the hell is that?" asked Belle.

"Dey are a crazy cult of radicals dat tink suicide at the right time gets dem into heaven."

Reaching the door to the containment room, her heart beating twice its normal speed, Barb swung it open and then lunged for the woman in one desperate attempt to knock her over, chair and all.

The woman laughed, even as her body, shoulder first, struck the tiled floor with a resounding thud. Barb landed on top of her.

"You can't come where I'm going, Agent. None of you can. No one like you will enter the Gates of the Golden City. There's . . ."

Barb shoved the plastic ashtray into the woman's open lips, forcing it into her mouth, extracting a gasping reflex that wiped the smile from the woman's face.

Behind her, she heard Braxton swear, Belle joining him, a little shock in her voice as she yelled.

Barb knew without looking that Buford had exercised his brainwashed prerogative and would be dead in a few seconds. She couldn't let that happen to the Grimes woman.

Leaning close, she whispered in her very best I'm-your-friend persuasion. "Please, Rachel, don't try to bite down on that tooth. We can help you. We can get you out of this group and protect you from the people who hired you."

Grimes's cold eyes focused on her face. Barb had to control the chill brought on by the pure, unadulterated hatred coming from the woman.

Instead, there was a sudden pressure against the ashtray and then an almost inaudible sound of breaking glass.

The woman smiled, then suddenly thrashed to the left, as much as her bindings would allow. Her eyes rolled up deep into the recesses of her head, white foam and spittle forming on her thin lips. Then the woman died.

# CHAPTER-29

The small, well-designed interview room in the west wing of the ADX prison was secure and impregnable, like the rest of the prison.

As it should be for a facility referred to as the Alcatraz of the Rockies.

The clean, stainless steel décor was completely void of anything that might be molded into some sort of weapon in the hopes of escaping the inescapable.

Ironically, the guards didn't carry weapons of any kind, not even nightsticks or riot-control clubs. They were, however, the most thoroughly trained federal prison guards in the world. Most were experts in more than one martial art; and they all were in exceptional physical condition. He supposed he would go that route as well.

A well-built guard opened the door to his right, and Sophie entered, smiling. She plopped down in the chair next to Manny.

"Damn, Williams, this place is absolutely full of eye candy."

"Is that right?"

"Some observant King of the Profilers you are. Hell yes, man. I mean, I'm in mourning, but I sure ain't dead. I think that last mass of muscle stared at my rack, more than once too."

Classic Sophie Lee. For once, her sexual innuendo was a welcome addition to their conversation. Yet another indication she was making the adjustment to her heart-breaking loss.

"Well, they are restricted to looking at mostly men all day, so who can blame them for an extra look?"

"Yeah, good point, especially hot Asians. Hey, speaking of that whole men and women thing, how did Anna end up here? I thought this was reserved for the male scums of the earth."

"It is, mostly. It used to include women, then was changed to an all-male prison. Since they're truly able to keep the population isolated from each other, there have been some special circumstances that allow for woman inmates to be admitted."

Folding his hands and placing them on the table, he continued. "Anna fits that special description, particularly after her behavior shift and given the nature of her situation, and her IQ . . . it was thought best to bring her into this one.

"It helps that Florence is forty miles south of anything remotely close to a city. If she did figure out how to escape, which would be like trying to fry an egg without heat, she wouldn't get far."

"So in short, the Feds, and you, think she's smarter than the rest of the pieces of shit in this place?"

"That's true as well. But that was all secondary to having secure access to interview her. That's been successful as far as the program designed for her is concerned. She has allowed over seventy-five interviews from almost every renowned psychologist, psychiatrist, doctor of human behavior, and law enforcement profiler in the world."

"She must feel like some reject from Pinky and the Brain with all of that research and questioning. I suppose she had to endure a few physicals along the way as well," said Sophie, disgust tinging her words.

"That goes without saying, but she can—"

The double doors leading from the holding cell into the interview room opened, and Anna Ruiz entered with a strapping gray-clad guard on each side of her. They were accompanied by the clanging of metal against metal as the chains on her wrists, leading to her ankles, spoke while she shuffled forward.

Her green eyes met his, lighting up like the proverbial Christmas tree. He returned her grin with an affectionate one of his own. All things considered, she looked like she was doing well. Certainly better than the last visit almost six months prior.

"Knights in shining armor don't take this long to rescue the fair maiden, do they?" she asked as she tumbled into the steel chair across from Sophie.

The guard on her left told her to mind her manners, then shoved at the back of her head, hard enough that her forehead almost hit the table.

Five seconds later, Manny held the guard's chin in his hand, bringing the big man's face close to his. "If you ever do that again, son, you'll be walking a beat in Ithaca, Michigan. Do you feel me?"

The guard nodded, his eyes as wide as hubcaps. "Yes sir. Just keeping order, that's all."

Releasing the guard, Manny stepped back. "You let us worry about that. Now take off the bracelets."

"No can do, against policy," said the other guard.

"I wouldn't piss him off anymore," said Sophie. "He ain't as badass as me, but he'll pull your tongue out your dick if you keep this up."

Manny flashed his ID. "This says we don't have a policy."

The guard looked at the clearance level of his ID, shrugged, and removed the shackles. "Your ass, Agent. We'll be outside when you need us."

The two men left the room.

"Dang, Sophie, that's a bit much, don't you think?' said Anna, the bounce in her voice undeniable.

"Hell no. These people need to know what's what." Sophie glanced at Manny, then back to Anna. "So how are you doing, girlfriend?"

"Hanging in there, mostly. I'm hoping against hope—every second, by the way—that you will get me out of here today. You did bring the limo, right?"

Her wry smile told Manny more than her words. Reminding him once again that he had never seen such a reversal of functional psychology in a single person. It was little wonder that she was the focus of much study.

"We're working on that."

"I know you are, Manny. I know it."

Her face softened as she turned in Sophie's direction, rubbing her synthetic hand covered by the black glove. She'd lost it during her encounter with Caleb Corner, Josh's brother.

"We're isolated in here, but I get information because of the computer work I do. I'm sorry beyond words to hear about Dean, Sophie. I've been thinking of you, praying too."

Sophie nodded slowly. "Thank you. I'm a little better. I just wish prayers worked the way I want them to," she answered softly.

"I know, but every notch upward helps. Better is still better. I know a little about that."

"I suppose you do. I'm on the road, but it'll be a long one. So thanks again."

Anna looked down at the table, her arms extended at her shoulders before she finally rested them on the table.

"I suspect you've got some questions for me, right?" she asked.

"We do. We've talked about some of the serial killers and other various categories of psychopaths before, but we need to focus on a certain type of individual this time."

"Fire away."

"Terrorists. Domestic terrorists. In your prior contacts and communications, did you run into anyone who might have an affinity for, maybe even evolve into, that type of expression?" asked Manny.

She tilted her head. "You're not working the BAU any longer, are you? Or is this a side trip to better understand the land of the deranged?"

Sharp as ever. "No, we're not exactly in the BAU these days. We've graduated, I suppose. We are involved in the next level of bad guys versus good guys. We're now part of the CTD, a newly created special unit."

"Counterterrorism, huh?"

"Yep," said Sophie.

Standing, Anna then paced from one side of the room to the other before eventually returning to her seat.

"Tell me what's going on, okay?" she asked, her voice quiet and subdued.

Manny gave her details about New Orleans and what they'd run into, with Sophie filling in the blanks.

After they finished, she sat still, hands now in her lap, obviously contemplating what she had heard. But it went deeper. It was more like sorting out information and filing it in a specific order, but with more intent, more insight and intuition on how that information worked. It was interesting to watch, even after seeing it a few times.

Finally, Anna leaned back against the chair, watching his face. Her body language told Manny she wasn't at ease.

"What's wrong, Anna?"

She shook her head. "I don't know if you could actually call something wrong that is as nebulous as knowledge can be. Knowledge just is. It's what people do with that knowledge, right?"

"That's a true statement. Please explain why that matters in this situation."

"I will. Give me a few minutes to tell this story."

"Deal."

"There was this one killer I wrote to when I was seventeen, just a month before I turned eighteen. He was in a prison near Houston, Texas. On death row, I believe. He'd been arrested and convicted for brutally killing thirteen Mexican immigrants with a pair of machetes in a camp just outside San Antonio."

She leaned in over the table. "As you might imagine, after he'd finished his spree, the area was a complete mess. I had managed to find some pictures on a couple of those creepy hard-to-find websites. Not pretty to me now, but back then that was a different kind of party for me."

Anna brought her knees up toward her chin. Manny noticed she no longer attempted to hide her artificial hand.

"Anyway, I started to notice a pattern. I finally got a copy of the transcripts of his trial—to see if the pattern was random or intentional."

"I remember that guy. Alvarez, right?" said Sophie.

"Yes. Victor Alvarez."

"Go on," said Manny.

"He had killed those people in a certain order. Doing it in threes, until the last group. He obviously had to murder that last group in a four-person order."

Manny ran his hand through his hair, causing Anna to radiate a warm smile. "I know the wheels are turning when you do that."

"Yeah, guilty as charged. Let me guess about that pattern. As subconscious as it probably was, he likely sectioned and categorized them mentally into types, taking out the most dangerous to his mission first, then the others."

She nodded. Her smile had dissipated into a far more serious countenance. "You're right. The three children and two elderly women in that camp were killed last. After he'd taken out the other younger, stronger adults."

He watched as she exhaled, her eyes wider, her heart rate obviously accelerated. The nervous little rubbing she often did with her normal hand touching her deformed limb made a reappearance.

"Moving forward, I sent him five letters, spaced exactly seven days apart. I told him what I'd observed at the crime scene and kept asking him to tell me what he was thinking before, during, and after his massacre. That I was struggling to make sense of what was going on in my head and, if I had one, my heart. I even asked him if he thought we were demon possessed."

Sophie was on the edge of her seat at this point; Manny nodded for Anna to continue.

She swallowed, appearing a little uneasy, then said, "He finally sent me the first letter. He wanted naked pictures of me in different angles. Hell, that was an easy thing for me to do for him because of who, what, I was and couldn't have cared less if he saw my body. So I sent him what he wanted." Anna touched her lips. "Can I get some water?"

Manny walked over to the steel water fountain against the far wall, drew her some water in the paper cup, and took it to her, his mind racing with possibilities.

There was a certain narcissism to everyone who walked the planet. He supposed it fueled or was fueled by a rainbow of emotions, needs, and situations. Survival, acceptance, and empowerment covered what most people needed.

In killers who had done horrible things on a hideously grand level, that sense of self-importance was elevated to the point that, eventually, they had to tell their story.

Yet, they also had to make sure they had a level of control first. He'd seen it a hundred times. By giving Alvarez what he asked for, Anna had given him, knowingly or not, the platform of control and dominance he needed.

Alvarez had begun to look at this young woman as his in almost every way. Manny suspected Anna had realized that—again, knowingly or subconsciously.

She drew from the cup, set it down, and moved her gaze from Manny to Sophie, then back to Manny, holding his attention.

"You are still not like anyone I've talked to or written to over the years in terms of how you think and piece details together. Do you already know what's next?" Anna asked.

He shook his head. "Not exactly. I have some ideas. I know this type of binge personality. And I know he would think of you and him as intimate. That he could trust you because he saw you as his, as far as a concept like trust goes with people like Alvarez. So tell us what's next."

But even as Manny finished his request, he felt the anxiety grow in him. Predictability to some extent was something he could profile in most; yet, in a few people, there was no such thing as predictable because of their own psychology. In those cases, even those people didn't know what was coming next.

Those few souls like that, who were riding on the devil's cape, made him more than nervous. He felt he was about to hear about such a man.

Anna continued. "A few weeks later, I got this ten-page letter from him. For the most part, it was a bit unorganized in its content and purpose. He'd talk about himself and how he'd settled in to prison, his physical conditioning, and then how well he was doing taking classes from the local college. Then *boom*, he'd write a line and say something about one of his victims. Always in first person. For instance, he wrote, 'The big man Eduardo fought hard, and I felt bad killing him, but it was him or me. I was able to save us.'"

"Rambling isn't that unusual with those sick bitches though," said Sophie. "But what did he mean about saving us?"

"Delusions of a hero?" asked Manny.

"I think you're right about that. That was my best guess. But that wasn't all. Anyway after about the fifth page, I realized he was writing in a pattern. Bizarre and unnerving, but he was doing it nevertheless. And I think he was cognizant of it."

"What was the pattern?" asked Manny.

"There was a design of words in sentences that began to speak to me. Like every third word was in a certain order. Anyway, he wanted me to know that he didn't regret what he'd done and that I shouldn't feel badly about how I felt, or something to that effect. He was telling me to do what I was designed to do. And—"

Anna stopped, staring down at the table, her eyes moist.

Manny waited for what was next, his pulse racing.

It took a few moments for this young woman, who was a psychological paradox, to finish, but she did.

". . . And to finish what I'd started. That he'd help as would the others to whom I'd written letters, and even those who thought on a grander scale, so to speak. He said there would be words that I should look for. That they would set me free and help me down the path."

Sophie sat back. "Damn, you got all of that from a disorganized letter?"

"I did. It wasn't hard when you recognized what he was truly thinking as he wrote. I mean, most people in that same psychological boat understand the lingo. Trust me on that."

"Did you embrace his instruction?" asked Manny.

"Yes, I did. At first, anyway. I was thrilled that I had some positive affirmation that I wasn't . . . well, you know, unusual. But eventually I evolved into my own expression, acting out what I'd become."

Manny stood, pulled his chair over to her side, and sat close. She followed him with her eyes. They never left him.

*Here we go.*

"Anna. That evolution is what I'm after. What are you leading up to here? What others? What grander scale?"

"I'm getting there. I received a few more letters from him, but didn't really care anymore. We both had gotten what we wanted, more or less. Then one day, I get this package from the States. It was the size of a large manila envelope, sealed, and I had to personally sign for it. It had come from Miami, but I already knew whoever sent it wasn't from there. No one in that world would send mail from where they lived."

"What was in it?" asked Sophie, learning forward again, hands clasped on top of the table.

Anna sighed. "It had fifteen printed articles about serial killers and what they'd done. A few pictures of their victims, and two from executed killers. Stuff I'd seen a dozen times. But the last article wasn't an article but a letter of sorts. Maybe even the beginnings of a thesis. It laid out profiles of mass murderers like Manson, serial killers like Bundy, and terrorists, from suicide bombers to people like McVeigh."

"So? Anyone with an Internet connection could pull that junk," said Sophie.

"That was my thought until I got to the last page. Whoever sent this wrote two paragraphs on justice—that true justice wasn't governed by laws, rules, or someone's psychology, but by a universal moral absolute. A higher righteousness with no boundaries. Justice and vengeance were unalienable rights that we should all be free to express, no matter the price. No matter what some politicians claim is the law of the land."

Manny rubbed his face with his hands. The long day was beginning to catch up with him, yet Anna's story was offering new life to his thoughts regarding the killers at the warehouse. "What else did the letter say?"

"That was about it. He drove home his point again then ended it."

"You said he," replied Manny.

"Yeah, he signed it Mr. R."

Sophie broke the short silence. "What does all that mean, Anna?"

"I don't know. I mean his take was different, you know? But it feels like the kind of people that could do something epic."

"Yet still a psychopath because he believed his version of whatever justice he was contemplating was the true way, no matter what that entails," said Manny.

"That's true." Anna's voice was softer now. She reached across the table and laid a hand on Sophie's hand, then her other hand on Manny's arm. "You could have figured a lot of this out on your own, so why are you here, really?"

Sighing, he patted her hand. "I had to be sure I was right. That you are what we need."

"Need?"

"I'll explain later. After we get you out of your cell."

# CHAPTER-30

New York had never been his idea of a lovely place to live, ever. The City that Never Sleeps was just that, enjoying what it hid in the dark. It allowed people to indulge in practically every perversion known to mankind, and then some. Any hour of the day, any day of the week. That somewhat disturbing fact alone appealed to many. In fact, he'd seen many of those vices, intimately. Some he had enjoyed immensely, some of those way-out "experiences" had earned the one-and-done label.

He was far from prudish, but even he had his limits. Yet, he was sure he could still curl the hair of a priest during an extended period of confession.

"No one is perfect, I hear," he whispered to himself.

Entering Central Park at the West 90th Street entrance, near the trail leading across Park Drive south that eventually would take him to the reservoir, he stopped. He then lit a large Cuban cigar and exhaled, taking in the rich aroma as it swirled near his bearded face. He reflected on how the aroma was indeed rich to him, yet others would turn green after only a few whiffs.

Again, the diversity of people, and their particular tastes, rose up in his thoughts. That included what people toiled at to make their miserable livings.

Accountants, lawyers, doctors, mail carriers, taxi drivers, whatever—they did what they did to make ends meet, but aspired to little more than that. He was one of the exceptions, however, who enjoyed the idea of what he did each and every time he did it.

After taking another long draw from the cigar, he continued his walk toward the water.

He supposed there weren't many capable of doing what his vocation required, which kept him in demand and filthy rich. It had taken a few months for his clients to realize he was in the game, thanks to some subtle posts in a few chat rooms on the Darknet. But success was success no matter the path, his old, strung-out mother used to say. At least he took something from her retched existence. He still remembered that unintentional wisdom even after he'd blown her head off those years ago.

Two fast-walking old farts dressed in wild-colored walking suits cruised past him as he turned left onto the path running along the lake.

He wouldn't be caught dead going to bed in apparel like that, let alone in public.

Some people just have it coming to them.

The sun was now much lower in the sky as the shadows from the newly leafed trees lengthened across the path. It was almost time. He knew that because his heart rate was rising like it always did. Always.

After another hundred yards or so, he stepped over the short wooden fence and settled against one of the large oaks with a partial view of the reservoir. His vantage point also allowed him to watch the wide path in both directions. That would be important shortly.

Several folks jogged, ran, or walked past him. No one said hello, or for that matter, acknowledged he was there, eye contact or not. That good old New Yorker unfriendly behavior toward strangers would work to his advantage this evening.

Five minutes later, with the shadows threatening to strangle the remaining light, a couple walking very close together, lost in their own world, strolled leisurely in his direction. They must have thought this setting, this late spring ambiance of Central Park, was created just for them. That was what lovers thought about beautiful places. He had too, once upon a time.

When they were twenty feet away, he stepped onto the path, dropped his wallet on the cinder surface, and began to walk away from them.

A moment later, he got the response he'd anticipated.

"Sir. Sir. You dropped your wallet," said the young man.

He turned, surprise on his face as he frisked himself. He shook his head in mock disgust. He then walked toward the couple, smiling, his hand deep in his jacket pocket.

"Thank you so much. It would have been a long trip back to California without my resources. I appreciate your honesty. Not everyone would have done what you did."

The young, dark-eyed woman returned his smile as she looked up at him. "We're from Michigan, and we understand how it would be to not have your money. Besides, our parents taught us not to take what isn't ours."

"Yep, she's right about that," chimed in the thin young man.

One last glance around confirmed they were alone, at least momentarily. Not that it mattered to him, not tonight.

"Thank you. Did your parents also teach you not to talk to strangers?"

"Well, when we were younger, but I suppose we can make that call on our own these days," she said, her smile now gone.

*You know what's coming, don't you?*

"She's right about—"

Smiling still, he pulled the Smith and Wesson that he had been given from his pocket and shot both of them between the eyes.

# CHAPTER-31

"It'll take at least two to three months, if then, Manny. Even I can't get that changed," said Josh.

Manny squeezed his phone harder, standing in the prison's waiting room. "It's a matter of national security, right? Did you tell your boss that?"

"Of course. But it's not going to happen like you want. Come on, Manny . . . she's a convicted serial killer. You get that."

"Was, Josh. Damn it, was."

"Lots of experts agree with you that she's no longer a public threat, but some don't. Besides, you know how it is when you ask the Bureau, the CIA, and Homeland Security to do something together that they've never done before. It takes time. Period. They want to take it slow with her. She'll have to prove herself."

He fought the urge to go off, knowing it wouldn't make things any better. Manny exhaled.

"What about this carte blanche access to whatever we need to solve cases?"

"Even carte blanche has a limit, Manny, contrary to popular opinion. We have to think of something else until or if she's released," said Josh.

"Final answer?"

"Yes. Nothing I can do."

"Okay, but I think this is bullshit, in this day and age, when politicians get away with felonies every week."

"Politics? Now? Come on, Williams."

"Just showing the irony here. Let me think about this."

Sophie nudged him as they stood inside the warden's plush office, looking out the huge picture window. "If it's a no-go to get her out right now, then ask him if we can set up a couple of computers for Anna with unlimited access to everything Dough Boy has."

"Did you hear that, Josh?"

"Yeah, I did. I'm sure I can at least make that happen. Especially since she's had some freedom in that respect anyway. We'll also get her into one of the offices on the warden's wing so she can set up. I'll call him in a minute. He won't be our number one fan regarding this. I'll also have a couple agents drive in from the Denver office to stand watch over her. I don't want the warden to use his guards for that kind of thing."

"Okay. And as far as the warden, we can't make everyone happy, can we? I want her to have unlimited cell phone clearance too," said Manny.

"I don't see a problem with that either."

Sophie clapped her hands. "About time something went our way on this one."

"True," said Manny.

There was brief silence as he heard Josh take a breath.

"What?"

"Nothing. I just want to make sure you're positive this is a good thing. Both of you. I'll say it again. It's not like Anna knocked over a grocery story with a water pistol."

"We're sure. I'll take full responsibility for this. If that's what you need."

Josh laughed. "Your workaholic butt always takes responsibility, but we'll bear this one together. All three of us. I'll make some calls then let the warden know.

"On a side note, we still don't have much to go on here. I'm waiting for Chloe and Alex to finish their work. I will say that they believe it's the woman who shot Brooks. I, oh, wait, I'm getting a call from Barb. Get your asses to work. I need ten minutes to make this happen."

Josh hung up.

Manny stuffed the phone in his pocket. He felt a little better. It wasn't like having Anna right at his side, where he could read her body language, but this arrangement would have to suffice for now. And, like it or not, he *did* understand the reasons for not releasing her, but someday, it would happen. And he'd be there with open arms.

"I'm going to pee and get a candy bar, then we can go see your buddy, the warden."

"I don't think we'll be pen pals after this one," said Manny.

A few minutes later, Sophie reappeared, finishing a chocolate bar the size of a Buick. "Okay. I'm ready."

"You should be."

"Don't give me shit. I have needs."

"I see that. Let's get this rolling."

"I'm with you," said Sophie.

They exited the mahogany door and were admitted into the administration wing. The warden, Robert Massey, a tall, distinguished man with graying temples and a cleft chin, awaited them.

"I got the call from your boss, and then mine. I'm going on record as hating this idea. She should be in her cell. What do you want?" he asked, an air of distrust in his question.

Manny stepped in front of him. "Listen. I get you don't like this. I suppose I wouldn't either, given your position, but we know what we're doing."

He shrugged. "You're right; I don't celebrate the fact that she's killed men in horrible ways. Not to mention, I've seen a few of these psychos in my time and know just how deceptive they can be. I'm not nearly as trusting as you regarding this miracle metamorphosis she's apparently undergone." The warden raised his hands in apparent surrender. "But, as you say, you know what you're doing. So again, tell me what we can do for you."

Manny and Sophie explained in detail what they needed.

Massey sighed. "I have an empty office overlooking the south wall. It has a two-month-old desktop with all the latest bells and whistles, according to our IT gal, including a twenty-five-inch monitor. I can have one of our laptops added to the mix if you want. We've got new iPhones for emergencies. She can use one of them."

"That will be fine. I suspect she'll want to have two computers to work from. I'll also need to have every restriction released from your IT security in terms of accessing databases and websites."

Massey's frown grew. Manny could see that his rope was near the axiomatic end.

"That makes me extremely uncomfortable, agents."

"Why?" asked Sophie. "Porn issues?"

The warden didn't smile. "That's possible, but we have extremely sensitive information regarding the facility's inmates, past and present. She's still an inmate, and no matter what you think, I don't deem her as trustworthy, or that trust you have for her as a priority, especially given what's stored in our system."

Manny felt his own patience slip. He sensed the clock ticking more than saw it. His next step put him face to face with Massey.

"I don't give a rat's ass about your concerns regarding your damned search histories or even what dirty little secrets you may have hidden in your system. This woman can help us find a potential threat to the people of this nation. That's our damned priority, got it?"

The warden never flinched, but it was obvious his anger was reaching a boiling point. Manny watched as he struggled to keep control, then did. "I understand. Just know if any shit hits the fan, political or otherwise, it's all on you and your agency. I'll be covering this facility's ass by posting guards at the outside of her, even with your agents being on the inside, until I get the word to put her back. I'm not jeopardizing the security of this facility for some potential threat that you can't even verify."

He reached for the phone on the nearest desk and hit the intercom. "Lois, come in here and help these Feds. Give them whatever the hell they want, and get me two guards just starting their shifts to bring Ruiz up here."

He then stormed toward his office. At the door, he spun around and pointed a finger at Manny. "You better make sure this works, Agent." He slammed his door.

Sophie looked at Manny and offered a smirk. "Damn. You sure know how to win friends and influence important people, Williams."

"Yeah, or just maybe that boy's underwear is too tight. Either way, Anna's on her way up here. We need to get her hooked up, and now. She has to get to work on the whys and whos and wheres—"

His mind locked up the next word he was going to speak. He swore.

He'd missed details and concepts a time or two over the years. But he was pressing hard to think of a time he'd assumed something so basic, so elementary in police work.

"What's the matter, Williams? You look a little pale," said Sophie, concern obvious in her question.

"In all of this data analysis hype, that would help identify potential candidates, we never went back to the most basic question. We just *assumed.*"

"What is that?" she asked, a scowl painted across her face.

"I have to make a call."

"Okay, but what's going on, Williams?"

He shook his head. "Sophie. We spent a lot of time on why and who, but never really spent time on *where* the terrorists might truly attack."

# CHAPTER-32

Sitting at the small desk, he glanced at the hotel room's clock. It displayed 8:45. He returned his attention to his Cajun shrimp entrée from the Red Fish Grill. The head chef deserved every penny of his salary and maybe more. The spice was right, and the shrimp perfect.

On top of that, the restaurant's famous double-chocolate bread pudding dessert, its incomparable aroma flooding the room, was patiently waiting for him to finish his shrimp. It wouldn't be long.

It was an interesting thread of words that had entered his thoughts.

Rhodes looked over his shoulder at the ornately decorated king-sized bed. There would be no Lucretia, with all of her assorted appetites, wrecking his sleep pattern tonight. Never again, as a matter of fact. The brief, but real tinge of loneliness and remorse reminded him of what he'd done. Then the emotion was gone.

His sheer will and purpose made that kind of compartmentalization relatively easy. Lucretia's elimination was simply the latest in a long line of sacrifices he'd endured to reach this point in his journey.

Pushing the plate aside, he opened the dessert container, the white and dark chocolate still warm, and then poured them skillfully over the bread pudding covered with melting ice cream. He devoured it all, right down to the last morsel.

Rarely had he gone this long without a good meal, especially in the Big Easy. He'd had a busy two days, however, so it was understandable.

He rose from his chair and sauntered over to the window, the Superdome clearly in his sights two blocks over. The city was still beautiful, even with the adaption of modern architecture and technology. What was the old saying? "You can take the boy out of the country, but you can't take the country out of the boy." He supposed that was true for cities as well. New Orleans would never rival New York in size, but held its own special niche for travelers.

New York. Things should be gearing up there about now.

He smiled at that.

"More than normal," he whispered.

Rhodes stripped off his clothes, turned down the sheet, and crawled into bed, his mind winding down as he did. He'd need a few hours of rest tonight. He wouldn't get much over the next twenty or so hours.

Then again, he wouldn't need much.

# CHAPTER-33

The jet ride back to New Orleans had been relatively quiet, and now they taxied along the tarmac.

Manny glanced at Sophie. He'd managed a few minutes of sleep, but this woman was in full-bore REM mode. The stress of events in her life and the long day had finally caught up to her. The sleep would do her good.

But his brief nap wouldn't cut it for long. After the next meeting with his team, they would all have to get some serious rest. Everyone was running on empty. They wouldn't be able to function without a few hours in the sack. With the exception of one.

Anna wouldn't sleep, as her prison history indicated. The woman was borderline "non-24-hour sleep-wake syndrome," according to the prison's records. Maybe that, or, as he knew, the gifted needed less sleep. Or she'd be too excited to sleep.

Regardless of the reason, he suspected she'd be researching every conceivable Internet avenue involving the parameters that he and Alex had given her.

They were particularly interested in likely locations for a terrorist attack that would do the most damage in and around New Orleans, if that were truly the target area. He shook his head. Was there even an intended attack? Was this just circumstantial bullshit?

*There is a target, though, isn't there?*

The murders in the warehouse weren't anything but a setup by the killers. That was a fact in his mind.

He felt his heart grow sick. He'd never had so many questions without answers in any investigation.

The jet stopped in front of a mobile stairway. He felt Sophie's hand on his arm. "Wow, I must have gone out for a while."

"You did. Don't worry, I won't tell people about your walrus imitation when you snore."

"Bite me, Williams. I'm a lady and don't snore. Get me?"

He laughed. "You're right. What was I thinking? I guess the video on my phone is a complete lie, right?"

She stood, then bent close to his face, fire in her eyes. "Listen, Agent. If there is a video—if you were actually able to figure out how to do one—it had better be gone from your damned phone before we get to the hotel's conference room. Do you understand?"

"Why, yes. I think you've made yourself perfectly clear," he said, raising his eyebrows in mock fear.

"Good, now get your tight ass off this heifer. I've got to pee before we get to the SUV."

"Okay, but why don't you use the jet's restroom?"

"It too small for my taste. Let's go."

Twenty minutes later, they were on the way to the five-star hotel conference room Josh had booked on Canal Street. They drove in silence for another fifteen minutes, the long day catching up with them even more.

Still, Manny ran the details over in his head, again. Could there have been a stranger day and a half in this new world they'd chosen to work and live in? Six deaths brought them here to New Orleans with no real affirmation as to why, other than the identity of five of the victims and their histories. Throw in an attack on their lives, breaking the team up then putting it back together, and an assault on a detective whose husband had been one of the victims. Then a quick flight to Colorado to recruit a brilliant ex-serial killer to help sort out cyber information that had once sent her careening into the very darkest realms of human nature. And they weren't done yet.

Yep, a good night's sleep sounded really incredible.

As they exited the highway, Manny felt Sophie's eyes on him.

"What?"

"Can she do this? I mean, really do this?"

"Anna? Yes, she can. She understands that world and its way of doing business. If you mean, once she's free, will she revert back to the killing machine she once was? No. Unless she's done the most complete snow job ever recorded, which isn't truly a possibility in my mind, I'd say she's good to go."

"Yeah, I wasn't so sure until this last trip. The girl has a heart and saw my pain," she said softly.

"She did. Not exactly a trait of an active serial killer."

"That's what I thought."

Sophie turned on Canal and then pulled in front of the eight-story hotel displaying some New Orleans fabled architecture, including iron-railed balconies decorated with beautiful flowers and plants. Even at ten thirty, the lights along the street and on other buildings helped to provide a clear view.

"Pretty place," said Sophie.

"It is."

She jumped out of the SUV, motioning for Manny to get it in gear. "Okay, the scenic tour is over. Now let's get something else to eat and get this meeting going. Dough Boy's email said they had something to discuss, *and* we have to find out what happened to those weirdos who attacked us."

"Wait. You're hungry again? You just ate on the jet."

"Yeah, but now I need dessert and maybe another sandwich. Being back in the saddle has made me hungry."

He shrugged. His partner had lost weight after Dean's death, so it was good to see her take another step away from that hell.

"Sounds like a plan. Josh probably has that handled. Let's get inside."

Walking past the valet's desk, she flipped the keys to the attendant. "That's a government vehicle; behave your ass when driving it."

The young lady frowned, then smiled. "Yes ma'am. I surely will."

Manny and Sophie entered the hotel, banked left down the wide hallway. Josh was standing outside the door with Chloe on one side, Belle on the other. Their conversation was animated, to say the least.

". . . I don't give a shit about all that," Josh was saying. "You've got a job to do and you need her help to do it."

"You can't just pull rank like that," said Belle. "I thought we were in this together. All of us."

"That girl has it right, don't ya know," said Chloe, arms folded across her breasts in one of those poses that made even Manny uncomfortable.

Belle shifted her weight, throwing her hands in the air. "Why would you do this?"

"Whoa. What's going on?" asked Manny.

Josh exhaled, then started to speak.

Chloe raised her hand. "Wait."

She then wrapped her arms around Manny's neck and kissed him. Then she pulled him closer and kissed him again.

Her full lips were warm and full of that electricity the two of them had experienced from the beginning. It was difficult for his thoughts not to run to later when they'd be in the hotel room, together and alone. He wasn't going to get as much sleep as he'd thought.

"I missed you too," he whispered.

"You did. I can tell. But that kiss was so I wouldn't kick the hell out of *your* friend," she said, glaring at Josh.

"Thank God," said Sophie. "I thought I was going to have to send you two to your room early."

"Still might have to," said Chloe, a wry smile contrasting the subtle anger in her eyes.

"That aside, what's going on?" asked Manny.

"Let's go back inside the conference room," said Josh.

They filed in behind him. Manny closed the door and saw Alex, Braxton, and Barb sitting around the large round table. None of them were wearing what he'd call a positive expression.

"Hey, Manny and Sophie, good to see you," said Alex, giving a wave with his prosthetic. "Forgive me for not getting up. I'm tired and the weight of the bullshit that never stops coming is keeping me in my chair."

"I'm afraid da mon is right dere," said Braxton, exhaling.

Barb waved and offered a tired smile. "True dat."

He frowned and turned in Josh's direction. "Spill it, Josh. What's going on?"

"We've got another problem. A big one."

His stomach jumped. He hated it when Josh spoke like that.

"What would that be?" asked Sophie.

Josh twisted his neck, trying to relieve the stress. "It seems we have six murdered people in New York, all by the same killer. Belle's BAU, Chloe, and Barb are being ordered to get there by morning."

# CHAPTER-34

What the hell else could go south on this case?

Manny chose to get past the idea of his wife and Barb being assigned to go with Belle and concentrate on what happened in New York. He understood why Josh wanted them to go. Belle's new team was hardly a team yet and lacked serious experience in the field. He also knew, after they'd gathered some facts, that there would still be plenty of time to change Josh's mind.

"A spree killer?" asked Manny.

"It appears so. He even left a note, a message at each scene."

Manny's stomach did a full flip. "A message?"

"Each one says **'Catch me if you can.'**"

"Shit. That's an issue. Obviously, because of the six dead in a short time, he's not done with whatever crusade he's on," said Manny, plopping down in the nearest black leather chair.

"I'd say that's right," said Belle. She moved to the table, sitting on the edge. "I want to help here, more than you all know. After I thought about it some more, and that doesn't mean I like it, Josh is right—this time anyway. The ACTU isn't my unit, and I need to go do my job."

"You do," said Manny.

"I'm just not sure my three folks are ready for their first case. They're very good, but they're just now wrapping up their weapons training. They've still got a full eight hours of briefing to complete on profiling. They need more time."

Josh nodded. "And that's why I'm sending Chloe and Barb to help. It's the right thing to do. I hate doing it, but adding Anna in the research arena helped me make the call. Besides, Bureau and Agency policies aside, it's the right thing to do for your families."

"But now we do that whole divide the team again. I think that's still dangerous here. We're still so in the dark about what, and who, and where, never mind why," said Manny.

"I think we can clear up a few things during the meeting. Meanwhile, we have crimes that need to be solved in New York," said Josh, his voice rising. "Belle's people have to go there, and she needs experienced agents to help. It's that simple."

Manny started to protest again, that they also needed Chloe and Barb, but realized Josh was probably right. And who was to say what was more important here? Plus, if they needed more support here in New Orleans, they could draw on the considerable presence of the Feds in New Orleans.

He put his hand on Chloe's. "I'm good with it, as long as you are."

"Well, I wasn't, but I am now, sort of," answered Chloe.

He glanced at Sophie. Her gaze met his, her chin jutted out. "In case we all get our butts blown to Kingdom Come or get infected with some germ-warfare agent, somebody is still left, right?"

"Exactly. And there won't be any more discussion. The three of you leave in the morning, bright and early," said Josh.

Sophie then reached out and touched Josh's arm. "I think you're smart here, even though I don't like it either. I will say though, surviving when your spouse doesn't ain't all it's cracked up to be."

In a complete impromptu reaction, Josh drew Sophie to him and hugged her fiercely, emotion showing across his strained face. "Yeah, that's true. And I've lost too many of you already. It's not just about the survivors of a family like ours. It's about all of us who can't do this job without the rest of us."

After a few moments, Sophie patted Josh on the back, then kissed him on the cheek. "Thanks, boss. I sometimes forget that." She then held him at arm's length. "You're going to have to stop being so damn emotional. It's not becoming for someone who is as manly hot as you."

Josh nodded, smiling. "I'll do better. I get like this when I'm tired and frustrated."

"Tell me about it. Now let's get this meeting going. Plus, I'm hungry. Let's get some of that Cajun gumbo, burgers, and dessert up here. Like chocolate cake and ice cream."

"Will do," said Josh. "Sounds good to me too."

Ten minutes later, Josh had finished briefing them on what had happened to the two God's Hand members.

"So we got IDs?" asked Manny, shaking his head at just how wild the aspects of this investigation were becoming.

"Yep, but that was about it. Lots of these cult members, especially ones as radical as this one, try to wipe out their past and get far away from family and friends. It's like they drop off the face of the earth. Neither had anything in their recent profiles that will help us. I did take the liberty of sending their names to both Anna and our tech staff to see if something comes up.

"Until we get more, if we do, all we can really say about them is that this group has had members do this killer-for-hire-to-better-the-world attack before, but we've never been able to pin any association with God's Hand leadership from those incidents," said Barb. "They seem to be Teflon, but we're still digging."

"No cell phones, I guess?" asked Manny.

She shook her head. "No electronic trail at all, at least so far. I wouldn't get my hopes up either. I've seen how some of these groups operate. They just don't leave trails on what they do and how they do it. Like Alex said, we're still looking, though."

"What about the woman in the lake?" Manny asked, looking at Alex.

"Glad you asked," said Alex, his eyes red with strain and apparent fatigue. But he was still wearing that got-something grin.

Manny sat up a little straighter.

"Her real name is Lucretia Doucett. She went by a few other aliases but didn't go through any effort to hide who she was, at least that seems to be the case because she was easy to identify."

Alex shifted in his chair then slid a stack of thin files down and over to the members of the team.

"This file has background info on her as well as a copy of the initial autopsy results. I'm not going to bore you with details that you'll forget. But there are a few things you should know."

"Fire away," said Manny.

"Okay. First, she is an expert shot. She attended several shooting schools and seminars, plus she won nine different competitions, including the big one in Atlanta put on by the United States Practical Shooting Association, four times. Twice with perfect scores."

"Handguns?" asked Sophie.

"Yes. No one else was close," said Alex. He paused to sip his coffee.

"I think that falls in line with Sophie's and Manny's theory that the killer was an expert shot. This woman would have fit the bill," said Chloe.

"That's a great start for identifying the warehouse killer, but we need more," Manny said, hearing the guarded excitement in his own voice.

Barb got up from the table, walked over to Alex, and kissed him flush on the lips, and then returned to her seat.

"What was that for?" Alex asked.

"Because you're the best, and you've got more on her. I know you do," she answered with a wink. "And there's more where that kiss came from."

Alex cleared his throat. "We can discuss my rewards later. Anyway, it seems she also owned four different handguns, two of them Beretta 92s plus a Glock 22 and a Smith and Wesson .38. She could have owned more, but these I'm sure of. She had to register them with that USPSA to compete."

"Okay, but how does that help?" asked Josh, rubbing his face.

The Cheshire Cat had nothing on Alex's grin. "Well, it seems they also have to register the kind of ammo they use and do a ballistics profile to make sure the ammo falls into their competition guidelines."

"Don't tell me one of those matches the crime scene in the warehouse," asked Manny, standing.

"Better than that. We got a match on *two* of her weapons."

"Two?" asked Sophie.

The knock on the door interrupted Alex's answer. Braxton jumped up and opened the door, waving in the waiter from the hotel's restaurant. The waiter wheeled in a cart that exuded the very aroma of heaven itself, filling the room with spices and chocolate.

Walking over to the metal food cart, Manny stood in front it, blocking it with his body.

"No eating until you answer Sophie's question."

"No problem. I'll make it simple. The Feds investigating those five murders in Florida and Louisiana from a few years ago that you sent me the file on will be happy. One of those guns was used in each of those five murders."

# CHAPTER-35

Leaning back in the soft microfiber chair, Anna glanced at the two agents sitting on each side of the door, earpieces in, sunglasses covering what she knew were curious stares. Freak shows were hard to come by these days. She'd probably do the same thing in this situation.

She turned back to the computers on the desks, determined to ignore the guards, and picked up her can of cola. The bright red and green colors seemed to have her mesmerized for a brief moment. It had been years since she'd had a can of anything.

They didn't trust her, and the rest of the incarcerated population here, with cans because they could be used to make a weapon, make an escape. She snorted. Where would she have gone? She didn't think even she could escape the fortress of hell without help. Not that she hadn't planned a couple escapes in her mind. But her ace in the hole, her white knight, had come through, at least somewhat, like she *knew* he would. No escape necessary.

In the end of this mortifying process of admitting her past and becoming human, Manny Williams had trusted her. Her. Was there anything more liberating than the trust of another? Especially given her history.

She closed her eyes, smiling. Liberation came in many forms, but she seriously doubted if anyone had ever enjoyed theirs more than she. Even if it was only for a day or two. She knew someday it would be for good.

The lone tear began its deliberate track down her cheek. She felt every millimeter, the warmth, the moisture, and above all, the purpose of that tear as it bore deep into her heart of hearts. Something she swore she didn't have those years growing up—a heart.

Her hands began to shake. She stopped them with a will she forgot she had.

A moment later, she laughed out loud. It sounded strange, shaky, and she loved it.

Emotion.

Good God in Heaven, she loved the array of emotions that she, Anna Ruiz, could call her very own. No person or thing could ever take those away. Ever.

After one long draw that drained the can, she set it down and then leaned forward toward the screen on her right.

The other one, the laptop, was working through a program she'd written to locate keywords Alex and Manny had provided for her that might give them a clue as to where an attack might come. Including the names of buildings, business centers, financial institution, local landmarks, and even prominent people.

She'd try, but that request was easier asked than accomplished. She had a few tricks up her sleeve, however.

Alex had given her another list and explained that they were Internet sites and URLs that had showed up in Amy Brooks's husband's search history on the couple's two computers. Identifying what words and sites would be considered unusual had been a trick in itself. She'd gone to each one that he'd accessed more than three times in the last year. She hadn't seen anything out of the ordinary with that search.

He'd visited some nutrition gurus, a few gun sites, researched a tattoo design he apparently was going to add to his arms, a few travel locations, and some local New Orleans nightclubs.

He'd spent considerable time on a few of them; she wondered if he may have been thinking about changing jobs as a bouncer. If that were true, those websites seemed like more normal visits to her. It was what most people did when they were unhappy with their job or needed to make a step to better one's life. She wrote them off and waited for what her program was designed to do: extract the sites he'd deleted from the subdirectory hidden deep in the computer's memory.

Most people thought once a URL was deleted from their machines, it was gone, but nothing was further from the truth. The info was still there; one simply had to know how to find it.

Police departments and government cybercrime agencies were becoming more and more proficient in that task, but some Internet carriers did a better job of protecting their customer's privacy than others by not allowing police access without a court order, and even then, it could be difficult to get to. That was where her program came in.

It wouldn't take long before she knew exactly where he'd been in Cyber Land over the last year. She hoped there would be some kind of clue as to what was going to happen, where, or even if anything was going to happen.

Manny had told her it was a stretch, at best, but cases had been solved with less. They just had to know what they were looking at. That's where she came in.

Moving a little closer to the large screen displaying a blank page, cursor flashing in the corner, she exhaled. This next journey wouldn't be so easy. People could go to great lengths to protect their worlds. The Darknet typified that to the nth degree.

It wouldn't do well for someone who had just ordered a hit on their wife to be exposed by sloppy programming or a breakable security code. Not to mention how that would affect the hitman's future business.

In this case, if a domestic terrorist wanted to network in order to accomplish his task, then the terrorist would need knowledge on how that was to be done. That meant proficiency at Internet protocol and deep security.

The Darknet had its share of perversions, mostly illegal, but she suspected high-level intel regarding complex security that would be—

The laptop's sharp alarm pulled her away from the PC screen. The huge smiley face, sunglasses resting above rosy cheeks, told her to touch him and she'd be rewarded.

She smiled; touch him she would.

After she tapped the screen, a list of URLs, green against a dark background, filled up the page then continued to scroll downward for about thirty seconds. After it stopped, she touched the screen again to get the visited pages to display in chronological order, newest to oldest—6,756 total sites visited. Anna whistled softly.

"Wow, you've been far busier than Manny and Sophie thought, haven't you, Daryl Brooks?" she whispered.

She stared at the desktop screen, longing to dive into the Darknet arena, this time with a purpose far nobler than five years ago. But she had some hardcore information to focus on now.

After one more longing look, she reached for the laptop and placed it on her thighs. She then began the process of looking at each entry. After three pages, she noticed that Daryl had visited an email page that was different than his current email account. She cut then pasted the URL into the browser box and hit enter.

The new email account flashed its header across the screen, the login information for Brooks already in place. He called himself Juggernaut16 and used his wife's full name as a password. So much for supposedly secure email sites.

Clicking on the "in" box, she watched as twenty-seven messages showed up in the spam folder, three new messages, and eighteen read messages.

She read the headers for the new ones, then five of the read entries, then stopped, moving closer to the screen.

The next read email down had a blank subject title, but the email address was from someone called Dreamer666. Dated two days before the warehouse killings. The name wasn't all that original, but the meaning was clear.

Anna clicked the email and it popped open. She read it.

**Are you ready? We can do this. I've found out a couple of things about Wanger that may lead to something else entirely. I don't think he's quite what we or the agency thought he was. I'll tell you when I have more time. Be there and be ready. This could be what we've been waiting for.**

**FB**

Anna tilted her head and read it again. She frowned.

*What the hell does that mean?*

Like a lightning bolt, the truth of the email struck her.

She reached for the cell phone, planning to call Manny, but the phone wouldn't turn on. It appeared to be dead and needed charging.

"Shit."

She got up from the chair, ready to ask one of the guards for their phone, then thought better of it. They'd just refuse her anyway.

Reaching for the phone's box resting on the metal desk near the door, she removed the charger, went over to the phone and hooked it up, bending over to plug it into the power strip under the computer desk. Her hair falling in her eyes and the long sleeve from her sweatshirt both got in the way, twice.

"Damn it."

After the third attempt was finally successful, she stood up and laughed out loud. She'd actually gotten angry and frustrated—not something someone with her past had experienced often.

The clock on the corner of the computer said 12:10. Fine. It would take at least ten minutes for the charge to be full enough before she could make one call. She hated waiting that long, but she still didn't want to ask one of the guards to lend her a phone. That could be a can of worms best not opened.

She thought about forwarding Manny the email, but thought better of it. She wanted to explain to him what she saw, plus the Feds's security system would probably delay the inbound message until they could verify the source. And a prison probably was on their no-no list to receive communication from.

After plopping down in the chair, she put her feet on the desk and began tapping her finger impatiently on her leg, wondering about the email. What agency? Did this have to do with the warehouse? Most certainly, right? Who was FB and why was he or she contacting Daryl Brooks like this? Why—?

A familiar buzz interrupted her thoughts as she glanced at the laptop. She did a double-take.

Daryl Brooks had just received another email.

Dropping her feet to the tiled floor, she reached for the mouse to click the message, then hesitated.

Slow is better. Always.

Taking a deep breath, she read the header of the email. It said 'Vacation Information' and the sender's address started out with 'No-reply' then 'getawaytrips@sailme.com.'

Anna relaxed and hit the mouse's left button.

The screen immediately turned death-message blue, except for five words in the middle. **WE SAIL IN TWO DAYS.**

# CHAPTER-36

Manny nodded toward Alex. He thought he'd be more surprised, but somehow, he'd known that Lucretia was the killer of those five men throughout the south four years ago, hadn't he? His conversation with Sophie in the SUV said so. Sometimes Alex's definition of intuition was true. Facts are the building blocks for it. Some people have a better knack than others at using those facts.

"What files?" asked Josh.

"There were these cold cases a few years ago that got my attention. I'll explain more later. What else, Alex?"

"You can all probably guess what's next. The woman's gun was definitely in the warehouse and used to kill four of those people."

"So, given the wench's history, Lucretia probably was there too," said Sophie.

"It be a good bet," said Braxton.

"Okay, let's get to brass tacks, but I need to eat first." Sophie got out of her chair.

"Yeah, hard to concentrate on an empty stomach," said Barb.

Manny stepped away from the food cart and watched as his team filled their plates, Sophie leading the way.

Fifteen minutes later, the eating frenzy involving spicy gumbo, cheesy au gratin potatoes, creole salad, and chocolate crème brûlée about over, Josh leaned back in his chair. "That hit the spot. Now I need some sleep."

"Heard that," said Sophie, finishing off her second dessert.

Josh turned to Manny. "What about those files?"

"The ones I gave Alex?"

"Yeah, those. Let me guess, recreational reading?"

He smiled. "I was researching some cold cases, hoping to get some more insight into Argyle a few years ago, and ran into a profile of five unsolved murders. Long story short, after getting Alex involved with the science, and comparing our current evidence with those cases, I believed that same killer could be our person in the warehouse. Especially regarding the marksmanship."

"Seems you were right," said Barb.

"It proves that the patterns in these type of killers are consistent. I only threw out the possibility. Alex's evidence comparison proved it," said Manny.

"Either way, it was good work. But we need to go to the next step," said Josh.

Manny's thoughts were already racing ahead to what was next on the agenda. Alex beat him to the punch, however.

"We're searching for any known associates to Doucett, but it seems she was a loner of sorts. No real family, she worked in the real estate business until three years ago, then pretty much nothing. At least so far."

"You mean she had no job?" asked Sophie, still nibbling at her plate.

"None that paid taxes at least," said Alex.

"So whoever she hooked up with took care of her, or she had a cash business," said Chloe.

"I'd bank on a partnership or relationship or something. Hey, she wasn't alone in that warehouse; that's obvious," Belle said.

"True. But she did have skills. Maybe Anna can find something on the Darknet that will help," said Manny.

"Yeah, the playground of creeps. Damn. It still boggles my mind that people can advertise their little specialties, like murder for hire, and not get caught," said Sophie.

"And you wonder why I'm not in love with that kind of technology. I do like the tech he's using now. He's going to run Doucett's image through our facial recognition software and see if we get a hit. There are millions of public and private security and traffic cameras out there. Maybe we'll get lucky," said Manny.

Josh looked at his watch, then stood. "Okay, if there's not anything else tonight, we're all going to get some sleep and hit it hard very early in the morning. It's been a hell of a day."

Manny raised his hand.

"Damn it, Williams, really?" said Sophie.

"I have two questions, then we can get some sleep."

"Workaholic," said Alex, grinning.

"I'll make it quick. Any luck on identifying the dead woman in the warehouse?"

"Nothing yet. We're running her in the same facial recognition search as Doucett. It is odd, though, that there's nothing on her in any of the FBI's databases. No fingerprints or DNA, nothing."

Manny frowned. Nothing *always* meant something.

"Did you try military and INTERPOL records? Maybe she wasn't a criminal."

Alex raised his eyebrows. "No, not yet. Are you thinking she was undercover?"

"Everyone has some record of their life. If you can't find fingerprints or DNA, then maybe those files are hidden or deleted. It wouldn't be the first time we've run into that. Right, Braxton?" said Manny.

"True. She might fit dat kinda hidden profile."

Alex tapped at his computer, then looked up. "Okay, since I didn't get any hits in the normal search databases, I've sent hers and Doucett's profiles to INTERPOL and the military's central ID databases. If they're there, we'll know in a few hours."

"Okay, one more thing. The people who attacked us, that God's Hand organization, when did they show up on the scene?"

"The first time we heard of them was about five years ago. They joined a couple other radical religious groups to protest the honoring of American soldiers at their funerals," said Josh.

"Some were arrested, but the leader of the group wasn't, choosing to stay away from the immediate area," said Barb, yawning. "Sorry, Big Boy, I'm ready to drag Alex to our room and hit the sack too."

"I hear you. Humor me. What's the leader's name?" asked Manny.

"It's not really one person. It seems to be a council of three with fictitious identities and profiles. We dug into them, believe me, but there just isn't much there. Besides, the CTD has pretty much signed them off as a threat to national security. They're more like the group in Waco twenty years back." Barb blinked, then shook her head. "Wow, I can't believe that just came out of my mouth. The fact they were involved in attacking you and Sophie should put them on the list. Sorry, Manny, I just didn't push that angle. Alex?"

"On it. We'll have anything and everything on them when we get together in the morning. Well, except for you three; you'll be on your way to New York."

Josh stood. "They will, and they'll need some rest. Go to bed, everyone. And turn your cell phones, computers, and tablets off. You need sleep."

Sophie snorted. "Yeah, like that'll happen."

"It works for me," said Manny.

"That's an order," said Josh.

"Yes sir," said Sophie. She then stood and saluted.

Manny watched as Josh tried to stifle the tired smile. It didn't work.

"Smartass. I'm going to bed. See you all at six a.m., right here. Barb, Belle, and Chloe, the jet leaves for the Big Apple at seven sharp."

Josh walked out of the room, and the rest followed, Manny and Chloe at the back of the pack.

They walked slowly down the hall toward the elevator, holding hands.

Five minutes later, they were in their room. Manny plugged in both of their phones, turned off the light, and climbed into bed next to Chloe.

The smooth feel of the cool sheets seemed heaven sent. Almost as much as lying close to his wife. Something he'd grown more and more fond of over the last few weeks.

There had been too many nights alone in hotel rooms over the years and that wasn't a good ingredient for most marriages.

A moment later, he pulled her even closer, feeling her heartbeat and the heat of her body.

"Are you sure you're okay with going to New York?" he asked.

"No. But I'll go for all of the reasons Josh said."

"Good. The timing is nuts though—"

Manny kissed Chloe and began to drift off to sleep. That idea was short lived. He suddenly sat up. "Damn it."

"What? What's going on?" asked Chloe, sleep in her voice.

He looked in her direction, the ambient light showing concern on her face. He shook his head.

"The timing for these murders isn't a coincidence."

Chloe groaned, then sat up beside him. "Come on, Manny, really? You think those six murders in New York aren't just a coincidence? That they are another distraction?"

"Think about it. Why now? Why today? The BAU hasn't had a case like this in weeks, and now three of you are leaving tomorrow to work this one."

"To what end is this a real problem? Even if there is some conspiracy, which is farfetched for even you to consider, what is the point, ya know? Separating us isn't going to stop our investigation in either place. We've already talked about that."

He sighed. She was right. What would be the point?

She kissed him on the cheek and lay back down. "I believe you're overthinking this. Put your brain to rest and go to sleep. You're wrong this time. It's nothing."

"You're probably right. I need some sleep."

Manny fell back and immediately felt Chloe's breast on his chest as she crawled close. She always felt good, even as tired as he was.

"I could take your mind of that stuff, for a while, don't ya know. Besides that, ya can't spend a night in New Orleans and not get laid." Then her hand moved lower. "Oh, is that a yes?"

"You're very persuasive. But I'm beat. Just wake me when you're done."

She moved on top of him, her hips resting on his. "I'll wake ya, man. I'll wake ya just fine."

Thirty minutes later, Chloe had fallen fast asleep, her mission accomplished. He'd been more than distracted with their lovemaking, yet it went past the physical. Even more so after Ian had been born. She'd always been intentional with the way they spent their intimate time together. Yet, after giving life to their son, the idea of making love had a much more pointed message—for both of them.

Manny rolled over and tried to forget New York, New Orleans, and even Sophie's battle with losing Dean. It took a few moments, but he was eventually able to follow Chloe's advice and relax. She was probably right anyway. He had been far from right a few times in his career. No one got it all of the time.

Turning on his other side, his hand on Chloe's hip, he closed his eyes. Despite the return of that persistent uneasy feeling that there was something more going on in New York, sleep found him quickly.

*** 

Manny's eyes popped open, the darkness still cloaking the room. It took a moment for him to realize his phone was buzzing. He hadn't turned off the vibration mode, only the volume button. Getting up, he stepped to the desk and picked up the phone. It stopped vibrating as he hit the answer button.

He refocused his eyes, looking at the number more clearly. The number wasn't familiar, but the 303 area code got his attention. His eyes darted to the time: 1:34 local meant it was 12:34 in Colorado.

Anna.

Before he could hit the redial, the phone began vibrating again.

"Anna?"

"Hey, Manny. Yep. It's me. Wow, you sound tired. Sorry about the calls, but I didn't think this could wait."

Her voice sounded alive, full of energy, unlike how he felt, yet it was good to hear that coming from her. She had something.

"What couldn't wait?"

"Well," she began excitedly, "I dug through some subdirectories and then ran a search on deleted URLs and other files. As long as they hadn't been replaced or zeroed out with a low-level file deletion program, something I fixed anyway because I wrote a quick recovery program—"

"Anna. Stop. This stuff isn't my cup of tea when I'm awake, and right now, I'm half asleep. Tell me what you have."

By now, Chloe was awake. She had turned on the lamp and was sitting on the edge of the bed.

"What's going on?"

"Anna," he mouthed.

Anna said, "Okay. I found an email that you want to read, then, waiting for the phone to charge, I got another one you *really* need to see. I'm sending them to you and Alex right now. It'll show up on your phone and his computer."

Manny was now fully awake.

"What does that mean, Anna?"

"I'm not totally sure about the first one. It looks like Daryl Brooks may have been undercover or something."

His mind played with that possibility, but sensed the second message was of more substance. "And?"

Anna inhaled a deep breath. "I think your terrorist is going to do something on a cruise ship."

# CHAPTER-37

"Keep the coffee coming," said Josh. "I feel like a wrung-out dishrag."

"Yes sir. I'll get two more pots," said the white-clad waiter.

"And croissants or doughnuts or whatever you have. I'm gonna need to eat again after having my beauty sleep disturbed," said Sophie.

"I will see what we have," then he hustled out the door.

Manny leaned on the table, taking another long draw from his cup. Caffeine at two thirty in the morning didn't change the fact that it was still two-thirty in the morning with three hours sleep. But he and this group had been here before; they would suck it up and do what was necessary, as always.

Josh rose, made one last attempt to wipe the sleep from his eyes, then placed both hands on the table.

"You've all seen the messages that Anna sent. She's going to continue to dig, but we've got to go with what we have for now. Thoughts?"

Every head in the room turned in Manny's direction, except Alex, who was concentrating, to the point of oblivion, on his laptop.

"I guess you're first," said Belle.

"I guess," said Manny. "Fair enough. I've got to put this in some sort of order. It seems obvious Daryl Brooks was working with or for that person, but the questions coming from that situation total about a million in my mind."

"Yeah, like for starters, after finding out who this FB is, what organization are they working for, and what was he or she and Brooks doing with that scumbag Wanger in the warehouse?" asked Sophie.

"That's a good start. I asked Anna to trace where that email came from, and she's trying, but she keeps getting hit with proxy sites bouncing all over the world every three or four seconds. She says it could take hours to days. She tried the same thing on the second email, but ran into the identical problem, only worse," said Manny.

"How about we talk to the directors of DEA, the Bureau, Homeland Security, CIA, INTERPOL, or whomever and see if they have knowledge of Wanger's people killed in the warehouse and this case?" asked Barb. "These folks know things, trust me."

"Already ahead of you on that one," said Josh. "I woke up some important people this morning. So far no one has anything for us. But I'm still waiting on the CTD director. He didn't answer his phone."

"I think we're doing what we can to find out what's going on with FB and Brooks. We need to move on to more pressing matters," said Manny, picking up his phone. "Anna thinks this reference could be a cruise-ship attack. I didn't think of that when I first read the message. When I saw 'we sail in two days,' I thought of something more private, like a yacht leaving a marina."

"Why that?" asked Chloe.

"I'm not sure. Just a first impression. God knows there's about a million chances to sail from New Orleans on any given day. I asked Anna why she thought it was cruise related. She told me that Carousel's *Ocean King* sails out of the New Orleans port tomorrow. It comes in about noon and then leaves about six. That made sense to me, after waking up more. I realized that if I were trying to make a spectacular statement to America in general, the cruise ship would be a better target than a smaller vessel. That must be what FB and Brooks, and their organization, think too. Who or whatever that is."

"Getting in touch with your inner terrorist?" asked Sophie.

"Something like that. Remember how we've talked about that. We have to try to think like them in every way. Anna helps with that."

"Do ya tink dat is what dese people have in mind? A cruise ship?" asked Braxton.

"Good question," said Manny, passing his hand through his hair. "I have to go with the theory that if it walks and talks like a duck, it probably is."

Manny had run that possible scenario over and over in his mind. Security was good at the ports, and the passengers and staff well screened, but he also knew where there was a will, things happened. He just didn't know for sure how someone could pull off an attack.

Hell, at this point, he was as unsure of an investigation as he'd ever been.

Gavin Crosby had told him years ago, when in that situation, to talk it out in front of as many people as possible. The adage of strength in numbers rang true.

"Having said what I said, let me go deeper and think out loud here, okay? There are things that don't make real sense to me."

"Damn. Williams is a little confused? I'm posting that on all of my social media accounts," said Sophie, grinning.

"Great. Can't wait to see it. Anyway, here goes. The message was clear that Brooks was to be ready to sail. But why him? Why did he get that message?

"If he was a part of Wanger's organization, who sent the message? They would know he's dead. You can say the same thing for any possible organization that had him undercover. Either way both of these organizations must know he's dead. Right? I don't get it. There's also another possibility, as far out as it sounds."

"Fire away," said Josh.

"What if he had been working all three sides?"

"You mean working with the people who bought whatever was sold at the warehouse?" asked Belle, frowning. "The terrorists?"

"Think about it. He would have a chance to hit on a payday so big he'd be secure the rest of his life. And, if it was done correctly, only Wanger and his thugs would know what happened, and they wouldn't be talking to anyone, would they?" said Manny.

"Dead men tell no tales, eh?" said Barb.

Sophie rubbed her fingers between her eyes. "Let me get this right. He double-crosses Wanger by giving the people who killed Wanger and his agency people inside info, makes it look like this terrorist group took them all out, and the undercover organization thinks the deal went south. Is that it?"

"Close," said Manny.

"Ahh, good God, Williams, you're making my brain bleed this early in the morning. Let me think."

"That goes for all of us," said Josh.

Manny poured more coffee for himself and Chloe while he waited for more ideas to be expressed, other than the one that was forming in his brain. Even after he'd said what he said, none of it rang true. But there was one more possibility, but how unlikely and bizarre would that be?

Talk about paranoid.

Belle rocked back in her chair, her dark eyes alive. "There are problems with all of these situations. Especially involving any undercover group investigation. I've seen a couple close up in DC. There is a designated communication time every twenty-four hours. I'd bet that any undercover organization would know he's dead. FB for sure."

"Right. Plus, the warehouse has been all over the national news," said Manny.

"True. But stranger things have happened," added Josh.

"You don't sound too convinced, cowboy," said Sophie.

He sighed. "I know. I'm not. And I don't think there's any chance he was working with the people who killed him either. To me, the fact that Lucretia Doucett, who helped kill six people, is dead means this group or person isn't in the loose-ends business, like Manny said yesterday."

"Assuming you're right on that, and these other theories we just talked about aren't right, where does that leave us? I mean none of this fits well. There are too many holes in all of it. So what else are you thinking, Manny?" asked Chloe.

Another good question. But that old saying about removing what you know for sure from any situation and what was left was the truth rang spot-on here. No matter how crazy it seemed.

"Let's get right back to basics. Who sent the message and why? It's a key to this."

"Who do you think sent it?" asked Josh.

"Let me answer that," said Alex. He had been glued to his computer screen up to this point, but now he raised his head, eyes dancing.

"Alex?" Manny asked.

"I think I know who sent the message."

# CHAPTER-38

Connie Corner rose from her king-sized, four-poster bed, went to the kitchen, and drew a glass of water. She hardly noticed the cold floor as she turned on the overhead light above the window. Cold was a state of mind, both inside and out, at least for her these days.

She headed to the front room to once again peek through the curtains to the street. At this time of night, the streetlights revealed just enough to tell her that Josh hadn't unexpectedly rolled into the driveway in the last ten seconds. She exhaled, her mixed emotions teasing both sides of her brain.

She'd always wanted him home, to be there for her and the boys. She remembered how wonderful it had been when he'd return home from a long bout with some sicko that his BAU had finally put away. Always with a gift for the three of them.

He was always safe and unharmed, unless one counted the mental damage of seeing what he'd seen. Regardless of that fact, seeing him come home had spawned tears of relief more than once.

Yet, *this* late evening, her feelings were on the other side of the board. She didn't want her husband of twelve years to be here. Not at all.

The situation would be hard to explain.

*He* would be hard to explain.

The next minute, his hands surrounded her middle as he pulled her close, kissing the back of her neck.

"You're awake again," he said.

"I am. And I'm glad you are. I'm always worried that you won't be gone before the boys wake up."

"I know. We've done this a couple of times, and it's been fine. Don't worry."

He kissed her again, and she felt the shivers go up and down her spine. It was hard not to compare this man with her husband, but it had been a long time since Josh had pushed her buttons like this. And after all, that was what counted.

She missed that intimacy with Josh, how it would bring her to a quick warmth. But no longer. Josh Corner had been replaced in every way except as father to Charlie and Jake.

"You're thinking of him?" he asked, still holding her.

"In a way. Not as a lover, but as a father to my children. He'll always be that."

"Do you think he knows about us?"

She pondered that, then answered, "He knows he and I are out of sorts, and it's happened one time too many for both of us. He . . . well, we have always been able to get on track before. But I think he realizes that neither one of us really want to do that again."

"You'll divorce him then?"

She instantly wondered what that might do to her boys. Protecting them was the most important thing on the planet for her. Yet, living like this, this tension, this fake happiness that the boys no doubt sensed could have far worse effect on them. She wondered if that was another lie she was telling herself.

"I'm not sure I want to think about that. When Josh gets home, we'll talk."

"I won't pressure you. Just know that I—"

His body stiffened, and he pulled away from her.

Connie spun around, fearing that one of her sons had gotten out of bed unexpectedly.

"Good evening, Missus Corner."

The man standing in her living room stood by her lover, gun to his head. She blinked to make sure what she was seeing was real.

The man and his gun didn't disappear.

"Please. The safe is open in the den. You can take all of the money we have. Just don't hurt anyone," she begged.

"Money? How novel. I'm not here to rob you. In fact, I've driven all the way from New York to meet you and your boys. But I didn't expect to find you with, how shall I say this, a guest?"

"What? Why would you do that?" she asked, disbelief still haunting her.

"Oh, we have a little ride to take."

"Ride? If you harm them, I'll hunt you down," said her lover.

"I bet you would."

The man with the gun then shot him in the head, blood spattering against the yellow wall.

She stood in shock for a moment, utterly horrified, then slowly moved her sights to the man with the gun. Her eyes were already filled with tears.

"What have you done? Oh God in Heaven, what have you done?"

"What was necessary."

Three steps later, he had her by her hair. "I'd hate to kill you and your family. I really would. So listen carefully. We're going to get your boys out of bed, and then we're going to take a trip. Do you have a problem with that?"

"No. No. Just don't hurt us."

He shoved her in the direction of the boys' rooms. "No hero-shit on your part, and you and your boys just might make it. Now go."

After one more look at the dead man on the floor, she did what he said, praying that she wouldn't go insane—something that would surely happen if her boys were harmed.

# CHAPTER-39

Manny sat back in his chair and waited for Alex to share what he'd found.

"All of your theories made some sense, but like Belle said, nothing fit well enough to make the best-case scenario. I prioritized about fifteen information and tracking requests about the email servers and Brooks's URL history to our forensic computer division at the FBI. Anna too."

"And?" asked Josh.

"I'm getting some feedback. First thing. This email was sent from a secure server, not truly a proxy, but one with big-time security. Once I figured that out, I asked for help and found out this was a timed email, scheduled to go when it did, some two days before."

"So no one had really sent it when Anna saw it?" asked Sophie.

"Right. Most systems let you schedule email up to a week in advance."

"Who sent it?" asked Manny. "FB or someone else?"

Alex nodded. "You guessed it, FB. It apparently came from a DEA server, routed through a New Orleans location a few hours before the shootings in the warehouse."

"So FB is or was a DEA agent?" asked Manny.

"We're sure of it. Her name is Flora Burns. According to my DEA friends, she was very active in undercover work and known for her ability to recruit help."

"So that's why we couldn't find anything in any criminal database or facial recognition files," said Josh.

"That's why. The DEA confirmed that she was after Wanger and was getting close."

"What about Brooks then?" asked Chloe.

"FB had prison contacts who would throw out feelers for men and women with certain skills, which isn't all that unusual. Anna is a case in point. Some of these people can and are willing to get down and dirty. She recruited Daryl Brooks with the promise of expunging his record and a fat paycheck if he helped her," said Alex, looking back at his screen.

"I think that will make Amy Brooks feel a little better and get her bosses off her ass. At least that ties up who our mystery woman is and what she was doing there. But the DEA had no idea what was going to happen at the warehouse, right?" said Manny.

"None. They thought it would be one last deal before FB had what she needed on Wanger. Obviously, our unsub spoiled that plan."

"Did you ask if they knew what Wanger was selling?" asked Barb, putting her hand on Alex's arm.

"I did. She only knew that it was highly volatile, and once she found out, she'd bring the whole thing down on both Wanger and the buyer. She guessed it was biological, just from the way Wanger was playing it close to the vest. She said he even had one of his people killed before the warehouse meeting for asking too many questions," said Alex.

Josh exhaled. "This is frightening on a lot of levels. We need to find out what this is and what the hell the plan is for the cruise ship."

The room grew quiet. Part of the mystery was solved, but they were still miles away from fixing the real problem. This person or group was planning to kill thousands, and they had to stop them.

Manny broke the silence. "I think we need to move away from this warehouse situation and go forward to what we should do with the high possibility of a cruise-ship attack."

"Based on what we have, we could make an educated guess for an attack on that ship coming in tomorrow afternoon," said Josh.

"Again, what should we do?" asked Sophie.

"That's obvious to me," said Belle. "We stop that ship from sailing. There's no way we can risk it going out to sea."

"Or, for that matter, going through an embarkation," said Josh. "Cruise security is good, far better than when we were on the *Ocean Duchess*, but if these people want to get something on board, it wouldn't be a huge problem."

"We can't risk the safety of anyone, but the flip side is that we won't have a shot at finding the suspect, or suspects, unless we go with business as usual and let the cruisers embark as planned," said Manny.

Josh shook his head. "You're right about better chances of locating the suspect, but we can't risk it. There will be five thousand people on that ship."

"I'm aware of that. I'm not saying we let it sail."

Sophie gave him a thumbs up. "That's smart. Just let them board but don't sail unless we find the dickhead or dickheads that want to raise hell here."

"Yes. I think we can set it up with security cameras, undercover people, K-9 units, our own people, NOPD, and Carousel's people. That should cover everything. We could also see how difficult it is to swap out as much of the ship's staff as possible to lower the chance that there is inside help from an employee."

"Dey can run security sweeps in da employee quarters too," said Braxton.

The bellhop wheeled in another cart of coffee, croissants, and breakfast sandwiches just as Josh stood up. He walked over, poured another cup of the rich-smelling brew, and then began to pace to the other end of the room, head down.

Manny knew that, ultimately, the decision regarding the ship was Josh's call. A burden he wouldn't want to bear himself. He got it. As good as law enforcement could be, one slip up and people died. Lots of people. Maybe even some of the people in this room.

After filling her plate, Sophie came back and sat down beside him, still watching Josh pace, agonizing over what to do.

"Josh?" asked Chloe.

"Yeah, I'm still thinking." He looked at his watch and turned back to the table. "One thing hasn't changed. You three are still going to New York. You have to. No matter what I decide, we can get this handled without you being here."

"What?" said Chloe. "You need us here. No one—"

She snapped her head around and bore two holes in Manny's face with those emerald coals glowing from her eyes.

*Here comes the Irish storm.*

"You told him what you thought about New York, didn't ya, Manfred Robert Williams?"

"I may have said something."

"I've got to hear this. What about New York? This better be good, because Chloe's right—we should stay," said Barb.

Josh exhaled a long breath. "Manny thinks it wasn't a coincidence that those murders transpired just before we got new intel about what could happen here," said Josh.

"Okay, that's paranoid for even you. You need another nap," said Sophie, crossing her arms.

"Maybe. But I feel like I'm right."

"Why in hell would you think that?" said Belle, exhibiting her own version of pissed.

"Think about it. Three sets of murders in random locations, yet still in Central Park. That's one of the most unusual escalations of a rage or spree killer I've seen. And that park has a very sophisticated security-camera system, as well as dozens of blues patrolling the area. It's a recipe to get caught, at minimum but he wasn't. That means he had a plan in my book."

"Go on," said Belle.

"Listen. It weakens us with you three gone, no question, but the timing isn't random. I'm telling you, it's not. And there's something else," said Manny.

"Pray tell, Manny. What else?" asked Chloe, the arctic having nothing on the chill in her voice.

"I asked Alex to request the initial ballistics reports from the NYPD. We also sent a couple of FBI reps over to look at the security footage from the cameras near the three crime scenes in

Central Park. They didn't have a lot of other information available yet, but they're sending it as it becomes available. At any rate, I got what I wanted to see from ballistics," answered Manny.

"Which was what?" asked Chloe.

Before Manny could respond, Alex said, "I don't know how Manny makes these jumps of logic and comes out smelling like a rose. But it appears he might be right," said Alex. "The ballistics show that the gun used to kill these people in New York, at least the first four, belonged to Lucretia Doucett."

# CHAPTER-40

The drive would probably take longer than he thought. Fourteen hours was an extended period of time, but would put him there with three hours to spare, give or take.

Complicating that eventuality was the whole idea of bathroom, gas, and food stops, the variety that could be dangerous to this kind of prolonged journey. Yet, it was something he had done before and more than once.

Besides, notorious risk came engraved with notorious reward. His kind of engagement, for sure.

Still, he'd have to keep his eyes open, three passengers were far different than one or two, but then again, he'd planned this trip over and over again, and would deliver as promised.

After that, he'd spend a few days in the Crescent City and enjoy all it had to offer. Given Bourbon Street's reputation, that could be interesting.

First things first, however.

He opened the front passenger door and gazed at the young boy staring back at him. His blue eyes bright and wide, the tear streaks almost completely disappeared.

"Do I have to repeat myself, or do you understand what's going on here, Charlie?" he asked quietly.

"Y-yes, sir. If we keep quiet and don't cause trouble, you won't hurt my mom or Jake."

"Right. Very bright for an eight-year-old. And how will we do that?"

"By doing what you say and not talking to anyone else."

It was hard to ignore the emotion in the young boy's voice. He couldn't tell if it was fear or hatred, then decided it didn't matter. Both would keep Charlie in check.

"Buckle up. We're going to leave."

Moving to the other side of the car, he opened the rear passenger door. Connie Corner looked up at him, her youngest son leaning on her, buckled into the middle seatbelt, already unconscious from the injection.

Her emotions were not nearly as masked as her eldest son's. *Her* fear and hatred were plain to see.

Interesting.

"What did you do to my son?"

"He is not harmed. I know what I'm doing. He'll be awake in about fourteen hours. I told you, no one else gets hurt here unless you force my hand. Give me your arm, then buckle up."

She hesitated.

"Now. I won't ask again."

Slowly, she stretched out her left arm. He then jabbed the needle into her upper biceps. The amber liquid disappeared into her pale arm.

"You'll be out as long as your son. It'll be easier for all of us. Old Charles and I will become friends. Just as a precaution, I want him awake for a while."

"What kind of precaution?" she said, already becoming drowsy.

"The kind that covers any contingency in the event you and Jake aren't able to go where we go. That's all you get."

She nodded and looked to the front seat. "Charlie?"

"Yes, Mom?"

"Do what he says and we'll be all right, okay?"

"Okay," he said meekly.

"Enough talk."

He slammed the door, got in behind the wheel of the Buick Enclave, and began to pull out of the driveway, the moon hitting the east side of the white colonial. A moment later they were on their way to US-64.

They'd made it down five miles of road before one last semi-expected reaction reared its head.

"I wish my dad were here," said Charlie, looking at his shoes.

"I suppose you do. That would be interesting. Now do what I asked and don't talk unless I say so. And don't worry; you'll see him soon."

He smiled as he thought about how that reunion might happen.

# CHAPTER-41

"Say that again," said Josh.

"You heard me. Those people were killed by a gun that shouldn't be there, in my way of thinking," Alex said.

Josh looked at Manny for his reaction. As usual, he didn't really have one. It appeared that he was already trying to piece the whys together. He wasn't alone.

"Why would that happen? What's the point?" asked Belle. "I mean, the killer had to know we'd find that out."

"Maybe the gun was stolen, and this is all some crazy-ass coincidence," said Sophie.

"Do you believe that?" asked Manny. "That would make this investigation much simpler."

Sophie tapped her fork against the china, then looked at Josh with an accompanying shrug. "No, I guess I don't. So, other than the obvious reasons for splitting us up—and we've been harping on that for the last ten hours, by the way, let's go back to Belle's question—what's the point?"

Looking down at his yellow notepad, Josh read a few of his notes. His eyes trailed to the lower corner of the pad, where he'd written Charlie's and Jake's names. Even here, even now, he wondered what was best for them. In his last argument with his wife, she'd pointed out he had no clue.

Was she right?

He shook his head. They'd talk when he got home, if they could be civil to one another for five minutes.

He looked back to his notes. Some had to do with the facts and some had to do with conjecture, which wasn't really his forte. Manny had been right when he said they needed to get back to what they all did well. Especially him. Starting now.

He stood. "Folks. We've spent more time meeting about this case, entertaining theories, analyzing information, etcetera, etcetera, than we've ever done with any other case that I can remember. Part of that's my fault. This ACTU may be new to me, to all of us, but I'm not new at putting investigations together. That's what I'm good at—organizing the team, pushing the best in all of us. I needed to remember that. You're all still the best resources available to me and part of the reason I took this job to begin with. I've underutilized you. Let's get this thing in motion."

He pointed in Manny's direction, then spread his hands, palms up. "Answer Belle's question and tell me what this is about."

His friend rubbed his chin and then looked up. "No holds barred?"

"None. Not that you ever did that."

"I have, at times. I won't now." Manny exhaled.

Was that a look of relief on his face? Josh thought so. He wondered what the man had been holding inside. He thought he was about to find out.

"I'm a little like Josh, in that I didn't know what we should expect here. In the end, I think I was right when I said there's not a lot of difference between the ACTU and what we did before, except the scale of the action.

"At first, I thought there was only one unsub. Then, as we went along, I thought more of an organization. I'm still curious about the God's Hand people and who they are. I suspect this isn't the last we've heard of them, but the context of an organization being involved here . . . well, frankly, it doesn't feel right."

"You think one person is behind all of this?" asked Josh.

"Yes. I think this man—and no question it's a man; the death of Doucett and the way she died sells that part for me—has a plan. I think it took years to put together. I think he didn't have money when this started, but somehow he accumulated enough wealth to pull this together. Every detail, every contingency, every facet has been thorough. I don't think a group pf people would have the ability to keep that kind of thing under wraps."

"I don't know Manny. What about those radical groups in the Middle East? That's a group that has done some bad shit," said Sophie.

"True. But the dynamics are different. The cowardly leaders of those groups simply send out orders to the soldiers. They don't need to be where the death and destruction takes place; they simply watch as young men and women kill themselves in attacks, and then they bask in the aftermath, taking credit for what happened. Most of that leadership, in fact all of them, wouldn't personally do what they order to be done. This case feels far different from that."

"How?" asked Barb.

"It begins with the warehouse, then with Doucett. Potential loose ends. There are probably more. Then there are the attempts to distract us. We've wasted time trying to deal with the attack on Detective Brooks, the breach at the safe house. Now New York, and the ballistics report. No organization would waste their people and resources like that."

Manny engaged in a long, loving draw from his coffee cup. "All of this sidebar stuff had me running in the wrong direction. The central idea, I thought, was why is he doing this? What prompted the whole idea of a possible terrorist attack in the first place?

"Then I realized I can't know that yet. We can guess, and we have, but we're not sure, not yet. The thing I can't shake in all of this is what he bought, or stole, in this case. I think that's central here. I researched some of the bioweapons on the bioterror information we have in our agencies. Only a few viruses or chemicals would accomplish what he might want to do on a cruise ship—and I'm guessing that's to infect every passenger and crewmember with something deadly."

He frowned. "Yet . . ." His voice trailed off.

"Yet what?" asked Josh.

"I don't get why he's letting us know what's going on here. He has to realize we'll figure it out."

"Ego?" asked Sophie.

"That, or he's not really going to attack the ship," said Belle.

"I've thought of that. I believe he will though. In all of his actions, I get a sense he's been, I don't know, honest with his goal. Not ego so much as determined. I think he was buying time through his 'distractions,' to get us off the trail for a while, true. But in the end, he'll try to get on that ship."

"Integrity from a man who wants to kill thousands?" asked Chloe, a look of disgust on her face.

"Oddly, the profile on this man says yes. He has a sense of justice and punishment. Not so much of a personal pleasure," said Manny softly.

Josh felt his pulse increasing. His friend hadn't pulled any punches. Plus, his out-loud thinking had a ring of truth. Again.

"So what do we do next?" asked Barb, watching Alex, speaking to Josh.

"This is what we are going to start with," said Josh. "I want Alex to research every incident that has occurred on Carousel Cruise Lines in the last five years. That means deaths, lawsuits, anything. Plus anything that might have happened in New Orleans pre- and post-cruise. Maybe we'll get lucky and can narrow down what's motivating this guy."

"Got it," said Alex, not looking up from his laptop.

"I want Anna to research possible illegal sources of any bioweapon marketing. Including anything missing from government facilities. The Darknet might shed some light on that. She also needs to connect with the CDC. I know for a fact they can help with that. Alex, please let her know what we want."

It was now his turn to exhale. He hoped this was going to work. They could use a break. He then glanced back at his notes.

"You three are still going to New York, and I don't want any shit about it. You might, just might, find something in the evidence that will help unravel this thing. Are we clear?"

"I can bring my team, right?" asked Belle.

"They're rookies, but good people, so yes. The more eyes, the better."

"Braxton and I are going to see if we can rekindle some old relationships with some of our high-profile snitches. Money and threats work, so maybe we'll get something there," said Josh.

He made eye contact with Manny. "You and Sophie have a hell of a job. You're going to meet with the cruise-line people and their head of security and lay out what's going on. I've changed my mind. I think we can risk an embarkation without a sailing. If we don't find the unsub or at least the biohazard, then we cancel the whole cruise idea."

"That's risky. What if they say no?" said Sophie.

"It's their decision, in my mind, but we have to impress that if we don't stop him now and go forward with shutting this cruise down, he'll try it again. You have to convince them that this is the soundest strategy," said Josh.

"We'll do our best," said Manny. "It would help if we—"

"Get the hell out of Dodge!"

Turning in Alex's direction, Josh began to reach for his weapon and stopped.

*Damn, boy, a little jumpy?*

Apparently he wasn't the only one startled. "Don't be doing that shit, Dough Boy. I about had a coronary."

"What she said," agreed Josh.

"What is it, Alex?" asked Manny.

"I was accessing some of the local security cameras around town. I searched for incidents atypical for crimes in this area of New Orleans. Which was tough, by the way. Anyway, I got a hit on a car fire on the west side. It was an old Chevy. Nothing special, but the program identified it as a vehicle seen near a cross street just after the warehouse killings. I then got a third hit, some two weeks ago near Canal and Bourbon."

Standing, he spun the computer around for the group to see.

Displayed was a relatively clear image that came more into focus by the second. The couple stood by the door of an old, gray Chevy.

Lucretia Doucett had her hand on the shoulder of an average-sized man with black hair and a mustache. Both wore wide grins.

"I think this is our suspect," said Alex.

# CHAPTER-42

No more sunrises. This was it before this journey was completed. The last one. That didn't seem quite possible, yet here he was.

There was an air of satisfaction, but also, surprisingly, a feeling of disappointment that his task was almost complete. He and this journey had spent every waking moment together over the last four years and change. Friends or convenient partners. Regardless, time spent was time spent.

After eating the bowl of fruit, he finished dressing and moved over to the large window revealing the Louisiana sunrise.

He supposed it was natural to become a tad nostalgic about the ending of such a partnership, wasn't it? Then again, can one grow evocative over such a complicated string of events that climaxed into this narrow window of time the next few hours would reveal? Did that really constitute a partnership as such?

"No matter. It simply is, no matter what you call it," he said softly.

He kept his eyes fixed on the horizon. How he loved the light. He'd spent years, as a youth and as a professional, trying to stay out of the darkness. However, it seemed to follow him like a desperate child, prying into his every thought.

Some would say it was destiny. Maybe. Was it destiny, what had happened to him? Or the incompetence and neglect of others that had left him on this journey?

He wasn't so sure. He bit his lip, trying not to replay memories he swore to abandon.

The memories had other plans.

Bowing his head, he'd chosen another direction. He'd had to, or his ideals would be for naught and the dark would win again.

After the terrible incident, the light finally did shine through for him, however. He saw the world for what it truly was. Satan's army couldn't be more stark, evil, and hideous in his eyes. That had to be true.

*Who allows that to happen to others?*

Rhetorical question aside, he understood who and even why. Yet, as his mother used to tell him, there will be repercussions to actions. To every action.

"And you, my friends, will find out what that means. And soon," he said.

With that, he moved to the bathroom. He turned back into the room he'd just left, looked at the bed, a hint of a smile tugging at the corners of his mouth. He wanted to see the looks on their faces when this one came down.

"Even you can't see everything," he whispered. He then began the arduous task of changing his look.

Everything had to be just right.

After all this time, he would do that. He would balance the scale. He would make things just right.

# CHAPTER-43

Standing near the gold, ornate, revolving door of the hotel, Chloe put her arms around Manny's neck and kissed him, then stepped back, the worry evident on her face.

"I love you. Keep yourself safe," she said.

He pulled her to him and kissed her again, then squeezed her cheek, grinning. "Don't worry about me. We'll be fine here. You watch your butt up there and don't do anything foolish. I love you too."

She smiled back. "Ohh, I'd rather have ya watching my arse than doing it myself. We'll be fine, like you say."

Then Chloe went through the door. Just before she got into the vehicle, she gave him her sexiest look and blew him a kiss. His heart jumped at that. Case or not, she was always able to get his attention.

Sophie called from behind him, "Better get your mind on task, Williams. No woodies when we go talk to the Carousel people. You'd have some explaining to do. Where's Alex?"

"He and Braxton are back in the conference room packing his electronics. He says he needs a faster, more secure connection, so he's going back to the safe house."

"Make's sense. Where's Barb?"

"Already in the SUV."

Manny turned around to locate Belle. She was forty feet away, standing close to Josh near the elevators. The two were engaged in an intense conversation. Belle suddenly put her hands on her hips, cocking her head in silent demand.

Josh put his hand on her shoulder, bent to her ear, and whispered to her.

She stepped back, slowly shook her head, and then turned on her heel, walking to the door.

"Everything okay?"' asked Manny as she drew next to him and Chloe.

"Nothing a good stiff shot of whisky couldn't cure. Sometimes I hate taking orders, but I'll make it. Are you two ready?"

"Yeah, we'll be fine," said Sophie.

"Okay. Good luck. We'll be in touch."

A minute later, the SUV was gone, and Josh was standing beside them.

"What was that about, between you and Belle?" asked Manny.

"Just some last minute instructions and a sharing of protocol," said Josh.

"That's it?"

"Nothing to concern yourself with. Sometimes receiving instruction can be tough."

"Been there," said Sophie.

"You have," said Josh, grinning.

Then the grin vanished.

"It's a little risky not putting this picture out for all of the local authorities to see. An APB might find this guy and save us some trouble," he said.

"Maybe. Then again, it might alert him to the fact we know who he is too. I'd rather keep it between us and the cruise line for now," said Manny.

"Okay, for a little while. But the more eyes the better, in my opinion," said Josh.

"Speaking of more eyes," said Sophie, "what if he's gone incognito and changed how he looks? We've seen that a time or two."

"I thought of that. In fact, he probably has done something like that. But that's where we come in. We have to be able to recognize his body type. His actions, his demeanor. We're trained for that."

"Maybe a trance would help," said Josh, cocking an eyebrow at Manny.

Manny grinned. "Hey, if it would help, I'd do it."

Just then, Alex reached them, Braxton in tow carrying a large wooden crate, his biceps bulging.

"We're ready," said Alex.

"Yeah, dat means I be ready. Dis boy loaded me up here," said Braxton.

"Hey, use it or lose it, as the saying goes. I don't want you to lose muscle mass or anything," said Alex.

"I think he's safe," said Josh.

"True," said Sophie.

"Okay, this is my cue. We'll take Alex to the house and then get on the phone. Maybe we can shake one of our informants loose and find out something about this man. Maybe even a little about what he is carrying. Let me know what happens at the cruise line. We've burned a few more hours, and it's only five hours before that ship comes in," said Josh.

"We will. We'll probably have to do a conference call or teleconference with their office in Miami. But once we tell them what's going on, we shouldn't take long to set up," said Manny.

"Good luck," said Josh.

"We might need more than luck," said Sophie.

Manny thought she might be right. Skill, intuition, and that enigma called luck only went so far. Maybe a little Divine intervention was in order. He'd take that.

Ten minutes later, Sophie and he pulled out of the parking garage, this time Manny was driving the gray Escalade while Sophie worked her phone.

"I could do both, Williams. You know that right?"

"Maybe. But this way I know I'll live a few hours longer. Besides that, I only brought so many pair of tighty-whities."

"Yeah, yeah. I'm driving when we leave though."

"Okay as long as you give me your phone."

She waved her small hand at him. "Whatever. Anyway, while Josh and you were getting everyone organized, I've been doing a little research of my own involving deaths and cruise lines over the last few years."

"Are you isolating the highest-profile incidents like death and injuries?"

"Yep. It's not as encompassing as Alex and Anna are going to do, but I can at least look at the high-profile stuff."

"So?"

"There have been eleven known deaths involving Carousel ships, plus two on their loading docks that we know of. I say know of because those folks who end up in those creepy little morgues on board aren't publicized, since those folks died of natural causes. Heck of a way to end a vacation."

"We've seen that up close," said Manny.

Sophie placed her phone in her lap, bowing her head.

"Are you all right?"

"Hell no. But I suppose I'll live. I didn't think I wanted to a few weeks ago. I guess that's progress. I was just hit with that image of Liz Casnovsky on the autopsy table, that fake rose on her chest, mangled by that bastard Argyle. It's the last true memory of her that I have. I remember the funeral, sure, but her body smack in the middle of that cold, steel table gave me more nightmares than almost anything we've gone through."

"Really? You never mentioned that to me."

"I know. I mean I was bopping her husband, and we were friends. How shitty was that? Throw in the fact that cruises are supposed to be beautiful and fun with dancing and sun and margaritas, not friends lying in morgues on those ships. It was that whole perfect storm of, what word do you use, dichotomies, that almost drove me nuts."

"All of that is true. But what can you do to change the past?"

"That's just it. I couldn't, but my past didn't go away, at least all of the time. Then along comes Mikus with that dumbass wardrobe and those deep-brown eyes and that whole on-his-knee . . . thing . . ."

Manny touched her arm. "Then you're suddenly saved, right?"

"That's it. Like Chloe and you," she said softly. "Now, well now, aww piss, I've got to find a way to start over, sort of, and I worry if I can stay sane enough to do it."

"Like you told me, one day at a time."

"What the hell did I know? I was trying to make you feel better."

"It was the right wisdom though. Let's get off that road for now, okay? Eleven deaths, right?"

"Right. Three were from drunks diving off the ship and were never found. Four were apparent suicides. They took dives off the back. If the hundred-foot drop didn't kill them, then they would have drowned.

"Two more had to do with cruise-ship employees raping and then killing their victims. Nasty stuff there. But how do you know what you're hiring? I don't fault the cruise lines for that. People do what they do."

"What about the other two?"

"Oddly, the other two had to do with food allergies. One older gentleman died from shellfish he ate, the other, an eight-year-old girl, died from peanuts inadvertently mixed into an entrée."

"The dock workers?"

"Both crushed by loads of product or luggage that had fallen off some equipment. One malfunctioning overhead crane, the other apparently from workers horsing around and dumping a lift truck load squarely on a worker's head."

Strange how life and death showed themselves. Vacations that ended in tragedy, no matter the circumstances. Manny wasn't sure at all if he'd ever get his mind around the why.

"There could be a situation or two there that needs digging into," said Manny, then, "Yet, it seems like a long shot to me."

"Maybe. I'll send the info to Alex anyway. Stranger things, as they say."

The phone was still resting in her lap when the screen lit up and then began to ring.

It was Alex.

"What?" asked Sophie.

"Get your asses over to the Bayou Hotel. We've got another hit on our suspect."

# CHAPTER-44

Six hours to go. Right on schedule.

He glanced over at the young man in the seat beside him. He had fallen asleep, his head on his chest, moving back and forth ever so slightly whenever the vehicle changed lanes or hit a minor bump on the freeway.

The rearview mirror revealed that his mother and brother were out as well. As planned.

"Miles to go before I sleep," he whispered. He wondered if Robert Frost had ever made this much money, however.

That was all the time he had to concern himself with. Then he'd be on his way to wherever the money he'd earned would take him. Then what?

Glancing at Charlie again, he wondered if a family was in his future. Could he love someone else enough to marry and bring children onto this wretched piece-of-shit rock called earth?

Moving into the passing lane, he drove by an old geezer in a blue sedan that was two sizes too large for him. The old fart could barely sit up far enough to see through the windshield. How long before he caused an accident and killed someone? Who knew? But it was a probability, from his point of view.

He then steered back into the cruising lane, staying right at the speed limit. It wouldn't be good to be pulled over. He'd hate to kill another cop, and so soon after the man in Corner's house.

One more glance at Charlie gave him reason to pause.

Were kids the true legacy for men? To leave your mark in a set of genes handed down from generation to generation? He thought about that for a moment, then decided no. Legacies were left by actions, not children.

Six hours.

Then he'd work on his own legacy.

Who could ask for more?

# CHAPTER-45

Motioning for the trio of agents from the New Orleans FBI office to go to the rear exit of the hotel, Manny then pointed to the other two teams of three, sending them to each side entrance of the six-story building. There were four more agents at the front.

Thirteen agents plus Josh, Braxton, Sophie, and himself—that would be enough to put this one in custody. Especially given the circumstances.

"We're going in the front?" asked Josh as they huddled near the hood of the SUV.

"We do. We'll go in when all the guests have been evacuated. Maybe another five minutes," said Manny. "The manager doesn't like it, but she's reasonable and is cooperating. They were pretty much full because of today's cruise, otherwise we'd be ready to go already."

"Let's see it again. We have to make sure we know this man," said Josh.

"Dat be true," agreed Braxton.

Sophie reached through the window and pulled her pad from the front seat of the SUV, pushed the on switch, hit another button, and the elevator's recorded feed came to life.

The security footage clearly displayed the image of the same man Alex had found from the traffic system videos standing near Lucretia Doucett two weeks prior. His slim face easily recognizable, his hair and mustache the same. He appeared to be smiling.

He'd checked in late last night and hadn't left his room, according to security guards and the front desk. To top that off, the room keycard hadn't been swiped again either. Although the hotel manager had said those imprint records could be unreliable, the manager suspected the man hadn't left his room either.

"Do we really think this is him?" asked Sophie.

"Hey, at the very least, he's a person of interest. But my gut tells me he's in this deep. Yeah, I think it's him," said Josh.

"Manny?" asked Sophie.

"Yes. I think he's involved. And if we can determine if he killed Doucett, I think that seals it. Maybe he'll have the knife on him, and we can match it to the knife tip Chloe and Alex found in Doucett's body."

"What about whatever he took from the warehouse?" asked Josh. "I mean; I know the procedure. But what if this goes bad, and he uses whatever he has right here?"

"The good thing is it'll be in a hotel and not on a cruise ship. The bad news is it'll be us inside," said Manny.

"Great. I haven't even had any of those fried oysters at the Ocean Grill yet," said Sophie.

"Hungry again?"

"Yeah, and I think I got to pee. This job makes me nervous."

"It should. Me too. But that's the worst case, remember?" said Josh.

"You're right," she answered.

"Sophie, run it again," said Manny.

She did. Watching the surveillance video for the tenth time, Manny shook his head.

"Why are you shaking your head?" asked Sophie.

"It's obvious, right? Why would this man risk being seen in a public place? He looked right at the camera."

"He might not know that much about security cameras and systems. Besides that, I know I look at the camera when I'm in an elevator," said Josh.

"You're a cop though," said Manny.

He shrugged. "People look at cameras. We've all seen it."

Josh made sense. Not everyone knows about everything. Yet, if this was their man, he'd know, right?

"You're not totally convinced, are—"

The manager emerged from the front, herding nine more people toward them. After the guests had been ushered off the block, she returned. The round, pleasant-looking woman was perspiring, the beads of sweat high on her ebony forehead.

"It's clear, y'all. He's the only person left in the hotel. Room 202."

"Thank you. We won't be long," said Josh.

The worried look on the manager's face deepened. "You're not going to shoot my hotel up, are you?"

Manny smiled, despite the situation. "We've not done that yet. I think your hotel is safe."

"Okay. I don't trust y'all, but what am I going to do?"

"We'll take care of your building. You can sit over there behind those four agents. You'll be safe there," said Josh.

Josh nodded toward Manny and Sophie. "Braxton and I are going in first, you two will back us."

"Oh hell no," said Sophie. "I've seen both of you shoot. Manny and I are going in first. We've done this way more times. If this goes haywire, I like our chances better with me getting a clear shot."

"She's right," said Manny.

Josh opened his mouth. Sophie raised her hand.

"Don't talk. This ain't up for debate. Let's go, Big Boy."

Sophie took off for the double doors.

Manny moved to her side, trying to pray away the uneasy feeling that they would get more than what they'd bargained for.

# CHAPTER-46

Alex Downs rubbed his eyes then looked back to the thirty-inch screen positioned between the two smaller monitors. His lack of sleep was creeping up on him, but he'd be all right as long as the coffee and the energy drink held out. Josh and Braxton had headed off to the hotel from the safe house, taking every agent except four with them. They were as excited as he that maybe they'd located the man who was planning to . . . do what exactly?

Fill a ship with toxins? Maybe they were off track, and he planned to blow up the ship. Maybe he was just going to kill the captain and crew. Hell, maybe he only wanted to kick the chef's ass. Who knew for sure with these people?

He drank more coffee from his University of Michigan travel cup, the aroma as good as the taste.

Did it matter, at this point? With more than a dozen highly trained agents surrounding their suspect, he wouldn't have time to take a leak when they went into motion, let alone carry out some misguided concept of revenge, as Manny called it.

Alex couldn't stop thinking about what Manny still wanted him and Anna to do. What was his friend searching for? Probably nothing, yet sometimes he wasn't even sure Manny knew what he was looking for. That he would recognize it when he saw it.

"Don't overthink it, boy," he whispered.

Anna hadn't found anything concrete about missing toxins or potential illegal shipments of Class A bioweapons. Even the CDC hadn't been able to help much. Only to say they were certain that none of their stash was missing, but who knew about the rest of the world?

She was still looking, however. She had expanded her search to include international sources and had even gotten a little help from INTERPOL.

"It's a big world, Alex," she'd said as she hung up. She was right about that. People thought technology made the world smaller, but in a true sense, it revealed just the opposite to him. Seven billion people could generate an insurmountable pile of information. His searches were proof of that.

He'd taken the information Sophie had sent him about the various cruise-related deaths and refined it. There were a couple of wrongful-death lawsuits settled in the cases she had found, as well as a few others he had found. Money talks, no matter the situation.

He'd gone over each case and saw no connection to what was going on in New Orleans. None of the families associated with those deaths resembled their suspect, or Doucett, for that matter. There were no drawn-out, high-profile cases to dive into. Nothing that he could see that would draw attention to any of those cases.

He thought that wise on the cruise line's part. They had done the right thing, after the hell broke loose on the *Ocean Duchess* those years ago, and paid up. He was sure that they cared about their business, no question, but the cruise line had exhibited a concern for their guests and family members touched by murder and injury, and he respected them for that.

After he rose and poured another cup of coffee, he plopped back down and studied the large screen again. He'd input parameters for situations in New Orleans over the last five years that had to do with serious crimes.

The software had done its work, and he now had over two hundred cases to review. Alex sighed, then glanced down at his new left hand.

It wouldn't be his real hand, ever, but by the hour, he was feeling more comfortable with it and what it could do. The doctors said the nerve graft would take time to work, and it wouldn't be complete, but it would allow him some feeling eventually. He still marveled at the progress in the medical arena and was grateful no matter what usage he regained.

It didn't look bad either.

As he began scrolling down the long list of murders, robberies, and assaults that fit into his parameters, the small screen on his right flashed a message that he'd gotten a hit on another security-camera feed. He scowled.

It must be something from an old file, because their suspect was in the hotel. But why guess?

Leaning over, he hit the "enter" button.

There he was again. His white fedora was pulled down on the left side, covering part of his face, but there was no mistaking the image of their unsub. It must have shown up after one of their camera sources updated their video files. Some companies and storefronts took weeks instead of hours to comply with security decorum mandated by law enforcement.

The black banner on the bottom of the still image gave the location: Poydras Street and Convention Center Boulevard.

Alex sat up so fast he almost fell from his chair. The time stamp was less than twenty minutes ago.

# CHAPTER-47

Standing near the elevator, after ascending the two flights of steps, Manny watched, weapon raised, as Josh and Braxton stood on the left side of the red door with the gold 202 displayed.

Sophie had taken a closer position, giving her a better angle to the front of the room. Given the narrow hallway, that made sense. Moreover, there was no stopping her when she got it in her head to go forward with what she saw.

Yet, he didn't see that as recklessness, rather her ability to size up the dynamics and angles of a situation like this. She was as good as anyone.

They had agreed, if anything was remotely off, they'd shoot now and ask questions later. Josh thought it was the best way to ensure as many people as possible stayed alive. Manny reminded Josh that not every circumstance was identical. What if this wasn't their man, as unlikely as that was? But Josh stuck with his first order. Kill the bastard if he looks cross-eyed, then let God sort out who was who.

Braxton caught his attention, then nodded that they were ready, the big man's face aglow with perspiration, matching his own. He remembered the old saying, "It's not the heat but the humidity." He almost laughed. Strange thoughts at strange times indeed.

"Let's kick some ass," whispered Sophie.

They moved silently along the blue and green carpet to the door, then they squatted down, one on each side.

Their eyes met. Sophie's were shining. The woman loved this part of the job. There was no denying that look on her face.

Adrenaline rush for him, no doubt. Love? He thought not.

He shifted, Glock in his left hand, keycard in the other.

*No reason to wait a second more.*

Manny rose from his crouch, raised a hand to swipe the entry card through the door sensor . . . just when the handle turned and the door swung open.

The smallish man, dressed in shorts and a red t-shirt barely had time to widen his eyes before Manny grabbed the front of his shirt and pulled while Sophie took his legs out from under him. The metal traveling case he'd been carrying flew several feet down the dimly lit hall, past Sophie's head, in the direction of Josh and Braxton.

Manny flipped the man on his face, and pulled his arms behind his back.

"Oww. That hurts. Who are you? What the hell are y'all doing?"

"Shut up. We'll ask the questions. Don't move your hands, or it'll be the last thing you do," said Manny.

"Okay, but I didn't do nothing," he answered weakly.

Sophie slapped the back of his head. "Did you hear the man? I think trying to kill thousands of people is something."

"What?"

Manny stood and straddled the man, his attention focused on the man's response to Sophie's statement. He seemed genuinely surprised.

By then, Braxton and Josh had gotten there. With one motion, Braxton lifted the man from the floor and stood him against the wall, holding him as if he were a doll.

Manny studied the man's face; he resembled the images that Alex had found, yet he didn't. But that could be because pictures from the security cameras weren't always great quality. Still, his unease grew.

"What's your name?" he asked.

Their suspect's eyes were as wide as saucers. "I wasn't going to kill no—"

"Answer the question," said Josh.

"Am-Amos Rivers."

"What are you doing here, Amos?' he asked, keeping his voice low.

The man exhaled, trying to calm himself. "I was watching this room for that other man. He gave me two hundred dollars to stay here and bought me food. When you ain't got no place to go, that seems like a good deal."

"What other man?"

"I don't know his name. He was about my size though. He brought me up here through the back door and told me to stay here until eight thirty, then to leave."

"He didn't give you a name?"

"He said Rhodes or something. I didn't care. The streets are a lot harder than that there bed."

Manny's uneasiness grew. This smelled bad and felt worse.

"What did he want you to watch?"

"I don't rightly know. He said I could have that case over there, then he said he had to go, and hit the door."

Leaning closer, Manny scanned Amos's face. He did resemble their suspect, right down to the mustache, but his chin was narrower, his eyes deeper set.

By now, that unease had grown to full-blown doubt. This man seemed to be telling the truth.

"What's in the case?" asked Sophie.

"Just some clothes, and I took a nice pillow. I'll give it back."

His worried expression deepened.

"And what the hell did y'all mean when you said 'kill thousands'? I ain't killed nothing but a few gators and a lot of bottles my whole life. I hate blood."

Josh had opened the case. "He's telling the truth about the clothes and pillow."

"Okay. Amos. You stay right here with my big friend. We need to check out the rest of your story," said Manny, his frustration rising.

"Josh, Sophie, let's go. I'm not feeling real good about this."

"You mean we might have been tricked here," said Sophie.

"I don't know yet."

*Yes, you do, Williams.*

Opening the door with the keycard, Manny pulled his weapon and proceeded inside, Sophie and Josh right behind him.

The queen bed was unmade, and there were black Styrofoam food containers on the small table to his left. The odor of spicy food still lingered in the room. The high-backed wooden chair near the table was empty. He could see no one else in the main room.

He bit the inside of his lip so he wouldn't lose his cool. Sophie stepped around him and moved into the bathroom, gun raised.

*No one here but us fools.*

"Clear in here," she said.

Josh dropped to his knees and lifted the sheet on the bed.

"No one could fit under this bed. No one there."

"Yeah, I think we knew that," said Manny through his teeth.

"Easy there, Big Boy," said Sophie. "We're getting close."

Looking out the large window, Manny got a glimpse of the New Orleans Superdome peeking out from behind two tall buildings, their lighted signs informing the world what they were about, Mercedes-Benz and all. He felt like they were mocking him. They'd seen what had gone on in this room, and he had no idea what that could mean.

"Close doesn't get it done here. I hate being steps behind this man. What he's doing, it just doesn't fit."

"With your profile? Hey, you haven't had a lot of experience with someone like this. We're all still learning," said Josh.

"That doesn't make me feel any better." He looked around the room one last time. "Okay. Don't touch anything. We'll get a forensic crew over here to see what they can find."

He turned from the window, heading out to speak to Amos Rivers again.

Why were they playing this chess game? Misled again. How had this happened? How did their suspect know they would find him? Furthermore, why all of this? He could have just stayed low-key and out of sight until the ship arrived.

*Too many question here. Calm down and concentrate on what you know.*

After stepping past Sophie and Josh, Manny reached the hallway just in time to see Braxton put his phone in his back pocket, his hand still on Amos's chest. Manny didn't like the look on his face.

"What?"

"After I saw dat you were done wit dat room, I called for backup to take Mister Rivers into custody for more questioning. But I tink he doesn't know any ting else."

"You're right. I don't think he's our man. We'll keep him for a day or two anyway," said Manny. "So why the look?"

"Alex has been trying to reach you. He says our man was seen by one of dos traffic cameras down by da river near da cruise port."

# CHAPTER-48

Belle looked at her phone, sipped her water, then went back to her phone, the sound of the droning jet in the background.

"What are you so interested in?" asked Chloe.

"Didn't you get Alex's email?" asked Belle.

"My phone's charging in the back."

"Mine too," said Barb.

"They got another hit on the unsub at a hotel downtown. It turns out that was a false alarm. Alex says Josh and the team think it was some kind of setup or another misdirection."

"Why?" asked Chloe.

"The man in the hotel room apparently isn't our suspect."

"They know that how?" asked Barb. "These weasels can be tricky."

"There wasn't any weapon of mass destruction in the room, and it seems the man was telling the truth about who he is. But the big thing is that

Alex got another video hit near the cruise port when our agents were at the hotel."

"Great. He could be anywhere in that area. When does the ship get to port?" asked Barb.

"Three hours, give or take," said Belle. Reaching down, she rubbed her knee, all the while rereading Alex's email. They were still about an hour out from New York and the first real case with her team. She was excited about it, or at least had been.

This new development in New Orleans was gnawing at her. She knew they could use the help of the women in this jet. More than that, she wanted to be there, maybe even needed to be.

"What's wrong, Belle?" asked Chloe.

"Nothing. We have our orders."

"But you think we should be in New Orleans."

"I said that before we left. But Josh made sense, and still does. We should see what's going on in New York."

Belle read the email again then put the phone on the seat next to her. *This is nuts. We have two profilers and another woman whose very job involved dealing with scum like this guy, and they were in jet going the wrong direction.*

*Orders are orders.*

Except when they weren't making enough sense on the inside, like now.

"I can't take this," said Belle, reaching for the intercom button to the cockpit.

"What are you going to do?" asked Chloe, grinning.

"The right thing."

The co-pilot's voice rang through the cabin. "Yes, Belle?"

"I don't care what you have to do with filing a new flight plan or whatever, but get our butts back to New Orleans, now."

"Is there something wrong? We can pull an emergency route change and stop if there is."

"There is. Now get us there."

"Will do. It'll take about ninety minutes or so once we're approved."

"Do it. We have a terrorist to catch."

"You're going to get your ass chewed," said Barb. "But I'm glad you made the call."

"Getting chewed out might be the worst of our worries," she said.

A few minutes later, the jet banked right, then right again.

She hoped she was wrong about the worst of their worries. No, she prayed she was.

# CHAPTER-49

"Do we have enough people here?' asked Manny.

"We have all of our folks. Plus twenty-five cruise-ship security people armed with his latest picture. That's almost forty people. We'll find him," Josh said. "I hated telling the cruise people about this situation over the phone, but what else could we do?"

"It's probably for the best. Sophie and I didn't have time to meet with them, so this is what we have."

Standing outside of the Audubon Aquarium, waiting for Sophie, Manny looked across the Mississippi River, then up into the late morning sun, and put on his sunglasses.

There wasn't a cloud in the bright, blue sky and the eighty-something-degree warmth was most inviting. Again, the contrast between what should be beautiful and relaxing and what was evil and fearful enveloped him.

Of all of the creatures on the planet, only mankind seemed to have that innate ability to screw things up. And right now, this Rhodes, or whoever the hell he was, was doing a great job of it. The ironic thing was that none of the thousands of people at this end of the French Quarter had a clue there could be trouble in paradise. In this case, maybe oblivion was a kinder place to be.

"So we have twenty teams working that grid you organized—good job in twenty minutes, by the way—and they know not to confront him when they see him, right?" Manny asked Josh.

"They've been briefed. Even if he's not carrying any kind of luggage or briefcase. Whatever he stole could probably be carried in his pocket, as risky as that would be for him."

"I'm not sure he's worried about risk to himself, especially if he truly realizes the magnitude of what he is about to do. Yet his behavior of trying to mislead and confuse us says differently."

"But we still don't know what it is, do we?"

Sophie had emerged from the restroom. "Sorry, guys, really had to drain the bladder. Must be nervous again."

"You're sure you're okay with this search? I get it if you don't want to do this right now," said Josh.

"I think so. I talked to Dean in the bathroom. He thinks I need to get back in the saddle. I think he's right," she answered. "It'll help balance the scales if we catch this guy."

"I like how Dean thinks," said Manny. "And, Josh, to answer your question, no. We have no idea what it is. I keep hoping we'll get some info from Anna or our intel people about what he might have. But nothing yet."

"That knowledge would help narrow down what he's planning," said Josh, donning his own sunglasses. "If he has a bio-toxin, then we handle it different than if he has a concentrated explosive like cesium, which explodes in cold water." Josh shivered then added, "If he got his hands on military-grade material like that . . ." He didn't finish his statement. He didn't need to.

"That's enough of the bedtime stories, Corner. Let's find this guy," said Sophie.

"Agreed. I'm hooking up with the security supervisor for Carousel's port at Iberville and Decatur. You two are starting at Canal, going past the casino, then taking South Peters to Poydras then looping back on Convention Center, right?"

"Got it. Good luck, Josh."

"You too. We need some here." He winked at Sophie. "Tell Dean we could use some insight."

"He knows."

Josh then turned along the river walk and disappeared around the building.

"Ready?"

"Born ready," said Manny, adjusting his earpiece. He then turned on the com near his collar. The familiar ambient buzz came into focus.

"Can you hear me now?" said Sophie.

Manny smiled. "I can, smartass."

"You get what you get."

"I could have done worse."

"Don't forget it."

Then the two of them circled the building, heading toward the casino up Canal.

They were about a hundred feet from the bright lights announcing the entrance to the casino when Manny noticed the woman in the red dress waving her hands in their direction. She moved in front of the wild stallion fountain and waved again. She then moved higher, to the top step of the marbled stairway leading inside. Manny looked behind them to see who she was waving at. No one was directly behind them nor reacting to her.

"Who the hell is she waving at?" asked Sophie.

"I don't know. It can't be us. I don't—"

Manny froze, grabbing Sophie's arm. That was no woman.

He recognized the face of the man in the last image Alex had sent them.

# CHAPTER-50

The drive had been an arduous one. Eating the way he had, stopping for toilet breaks, and worrying about whether he'd actually have to shoot one or all of them—it all had weighed on him.

But the distant bridge rising over the Mississippi, just past the New Orleans skyline, told him he'd done it. He felt a surge of pride.

This assignment had no doubt been the toughest of his new life. Particularly in light of his cargo.

He glanced to the backseat. Mother and son were still groggy from their last application of sedative. They'd be more alert within the next thirty minutes. All as planned.

That couldn't be said of Charlie. The young man had napped several times during the long trip, but when the day broke a few hours ago, he'd remained wide awake. He'd had to put him under.

Neither had hardly spoken before that. He'd counted that a blessing and curse. He didn't dislike the boy. In fact, he had no ill will toward any of them. He'd simply done what was necessary, and profitable. It was the American way. Capitalism at its finest, and in the end, well worth the varied concerns of this journey.

"Where are we?"

The question came from the backseat. Connie Corner was still sluggish, but making the anticipated return trip to coherence.

"I guess it won't hurt to tell you now."

He merged left to Interstate 510, then continued.

"We're in New Orleans."

"That's where Josh is," she answered.

"Correct, my dear. You're about to reunite with your husband."

# CHAPTER-51

Manny spoke into his mouthpiece. "Josh. He's at the casino."

Then he and Sophie took off for the waving man.

"Where did he, she, it, go?" asked Sophie, running beside Manny as they reached the bottom of the marble steps.

"I lost him when he ran behind the fountain." He stopped and searched, his heart pounding, his eyes scanning for anything red.

Peculiarities weren't unusual in cities like New Orleans or Las Vegas, but seeing their suspect wearing a dress was at the top of Manny's list of Weird Occurrences.

They hurried up the twenty steps, Sophie a few feet to his left. They reached the fountain, the fine spray touching his face and arms, feeling cool in the heat.

"Damn, Williams. You sure can pick 'em. I ain't seen that before."

"That's two of us. Go around that way."

After circling the fountain, they met on the back side.

Nothing.

Only dozens of people walking in and around the square, the buzz of conversation high. No one wearing a red dress.

Another desperate scan of the crowd offered nothing more than a sinking feeling . . . Rhodes had escaped them.

"Inside?" asked Sophie.

"Must be. But I don't understand that. He obviously drew attention to himself."

"Yeah, so how did he know who to flag down?" asked Sophie, turning in his direction. "How did he know us?"

He shrugged. "I'm not sure. Except to say I'm not that surprised. We've not kept a low profile since we got here. Look at what happened at the safe house. I can only say that he had to know that at some point we'd come looking for him down here. Other than that, I don't know."

"He could have sent a damn invitation."

"He did . . . with that image Alex found," said Manny, his mind racing.

"I'll give you that. What about the dress? He won't be wearing that anymore, will he?"

Manny shook his head. "No. We're being led around by the nose again, so I doubt it."

"We have to go inside anyway. Plus, they have security cameras in the casino," said Sophie, heading toward the green revolving door.

Manny started to follow her, then stopped. "Wait."

"Why?"

"It's too risky for this guy to go inside. Every exit is probably heavily covered by casino security, who, no doubt, is aware of what he looks like. Josh has plastered his picture all over the security network."

Sophie raised her hands in frustration. "This is making me nuts. So he didn't go inside?"

"I wouldn't have."

Scanning the area again, he took in the bustling street on the west side, then across the median, hesitated, looked past the colorful trolley car waiting on the track, then to the east side of the street.

He looked back at Sophie, realization flooding his mind. He finally understood where this was heading, he hoped.

"We have to get to the ship. He wants us there. He pulled us away from the port, and it worked. There will be thousands of people getting off and getting on that ship soon. We need to get there."

"Everyone to the port. Forget the casino," he said into his com.

He pulled out his phone to text Alex a quick message then stuffed it in his pocket.

"Let's go."

Sophie hurried down the steps in front of him, then they began the three-block race to the east side of the port, desperate to get there. Their suspect had run them in circles for one final stint. Manny prayed he had realized the truth in time. They reached the end of the first block and sprinted across Julia Street toward the port.

He hadn't been sure of much in this case, but he was sure of one thing now. Whatever this man was planning, the show was almost ready to begin.

# CHAPTER-52

That had actually been easier than he thought. He watched as the two Feds and three other search teams raced off toward the cruise port.

"America's finest, huh?" he whispered. "This country is in trouble."

Looking in both directions one final time, he stepped away from the large, iron pillar that supported the open-air shopping area on Canal, directly across from the north end of the casino.

Satisfied he was safe, he picked up the small bag concealing the flashy red dress and began walking across the street. Once he reached the opposite side of Canal, he dropped the bag in a trash container. It had served a purpose, then it was no longer needed. Just like people.

A moment later, he stood on the very spot the Feds had occupied. The smile came without thinking. No matter what happened now, once he went inside the casino, law enforcement would never reach him in time. They'd blown it, and he'd get what he came for.

He had pulled it off, as planned, right down to this moment. The message that his phone received twenty minutes prior, complete with images, told him all that was left for him now was to complete what he'd started those years ago. And he would.

Touching the small device in his front pocket, he inhaled the warm air, straightened his posture, and walked inside the casino.

# CHAPTER-53

After walking out of the front door of the old home located on the south side of New Orleans, he paused, then turned back to look through the wavy window of the faded wooden door.

He tilted his head to get one last look at the three people on the sofa, tied, gagged, and once again sedated.

They looked peaceful, like they were resting. Good. That was the image he wanted to portray. He had done his job. Thus, his reward awaited him.

He took one last look at his surrogate family for the last fifteen hours or so—and he did think of them that way; he'd protected them. Some may think what he had done was deplorable, and he knew it was illegal, but he wasn't a bad man. He'd been kind.

Yet, we all had to make a living and his skill at this type of thing would always be in demand. His bank account said so.

He turned and stepped down the dilapidated steps, each one creaking as he went.

Once on the ground, he moved to the '69 Camaro SS that he'd negotiated in this deal as a getaway car, in a manner of speaking. The SUV was out of sight in the leaning garage, but this baby wasn't. He smiled. Where was the fun in being totally under the radar?

After climbing in, he checked his travel bag. It contained an extra twenty thousand in cash, provided by his client to allow him to get to Los Angeles after a day or two in New Orleans. It was all there. He started the vehicle.

He punched it a couple times, the roar like music to his ears, before he backed out of the driveway flanked by scarlet bougainvillea.

There was no question he'd enjoy his time in good old NOLA, but he'd also enjoy his trip back to LA. It had been weeks since he'd been home. The rest would do him good. Especially after this trip. New York to DC then to New Orleans—it had been a tough road anyway he cut it.

Yet, he was feeling totally alive.

He rolled down the window as he reached North Causeway Boulevard and hit the accelerator. Fifty, then sixty.

Once he hit sixty-five, he heard it, even above the road noise. The muffled click as two pieces of metal came together.

Shit. He should have known. He hadn't checked for this.

It would be his final regret and the last thing he heard before the Camaro exploded into a fiery ball.

# CHAPTER-54

Strolling in like he owned the place, he nodded at the two guards, flashing the smile that had gotten him out of more than one troubled situation. The guards both returned manufactured, mechanical grins and went back to their own conversation.

Idiots. Nothing had changed. But it would shortly, wouldn't it?

The anger rose, and this time he allowed it. They, this place, had cost him everything. Innocence had died that night.

They hadn't been like the poor excuse for humanity that was here now. These lost people, who would rather play cards or stay at their machines to win nothing but a zeroed-out bank account, were as guilty as the owners of this piece-of-shit establishment. Most in the casino that night could have helped. They could have prevented what had happened, but they hadn't wanted to be involved. So be it. These people, here and now, would be involved. He could only hope there were some here that were here then.

Karma's a bitch.

Once he was done with this one, Las Vegas was next. Then just maybe he would do a cruise ship, as he had tricked the authorities into believing was happening today.

First things first, however.

Turning on the red and gold patterned carpet, the lights and sounds of the casino cascading from every direction, he moved to the huge display near the theater on the west wide of the building. He'd be safe there while he did what he had to do, then hit the side door, which would not be the case for the rest of the garbage inside the building.

One more left turn, and he'd be in position. This end was less populated at the moment. Excellent. That meant more people on the main floor.

His heart was ready to explode through his chest. Much like the Camaro carrying his last remaining loose end had surely experienced by now.

He reached into his pocket, took out the small black device with the red button square in the middle, and placed it in his left hand. Taking two more steps, he stopped to exhale and gather his wits. He needed everything he had to get this done and survive.

"That's far enough, Mister Rhodes, or should I say Gerhard Wanger?"

Rhodes spun around only to find himself staring down the barrels of four guns. Manny Williams stood beside his Asian partner, wearing a look that sent his confidence plummeting toward anxiety. But only for a moment.

Rhodes smiled.

# CHAPTER-55

Manny waited—the real Gerhard Wanger's smile taking some wind out of his sail. One look at his hand told him why Wanger was smiling.

"Put it down and you'll live," said Manny.

"I might say the same thing to you, agents."

Manny quickly glanced at Sophie, then Josh, then to the security officer Josh had been partnered with. "Don't shoot, yet."

"I'd say that shooting at all would be detrimental to everyone in this place," said Wanger, his voice calm and confident.

"That would mean you as well," said Manny.

Wanger quickly scanned the area. Manny saw realization. "I now know why this area is minus people. But that won't help them. When I hit this button, this place will be scorched from front to back. And to answer your question, yes, it would mean me as well. But that's a price I'm willing to pay. Are you?"

His face was giving away his deep-down thoughts. Manny suspected he would die rather than lose this standoff, yet there was something else going on with him.

"Explosives then?"

"The most volatile on the market. Once it mixes with cold water . . . well, *boom*. I suppose you guessed chemical bioweapons, but that's not my style. I want them all to pay, but I'm not cruel, Agent."

"Yeah, you sound like a saint," said Sophie.

"No saint, Agent Lee, just a seeker of justice."

"Let's get back to your question. No, to be honest, I'm not prepared to die. But I can tell you don't want to die today either, do you?"

"Of course not. But the alternative of you taking me into custody isn't in the cards, ever. I'll push this button, even if you all get a shot off and kill me. My reflex will send this place into a fiery hell like you've never seen. But then again, you won't see it very long yourselves."

"Maybe. We can't let you walk out of here."

"Ahh, but you can. First, before I show you and Agent Corner how that's going to happen, I have to commend you. How did you know I'd be here and not at the port . . . and how did you find out who I am?"

"Fair enough. I saw you on the other side of the street after we lost you in front of the casino, just the side of your face, mind you, and briefly, but it was enough. That's when I realized what you did was the last in a long line of deceptions. Pulling us along by our ears, getting us to go where you wanted had worked to that point. I figured if that's where you wanted us, you must have something else in mind."

"Go on," said Wanger, a bit of his arrogance waning.

"It became obvious to me that you never intended to attack the port. Seeing you still near the casino caused me to make an educated guess on what you truly had in mind."

Manny then motioned at the others. "Keep on him." He lowered his weapon and stepped forward.

"Far enough, Agent."

Manny stopped. "I just want to see the look on your face after I explain the rest."

More doubt crept into Wanger's shifting eyes.

*Lord in heaven, I hope I am playing this right, or none of us will make it out alive.*

"I texted my research folks for two bits of information, and guess what? We found what we were looking for."

"Which was?"

"I couldn't figure out why, two different times, you practically invited us to identify who you were by staring into security-camera feeds. The only way you'd do that was to make sure we knew what you looked like, albeit a bit different than your normal look with the mustache and black hair and the fedora.

"So we compared facial recognition run against the men in the warehouse and you, minus a few attributes, and guess what? Your face was a ninety-six-percent match to the smaller man you killed in the warehouse, the one we thought was the real Wanger. The cheekbones were almost flawless; the eyes were close but not right on. Nevertheless, it was obvious there were two of you."

Manny took a breath. "I believe you hired someone to be your double, paid for the surgery, then killed him and the others in the warehouse. No loose ends. But I still don't understand why you didn't do plastic surgery on yourself. I don't know. Maybe that's coming."

"You're smarter than I thought. That won't stop what's going to happen here."

Then with his right hand, Wanger slowly pulled at his mustache and dropped it to the floor. Then he pulled off the wig. Manny saw him as the real Wanger now. No question. But Wanger didn't stop.

Grasping his chin with some effort, the prosthetic came loose, revealing mangled scar tissue that looked like something from a horror movie.

"I'm not finished, Agent."

Wanger then reached up to the right side of his face and removed the eyes and ear prosthesis, revealing another patch of mangled flesh.

Manny stared. It was impossible not to.

"I see you now understand the gravity of my situation. I've had surgery, but not like you assumed. The rest of your hypotheses are close enough, Agent. It wasn't that simple to find someone. However, you'd be surprised what people would do for a million dollars. The process of integrating him into my business was difficult, but in the end, it worked out. It freed me to pursue other endeavors."

Wanger was beginning to perspire. Manny wasn't sure if it was because of his situation or because of what Manny was going to confront him with next. Wanger knew what was coming, no doubt.

"After realizing that you were trying to cover your tracks as Wanger—to get yourself and what you did for a living forever out from under the scrutiny of the Feds—we had to find out why. I mean, you could have done this without all of the killing, but then you'd be a wanted man. This way Wanger is dead, and you'd be a shadow that we'd never find, especially with your new look, whatever that would be. You'd be free to do whatever you wanted. That's when we found out what had happened in the casino's elevator five years ago."

Wanger's face contorted, then he regained his poise, most of it.

"I'm sorry for the death of your wife and son. I know a little about that. But it wasn't the casino's fault. That robbery went south, that's it. That's all," Manny said softly.

Wanger stayed completely stoic, except for the pain in his eyes that came and went. Pain that would never leave him, no matter what he did.

"You don't know a damn thing about it. People, including security officers, stood by while those bastards shot my family, one by one, then me, directly in the face, last. All because some dumbass hostage negotiator thought she knew what the hell she was doing. We ended up being the diversion that allowed those three men to escape. Us. My family. Just an innocent elevator ride to the hotel room we never saw."

His eyes deadened. It made Manny's stomach turn.

"We were going to have a grand time, Agent Williams."

"I—"

Wanger reached his left hand toward Manny, the threat obvious. "Don't speak about that again. What's done is done, and I'm here to right the scale."

"As you wish," said Manny.

"Now, I'd clap, but my hand is occupied. You are right on most of the rest of your assumptions. The orchestrated killing of the real Wanger was essential to my goals. I could have blown this place to hell, and I wanted to. But eventually, even as slow as you Feds can be, I'd be caught. The fact that the DEA had already been able to infiltrate my organization with Flora Burns and Daryl Brooks—yes, I knew about them—made that clear. I had to become more creative."

For a brief moment, Wanger looked past Manny and the others, toward the front of the casino. The stoic expression on the good side of his face now gone, replaced by rage or insanity . . . then back to control. The psychos they'd busted at the BAU had nothing on this one.

"You think you can evacuate this place before I kill hundreds? You're wrong. I, fortunately, have contingencies. As much as I hate to do it, I guess I'll go to plan B. Our time is done here, either way. So here's what's going to happen. We're going to make a trade."

"A trade?"

"Yes. I plan for everything, and this possibility came out of my worst-case scenarios."

Wanger reached into the front pocket of his pants and pulled out a phone, then looked at Josh.

"You are the leader of this group, Agent Corner. I'm going to toss you this phone, and I want you to look at the photos. Do it quickly."

Josh nodded nervously. He then fingered the phone as the rest of them watched.

Wanger's smile was particularly gruesome, given his face.

"You'll see the first one is of a dead man lying on the floor of your home. If you get the chance, I suppose you'll have to ask your wife about that situation. My guess is she might have been lonely or something."

"What the hell are you talking about?" snapped Josh.

"You'll figure it. Do you recognize the people in the next three images, Agent Corner?" He was almost cackling now.

It took a few seconds, then Josh looked up from the screen. Exchanging a confused look for unbridled anger of his own. He hurried toward Wanger, gun outstretched. "You son of a bitch. What have you done to my family?"

"Nothing, yet. And I suggest you stop right there, or none of them or us will live another day."

Manny grabbed Josh around the waist, Sophie helping, to keep him from killing them all. Josh finally stopped, but Manny didn't think it would take much to get him going again. If he were in that same situation, he knew he'd be going wild right now, worried about his family. Not to mention that first picture.

Taking the phone from Josh's hand, his heart broke. Charlie and Jake and Connie were propped up on a sofa in a room somewhere in New Orleans.

If the handwritten sign pinned to Connie's blouse wasn't enough proof, the split screen showed Josh's family's SUV in front of a city neighborhood watch sign that read the fine city of NOLA.

Wanger was warped, but Manny didn't believe he held any real ill will toward Josh or his family; they were simply a hedge against the unforeseen, like getting caught, like now.

He looked back to Josh. The man was doing all he could to keep it together. Manny knew he would. He had to.

"I suppose this den of sin is about empty now, kudos for you getting that far, but it doesn't change my situation or yours. Here's the deal. I trade this detonation switch and the life of Agent Corner's family for free passage out of this dive. You won't follow, you won't send anyone after me, and most of all, you'll stay inside this building for two hours exactly."

Just then, Wanger's eyes moved to look past Manny. His hideous smile worked overtime at what he saw.

"What if we don't like dat deal, mon?" said Braxton.

"He's got a good point," said Belle.

Manny turned to see them standing side by side, Belle's gun drawn, Braxton breathing fire, his hands clenched into large, ebony hammers.

"He really does," said Barb.

She and Chloe appeared to his right, posed like Belle.

He wished she'd stayed outside, as he'd asked when Josh told him that the three women had returned to New Orleans. But had he really expected them to listen? He wouldn't have.

Chloe smiled at Manny, then turned back in Wanger's direction. "Especially from an ugly bastard like yourself, don't ya know."

"Well, hail, hail, the gang's all here. And my looks are of no consequence to any of you. The bullets did what they did," said Wanger, trying to sound unaffected by Chloe's remark.

Wanger scanned his left, then came back to the right, making sure there were no more visitors to this dance, the nightmare smile returning. "If you don't like the deal, like I said, we all die. And you'll be responsible for killing three innocents, plus whoever else is still here. You must decide. I have places to be, or not."

"How do we know you don't have other devices that would blow this place?" asked Manny.

"You don't. Just like you don't know that I'll not kill Corner's family by setting off the other bomb in that room where they are, no matter what happens here.

"Just like you aren't totally sure I have a device in place that would blow this place to Kingdom Come. You really don't know anything. God forbid, you'll have to trust me.

"I suspect that pisses you off more than it scares you. Nevertheless, agents, that's the deal. And while you're taking thirty seconds to make that decision, I want all of your weapons, backup weapons, and cell phones on the floor. Kick them in my direction. I'm using caution, in the event you think you want to gamble on any of those situations."

"What about—" started Josh, his face filled with contempt.

"Enough," snarled Wanger, transferring his face into something from the *Walking Dead*. "Now. I'm done talking. No more explanations or conversation. Just do it."

Sophie bent over first, placing her weapon and phone on the floor and then slid them over to Wanger's feet, her hand running along her ankle. Slowly, like a mesmerizing domino trick, the rest of them followed suit.

"Good. That's using your heads."

Reaching into his back pocket, he pulled out a yellow sheet of paper. He tilted his head toward Josh.

"This paper gives you directions on where you will locate another document that shows you the address of the house where your wife and children are resting comfortably. There are also instructions on how to defuse the device underneath that sofa. Make sure you take care to do it exactly as I've written. Or . . . well, you'll be in my boat.

"I must reach the area where the instructions on how to defuse the bomb are located and make sure you have access to them. That process needs my special touch to work and give you access to those instructions. As you might guess, I've done it this way just in case you think you can pull off some heroic act right now. Your children might appreciate seeing their father again."

There was a wisp of emotion as Wanger's voice softened, some of his humanity still intact. Then it escaped into the recesses of his diseased mind.

"Now, all of you, on the floor, face down, facing each other in a circle. Once you do that, our little get-together will almost be over."

Manny had been forced into some unpleasant situations in his life, but nothing like this one. He wasn't at all sure that Wanger wouldn't still kill them, one way or another. In fact, if he were him, he'd get rid of them all, knowing he'd still be the subject of an international manhunt. Yet, what choice did they have? He was sure the others felt the same and had drawn the same conclusions.

Josh led the way, followed by Belle and Braxton. Manny moved to go next, then Sophie stepped past him, her hand brushing his. It was more than a brush as she placed something between his fingers.

Never missing a beat, he got down on the floor beside Sophie, both in the direction of Wanger's deformed face.

A moment later, Chloe and Barb were down, the circle formed as Wanger had demanded.

"Good. Remember. Two hours. If you leave that position before then, you'll kill Corner's family. Goodbye, agents."

Manny waited for footsteps moving away from them, but there were none. All he heard, at first, was Wanger's breathing. He thought he detected an air of relief in that breathing. Then he was sure of it. A moment later, he heard the subtle clank of gun touching gun.

That could only mean one thing.

No loose ends.

The man wasn't a man of his word after all. He was going to execute them.

Manny lifted his head, tapping Sophie as he did. Wanger's arrogance in believing that, no matter what he said, they would do what they were told, gave them a window.

As Wanger bent for one of the Glocks, his attention away from them, his left hand was clearly visible, loosely holding the detonation device.

Manny rose up enough to lift Sophie's second backup weapon and fired, hitting Wanger's wrist.

He howled in shocked agony, blood flying. The device he was holding skittered across the carpet, some ten feet away. Despite his injury, Wanger recovered quickly. He scrambled after the device.

Rising to her knees, Sophie threw the star. It buried deep into Wanger's knee, dropping him two feet from the glowing red button encased in plastic, a second scream of pain echoing through the casino.

"No. No. No."

By then, Braxton, Josh, Barb, and Chloe had gotten up and were rushing him.

Wanger rolled over on his side, one of the Glocks still in his right hand. He fired wildly. He didn't have a chance to shoot again before Braxton was on top of him, wrestling the gun away. Then he put him under with a right hand to the face.

Manny rose up and headed for Wanger, already thinking about what they were going to do about Josh's family, when Chloe yelled.

"Manny!"

He turned to see Sophie lying on the floor, blood pouring from the wound on her head.

# CHAPTER-56

Funny how things work out. Manny couldn't help but think that for the one hundredth time.

Not just in everyday life, but even when the extraordinary enters a person's life, like it does for all of us from time to time. That extraordinary event could be a good circumstance. In fact, he guessed it was mostly good for the masses.

But not always. Wanger losing his family and getting shot in the face had occurred in such an unfortunate way. Yet, Wanger's reaction, his grief, his rage, had led to more deaths than Manny could know. Who, other than Wanger, knew for sure how many people had died so he could get here, to this place?

He wouldn't be hurting anyone else, however. Not from prison, then maybe death row. He was so distraught at his failure that he was on suicide watch, his life's work an abject failure in terms of ruining the casino and killing hundreds in the process. Not complete justice for what he'd done and tried to do. The system worked, and Wanger would never see the outside again.

Manny changed his position and leaned with more of his weight against the SUV, his mind alive with more emotion than he usually allowed.

Compartmentalization was a good thing, mostly.

"You ready?" said Chloe, touching his arm.

"Yep."

"Before we do this, did you hear from Josh again?"

"I did."

Josh.

His boss and his friend had endured a most horrible hour just two days prior, only to find out there hadn't been a need for that kind of heartbreaking concern. Not all of it at least.

Wanger had screwed up, more than once it seemed. The photo he'd received of Josh's family had a date and place stamp showing where it had been sent from, something that Josh had noticed.

It had taken less than thirty minutes for Josh and the agency's bomb squad to get to the house on the south side, based on that information and Alex's tech help.

Another thirty minutes for the K-9 bomb sniffer, Buster, to be led into the front door and, as trained, checked out the area his handler had shown him.

Nothing. There had been no bomb at all. Only a gut-wrenching threat that Wanger had gambled would work. And, when playing on emotions like those, it had worked.

If the psycho hadn't thought he needed to kill the agents on that casino floor, he'd be in the wind now. Bad judgment for a man who had made a habit of making sound, cautious decisions.

He also wondered if, just maybe, Wanger had not actually put a bomb in that house because of Charlie and Josh and Connie, and what they represented. Maybe somewhere deep down, Wanger hadn't really wanted another man enduring what he had.

Maybe.

This case, and Wanger's thirst for revenge, had led to this moment. To standing in front of this hospital—the last place he'd seen Sophie.

Good God, why did this have to be so hard? Why did everything they did as a team lead to things like this?

He remembered a wisdom he'd heard once or twice about asking questions about which one already knew the answer.

"Let's go." He reached for Chloe's hand, and they began the trek across the hot parking lot.

As they reached the front, the automatic door opened.

There, rolling through the exit to the outside, being pushed by Alex in a wheelchair, sat Sophie Lee, the white bandage much smaller than this morning.

"I gotta get shot more often, Williams. This being waited on hand and foot works for me," she said, smiling.

"I think I can do without you being shot again, even if it was only a graze," said Manny.

"Hey, it was a little more than a graze. I think I'm going to have a scar. That's kind of cool. Even Dough Boy said so."

"I did. And don't call me Dough Boy. It still won't be as cool as this robotic hand, but hey, no one's perfect," said Alex, wearing a wide grin.

"You got me there. But I'll take it."

Once outside, she rose from the chair and gave Chloe a hug, then Manny. "Did everyone get home okay?" she asked.

"Yes. Barb left this morning. Braxton last night. Belle took her new BAU to New York, even though it still looks like Wanger had a hand in that. He's not talking about it though. She took off as soon as she was sure you were good to go."

Sophie lowered her head. "What about Josh?"

He ran his hand through his hair. "Let's just say it's going to get complicated. Connie told him about her affair. He's trying to get his mind around that. He blames himself."

"Yeah, been there," said Sophie.

"He's worried about the effect of all this on the boys to boot. He's at home for now. They've already set up counseling sessions for all of them, to deal with what happened at home and the trip here."

"You told him we're here for him, right?"

"I did, and he knows. Especially after your nine texts and voicemails."

"Good. And it was only seven." Sophie smiled, but tears moistened her eyes. "Did you tell him about . . . you know?"

"About the last, most incredible gift Dean left you? The one that shocked us all?"

The tears made a slow trek down her cheeks. "Yeah. That. That the doctors here found out about me. That I'm knocked up?"

"Pregnant," said Chloe, hugging her again. "You're pregnant."

"Okay. Yeah that. That I'm with child?"

"I did. He said to say he'd call and congratulate you in a couple of days. He also said it was about time, because your damn clock was ticking."

She laughed, wiping away tears. "I'm not that old."

"Yeah, you Asians never look that old," said Alex.

"Bite me. We're just hot longer than you white boys."

Alex bowed to her. "True, and I can't wait to see you as a mother. You'll be wonderful."

She tilted her head, then reached up to kiss Alex. "Thank you. I'll make Dean proud. I almost can't wait. But, c'mon. That's enough of this emotional crap for the day. I'm hungry again. Let's get some Chick-fil-A and then get the hell out of town. I love the heat, but this is messing with the curls in my hair."

"You don't have curls in your hair," said Manny.

"I rest my case. And I'm driving."

With that, the new members of the ACTU climbed into the SUV and headed for the airport.

Manny thought it the best feeling he'd had in weeks. There was no place like home.

*** 

Josh Corner stared at the file, his family problems on hold as much as possible. If possible.

He ran his finger along the last line of the second group of reports Belle had pulled for him and frowned.

The first background had been clean, as he suspected. Sophie Lee hadn't been involved in anything other than the normal everyday life of an agent. He even smiled to himself at the idea of her becoming a mom. She thought this job was tough.

He stared at the report again, making sure he wasn't wrong.

He wasn't. There was no question about what he'd seen and where it had come from.

He wouldn't have believed it. Yet, his cynicism had grown in leaps and bounds over the last few years. No matter how unlikely the tip he'd received, he had to check it out. It played true.

Manny Williams, his Manny Williams, had twenty million dollars in an offshore bank account, compliments of God's Hand. That seemed impossible. Manny Williams? He should just call him. But that was not how things were done in his new position.

He reached for his phone. "You were right. Now what?"

Fifteen seconds later, he hung up and dialed another number.

"Arrest him and bring him in."

Josh Corner threw his phone on the desk and left the room.

Thank you for reading Cajun Fire. I hope that you enjoyed the crew's new adventure into the world of domestic terrorism. It took a little longer to get this one out mostly because of the amount of research involved. And the fact that I was spending some vacation time away! ☺

Thank you, faithful reader, for your patience.

As always, please contact me and let me know what you think. I love our interactions.

rickmurcer @gmail.com

www.rickmurcer.com

Yours,

Rick Murcer

47926824R00215

Made in the USA
San Bernardino, CA
11 April 2017